Near Death Horizon

L.A. Morton-Yates

Synthesis Press

First published by Synthesis Press 2026

Copyright © 2026 by L.A. Morton-Yates

All rights reserved. No part of this publication may be reproduced, stored or transmitted in any form or by any means, electronic, mechanical, photocopying, recording, scanning, or otherwise without written permission from the publisher. It is illegal to copy this book, post it to a website, or distribute it by any other means without permission.

This novel is entirely a work of fiction. The names, characters and incidents portrayed in it are the work of the author's imagination. Any resemblance to actual persons, living or dead, events or localities is entirely coincidental.

L.A. Morton-Yates asserts the moral right to be identified as the author of this work.

First edition

ISBN: 979-8-9866022-8-8

To those who keep on running...

Contents

Acknowledgements	VII
Waking	2
Chapter 1	4
Chapter 2	11
Chapter 3	27
Chapter 4	44
Chapter 5	55
Chapter 6	70
Chapter 7	79
Chapter 8	90
Chapter 9	103
Chapter 10	112
Chapter 11	123
Chapter 12	134
Chapter 13	139
Chapter 14	146
Chapter 15	161
Chapter 16	166
Chapter 17	175

Chapter 18	183
Chapter 19	197
Chapter 20	203
Chapter 21	211
Chapter 22	221
Chapter 23	230
Chapter 24	242
Chapter 25	246
About the author	266
Also by	268
Excerpt from Bittersouls	269

Acknowledgements

This book, like many children now approaching their fifth birthday, was conceived during the longest days of the COVID-19 pandemic. While many people were unable to work during the lockdown, I was working in a clinical laboratory processing specimens to be tested for that very virus. I remember long hours, incredible stress, and the looming threat of burnout. So when my older sister Grace asked me to do NaNoWriMo with her, my first thought was, "why the hell would I do that?" After a little while, she managed to convince me that it would be good to pour my emotional state into a novel—a way to express the feelings that I saw growing in myself and those all around me. Feelings of isolation, of apathy, and of perseverance. I agreed, and in November of 2020, I wrote the first version of what would later become this novel.

Though it was what my mind needed at the time to process what was going on around me, I had no initial intentions of trying to polish that novel for publication. It was far too short, for one thing, barely 50,000 words, with nearly 10,000 of those being a suspiciously rotund epilogue (something my wife makes fun of me for to this day). But over the past several years, I was encouraged by a few key voices to keep working on it, to fill out the parts that were too skeletal, and to trim away the fluff that didn't drive the main narrative. Without those voices, this book wouldn't be sitting in your hands today.

First, and most obvious, I must thank my sister, Grace. Without her challenge to rise above what I thought I was capable of, that first draft would never have materialized. Her continued faith in my craft has driven me to bring forward not only this book, but several more that I one day hope to share with the world.

Next, I have to thank my wife, Julie, who has always been my biggest fan. Though I wrote *Bittersouls* specifically for her, she told me after reading the very first draft of this book that it was her favorite story of mine so far. If it weren't for her continual reminders that 'hey, that was a good book and deserves to see the light of day', I almost certainly would have left this novel to gather dust instead of putting it through its paces.

But even after all that encouragement, this book wouldn't be in the shape that it is today if it weren't for the efforts of my editor, Ceara Nobles. As always, she sharpened my prose and ironed out my errors, giving my words the edge that they needed to sing. Thank you.

I also want to thank my wonderful cover artist, César Pardo, who once again crafted an intriguing visual first contact for readers to experience. In all likelihood, it was his efforts that was responsible for you reading this page.

And to all my friends, family, and readers who have continued to believe in me as I pursue my craft. Thank you for that faith, and I hope you enjoy this journey. You are my 12,000.

Dust scraped between boot and glass as Rhett crested the ridge over the Stormshadow Hinterlands. It was strange returning to the region, reminding him of all that had gone wrong. He'd often wondered if the journey should have ended here.

Perhaps it still would.

Waking

{stellar boundary detected}

  {hypersleep system initiated}

  ...

  {begin waking process}

  ...

  {vanguard team selected}

  {loading data}

Designee 1

POD: *A-1159*

NAME: *Shamus McNeary*

ROLE: *Captain*

BACKGROUND: *Diplomacy, Leadership*

Designee 2

POD: *A-207*

NAME: *Sarah Galerkin*

ROLE: *Translator*

BACKGROUND: *Communication, PhD in Xenolinguistics*

Designee 3

POD: *B-1381*

NAME: *Markus Braaten*

ROLE: *Technical Specialist*

BACKGROUND: *PhD in Physics, PhD in Mechanical Engineering*

Designee 4

POD: *B-912*

NAME: Steven Caldwell
ROLE: Physician, Navigator
BACKGROUND: PhD in Astrobiology

Designee 5

POD: C-144
NAME: Henry Bischoff
ROLE: Security Officer
BACKGROUND: Lieutenant in the UENAF

...

...

{processing}

{processing}

...

{waking sequence initialized}

Chapter 1

Day -54

TRANSCRIPT BEGINS

Good morning, Henry.
 [sigh]
 [silence for 1.2 seconds]
 They... they asked me to record this. They told me it's best for people waking up after so many years of hypersleep to hear a voice that's familiar. One they feel comfortable with. It'll help you stay calm, they said. Help you to... reorient yourself.
 You're probably feeling pretty confused right now. Maybe a little lost. I don't really know the procedures for the thawing process, but I have to imagine you don't have a lot of room to move around. Try not to let it get to you, though. Just listen to my voice. Focus on what I'm saying. It'll all...
 [sniffs]
 It will all be okay.
 [silence for 2.4 seconds]
 You know, they did a good job, choosing you for the mission. I've never known a man as strong as you. They're going to need that out there, if I had to bet on it. I know they've said this is going to be a peaceful mission. Diplomacy with the Occassi has been successful since we first picked up their signals. And it's the next logical step—I

CHAPTER 1

know it is. You can't just... call someone on the phone all the time and call them your best friend. Eventually... eventually, you have to actually meet.

[sniff]

It's a good thing. I keep telling myself this is all a good thing. Allies, they are calling them. A partner species with whom we might one day quest for the stars far beyond our home systems. I just... I just wish they weren't so far away.

I wish...

I wish you weren't so far away.

[sob]

[cough]

I'm sorry. I don't think this is how I'm supposed to be doing this. I'm... I just...

Why'd you have to go, Henry? I miss you. Your son... he misses his daddy. He asks about you all the time. Asks when you'll be coming back. When he'll get to see you again. I tell him... I... I tell him...

[sobs for 3.5 seconds]

Did you know?

[sob]

Did you know we hadn't been chosen?

I'm sure you didn't. I keep telling myself that. You're a good man. You wouldn't want to leave us behind. But it's an important mission. There are only so many pods on the ship, and every one of them is supposed to go to the best and brightest. We have to make a good impression with the Occassi. I know that. I just...

We weren't good enough for them, Henry. I wasn't good enough. Didn't stop them from asking me to record this, though. As if I needed another reminder that I'll never see you again...

[sniffs]

But it isn't about them. No. This is for you. Henry. My husband. My love. My rock. I hope this message finds you well. I hope and pray that your mission is as peaceful as they've promised me. And I hope that, with the adventure of an alien planet ahead of you, you won't dwell too much on what you...

[chokes back sob]

What you left behind.
[cries]

TRANSCRIPT ENDS

Rhett didn't know when exactly he'd woken up. Like any sleeper after a long night, he came to gradually, only becoming aware of his awareness after the fact. There was a sound like a knock at the door, only harder. A demand to be let in, reverberating through the tank's walls, through the honey-thick liquid that suspended him. It began in short rhythms.

Three knocks. A pause.

Three knocks. A pause.

Then it grew more demanding. More desperate. Rhett couldn't tell where it was coming from. Still couldn't open his eyes. His eyelids were so heavy, the slurry around him so thick... He tried to move his arms but found murky resistance that overwhelmed his atrophied muscles. For a moment, he thought he couldn't breathe, but he found that air was still entering and leaving his lungs. There was something on his face. Something reaching into his mouth and down his throat. He almost gagged at the realization.

Rhett tried to focus. He could breathe. The tubing had to be helping with that. But where was he? He tried to remember, but his mind felt as thick and incongruous as the syrup in which he swam.

Three more thumps. A pause.

"Good morning, Rhett."

The voice was so sudden and stark in his ear that he might have jumped if there was anything solid beneath his feet.

"*Did you sleep well?*"

CHAPTER 1

Rhett forced his eyes open a crack and immediately regretted it. Though he clenched them closed again, the strange substance that surrounded him had already made its way in, leaving him hissing into his breathing tubes at the sticky, scratchy sensation.

Four thumps this time.

The voice in his ears laughed softly—a laugh he recognized. *"It's all right, Rhett. Just listen to my voice. I know you're confused, but that's going to pass, all right? Just focus on me. You know me, remember? Cynthia, your girlfriend?"*

Rhett tried to slow his breathing. Tried to calm himself. Cyn. Yes, of course he remembered her. How hadn't he recognized her voice from the start? They'd been together for almost six years, after all. Might have even been married by now, if she believed in that sort of thing.

Four more thumps.

"That's it. Good. Just breathe. I'm right here. Take your time. Hypersleep can really take it out of you, so just be patient with yourself. What matters is that you're safe. All right? So just breathe."

Rhett thought he heard another voice. This one was muffled. Distant. Somewhere outside the hypersleep pod, maybe? He couldn't make out what it said.

Five more thumps.

Cyn's voice laughed softly again. *"They asked me to go for a few minutes with this recording. Enough to make sure you could get reoriented. I'll admit that I've never been in hypersleep before—not yet, anyway—so I'm not sure what to go on about to... keep you company? I guess you'll be doing one of these for me, too, though. I'm sure... I'm sure that will be really interesting."*

Rhett tested his fingers, which seemed to move easily enough through the fluid. His arms and legs all responded the way he hoped. From what he'd been told, temporary paralysis of the extremities was among the possible side effects of hypersleep.

Four more thumps, softer this time.

"You know, I can't think of a time when you've spoken for more than a minute or two consecutively. You're always just so... efficient with your words. So concise. So...

blunt? Maybe I'll suggest they have my mother do my recording. Except that would involve them telling my mother that I'm leaving..."

Rhett clenched his jaw, trying to focus on what he last remembered. Leaving. He remembered leaving, didn't he? But leaving where? The knot in his stomach told him it was important. Whatever he'd left behind, he'd spent a great deal of time stressing about it.

The thumping came in a long stream this time, wavering in intensity but never pausing.

"It's all right, Rhett. I shouldn't have brought it up. It's an honor that you were assigned to the Occassus mission. And I should consider myself lucky—not all of the crew were able to bring their partners with them." Cyn clicked her tongue—a sound she made when she was thinking. "Imagine that. Reaching Occassus... a hundred and thirty-five years in hypersleep... and waking up alone? I know I won't be one of the first thawed when we get there, but at least I'll be on the ship. I just... yeah."

135 years. 135 years? Occassus?

Rhett's breathing accelerated, coming in quick gasps through the tubing as his mind searched for sense amid his jumbled memories. What was Cyn talking about? He understood that he'd been in hypersleep. That probably explained the tank and the sludge and the tubes in his lungs. But the rest... the rest...

A crashing noise sounded outside. The thumping stopped.

The ship. He remembered getting onto a ship. And leaving somewhere. A mission to Occassus. Yes, Rhett remembered now. They'd left Earth. Left home—forever. He was part of an expedition... or something. The memories were there, coming in disorganized bursts as he tried to piece them back together.

"*I should wish you luck, Rhett,*" Cyn's voice said. "*I don't know what lies ahead of you, but I do know you. Whatever comes your way, you'll be ready. And when it's done... well, I hope yours is the first face I see when I wake up.*"

Rhett shuddered at a screech of rending metal inches from his face. Light pierced his still-closed eyelids. His body surged forward as the cryogenic soup began to spill out, forcing a dull collision between his head and the inside of the tank. Whatever new hole had been gouged in it wasn't anywhere close to large enough for him to pass through. His skin tingled as the air bubbled in, brushing past like a hand lazily petting a dog.

A moment later, the tank's front half tore open properly, spilling man and fluid alike into the over-bright chamber outside. Rhett gagged as gravity yanked the tubes from his throat. Whatever they'd stuck in his ears to play Cyn's recording was ripped free just as suddenly. He collapsed to the floor, the weight of the clinging syrup overwhelming his atrophied muscles, and retched weakly.

"Who? Who...?" a gruff, masculine voice said. "You're... you're not Sandra."

Rhett clenched his eyes shut, then tried to open them. They still hurt, and everything around him was a haze of light and shadow.

A figure loomed over him. "Where's Sandy? You're... she was supposed to be here. She was supposed to be with me!"

"Rhett," he choked out, blinking desperately to clear his vision. "Corporal... Rhett Wethern."

"Tell me where she is! I couldn't... she couldn't..." The figure lurched down toward him, triggering a sluggish reflexive block from Rhett's left hand. It shouldn't have helped, but the figure's movements were just as awkward. "You did this, didn't you? Tell me where she is!"

Rhett tried to scramble away, his mind barely making sense of what was happening. The man lashed out again, but this time Rhett had his footing. He struck back, bypassing the big man's flailing arms and landing a half-decent punch to his left ribs.

The man grunted, stumbling back. He recovered enough to send a vicious glare Rhett's way. He was big—a good six inches taller than Rhett and thickly muscled. Probably another soldier. Like Rhett, he was completely naked from his time in the hypersleep tank.

Rhett blinked. This didn't seem right. Why were they fighting? He couldn't—

The man advanced again, wielding a wrench he had gotten from somewhere. Rhett raised his arm to defend himself but only managed to volunteer it for the brunt of the blow. He gasped as the bones of his forearms cracked, the heat of the pain sending shivers through his whole body.

Rhett stumbled backward, looking desperately for something to defend himself. There was nothing around except the bent metal piece that had been ripped off the front of his tank. The floor was grated, designed to allow the sludge from the tanks—and any other fluids that might have been discharged in the waking process—to drain straight through it. Aside from the tanks, there was nothing but gently curved white metal walls.

Rhett ducked to the side as the man swung again, trying to get close enough to grab the piece of metal. He managed to reach it, but the throbbing in his arm told him it was far too heavy to be of any use as a weapon.

The tank. If that piece could be broken off, then maybe…

Rhett dodged again as the man roared. The wrench smashed through a large Imageglass panel, sending sharp bits flying. Rhett snatched one up with his good hand, circling the big man as he tried to pull the wrench free from where he'd gotten it stuck. Maybe if Rhett was fast enough, he could—

Another fluid ran down Rhett's hand, thin by comparison to the sludge he'd been sleeping in a few minutes before. He frowned, staring at it as it made its way like a lazy river down the length of his forearm and dripped from his elbow. It was hot but quickly cooling. Its color…

The big man slumped forward against the tank he'd smashed open. He gurgled for a few seconds, hunched over, and the wrench clattered to the ground.

"Fuck," Rhett muttered, staring at the man's still body. He tried to let go of the shard of glass in his hand, but his muscles refused to obey. "Oh, *fuck*."

Chapter 2

```
MAZER BROADCAST
SOURCE: Earth
RECEIVED: December 14th, 2195
TRANSCRIPT BEGINS
```

Good morning, Captain. Crew. I hope this recording finds you well.

My name is Samuel Ivanchuk. I have recently been promoted to Director of the Extraterrestrial Treaties Administration, and as my predecessor did before me, I have been entrusted to keep the ES Votum informed about the status of the home they left behind.

At the time of this recording, it has been fifty-three years, four months, and nine days since your departure from Earth. Unless something has gone terribly wrong, you are all still in hypersleep and will remain so until you enter the Occassi system. According to the latest telemetry we've received from the Votum—sent over four and a half years ago now, due to the transit delay—everything is still working as it should. If luck holds, you'll be listening to this as part of long chain of similar recordings from myself, my predecessor, and likely my successor as well.

[clears throat]

Anyway. To the point.

You'll be happy to hear that Earth has continued to prosper. As it has a way of doing, technology has continued to advance in leaps and strides. In the past ten years, life expectancy has increased across the globe to just over 95 years. We've begun the process of terraforming Venus, and Europa has officially been instated as the farthest human settlement in the solar system.

That said, humans are what they are. There are currently two international wars in progress, although neither of them are between constituents of the United Coalition of Nations. In terms that affect the work of you and your crew, it is unlikely that anything will come of them, but any loss of human life is a tragedy.

We have continued to monitor frequencies entering the solar system, and our continued expansion of the Receptor Buoy Matrix has yielded a few more interesting finds. Only time will tell if these are real signals like the Occassi were or simple flukes of astrophysical phenomena.

As with previous broadcasts, the most popular and influential media of the last five years has been attached with this message. For your enjoyment, there are 67 virtu-films, 249 music albums, and 614 books being sent. It may take up to a week for them all to buffer into the Votum's system due to the limitations of Mazer communication, but as I understand it, there should be relatively little data loss, even at this distance.

[shuffling papers]

I'll also be including a few notes about the transition of the directorship, but I won't bore you with that now. In the annals of history, it'll be nothing more than a footnote.

As always, you have the best hopes and wishes of all those on Earth behind you. May your long journey come to a fruitful end.

Director Ivanchuk, out.

TRANSCRIPT ENDS

CHAPTER 2

Day -48

"He was an asshole anyway."

Rhett looked up from his meal, nearly choking on the bite. The tech officer, Markus Braaten, stood in the doorway to the mess hall, tugging at the thin hairs of his soul patch.

"What?" Rhett managed.

"Bischoff," Braaten clarified.

Rhett blinked at him. Henry Bischoff, the ExTA's first choice for security officer on the mission to Occassus, had been killed six days before in the hypersleep wing on deck 7. According to the Votum's anatomy scans, he'd been suffering from acute hypersleep mania at the time, which had driven him to first wake and then attack a dormant crewmate. Unfortunately for Henry, he'd selected the tank of Rhett Wethern, the ExTA's second choice for security officer on the mission to Occassus.

"I'm serious," Braaten said, approaching Rhett's table. "The man was *anything* but a people-pleaser."

Rhett pursed his lips. "I'm sure you know a lot about that."

Braaten laughed, strutting over to the meal vendor and tapping out a string of requests on the Imageglass screen. "For me, it's a matter of desire. If I want people to like me, they do. But honestly? Most of the time I don't care."

Rhett released a quiet sigh. For the past half hour, he'd been enjoying the silence of the mess hall. Though the ES Votum was a large ship—nearly a kilometer long, more than a dozen decks tall, and boasting over 12,000 crew in stasis—the constant stream of training, briefings, and re-acclimation therapy tended to keep the five people who'd been woken early for the mission in relatively close proximity. Moments of solitude were infuriatingly hard to come by, despite Rhett's tendency to wake before 0500 hours.

Braaten sat across from him and began the methodical preparation of his first cup of coffee—or, as Caldwell preferred to call it, 'cream'. "I'm just saying we're better off."

Rhett didn't answer. He stared at the reconstituted brick of eggs on his plate—already half-eaten—and wondered how he'd managed to make it that far.

"Listen, meathead," Braaten said, taking a sip from his aluminum mug. "I'm trying to give you a compliment."

Rhett didn't bother looking up. "I must have missed it."

"Heh." Braaten set his mug back down and took his first bite. He chewed for few seconds. "It's a diplomatic mission, right?"

Rhett set his fork on his tray.

"So we need people who... you know." He took another bite but didn't pause to chew it. "People who have control of themselves."

"And you think I'm that?"

Braaten shrugged.

"You watched the recording."

"The old man wanted my opinion." He was doing it again. Calling McNeary—the diplomat they had promoted to captain so they could put him in charge of the mission—'old man'. Rhett wouldn't have been bothered by it except that the man was barely thirty and that Braaten would say it to his face. "And sure, Bischoff didn't stab himself, but it was pretty obvious he had it coming." He took another bite. "How's the arm, by the way?"

Rhett stood.

"Hey. Hey!" Braaten gave him an incredulous look. "I just sat down."

"I'm not your friend, Braaten."

Braaten grinned, taking another bite.

Rhett ignored him, sliding his tray into the slot and making for the door. Just as he reached for the control, it slid open.

CHAPTER 2

McNeary stood on the other side. He was a robust man, especially for lacking any military service, but the softness of his cheeks and gut made his opinion on exercise clear enough. He glanced between Rhett and Braaten with his cool, calculating green eyes and pursed his lips. "Corporal." He dipped his chin toward Rhett. "A word?"

He must have thought using Rhett's rank was a sign of respect—an homage to the chain of command Rhett was used to operating under—but given that he was himself a civilian, it came off as grating instead.

"Sir." Rhett said the word as impassively as possible. At least it got him out of the room with Braaten.

He followed McNeary down a long corridor to the briefing room. The diplomat closed the door behind them.

Rhett waited for the man to say something. Instead, he simply studied Rhett like a treaty with suspiciously worded fine print.

"Sir?" Rhett eventually asked.

"Caldwell's given you a clean bill of health," McNeary said, never letting up his strangling gaze. "With all the usual caveats."

It made sense now to Rhett why the man would make a good negotiator. Right now, all he wanted was to end this conversation, no matter what he had to trade to do so.

"I'm fine," Rhett said.

"Is that so?" McNeary raised a red eyebrow. "I heard the end of your conversation in there with Markus. Seems to me like you aren't making much effort to integrate with the team."

Civies. Rhett rolled his eyes. "Braaten is..."

"Arrogant?" McNeary supplied. "Abrasive?"

"An asshole."

"He is. He's also brilliant in a way neither you nor I will ever understand."

Should have put him in charge, then. Rhett made a face at the thought.

"I understand your hesitation," McNeary said. "And under normal circumstances, given what you've been through, I think protocol would dictate that you get some time off to recover from it. *But.*" He raised a finger—an acting trick they had probably taught him in diplomat school. "These are not normal circumstances. We have before us the single greatest assignment any team of humans has ever had put before them. First contact is one thing, but a treaty? A permanent alliance with an alien race? It's the culmination of almost a century of research, preparation, and strategizing."

Rhett pressed his lips into a thin line. He sounded like Cyn's father. Always lecturing. Always trying to define what was what and how things should be. Rhett had thought leaving Earth would get him away from that.

"Corporal, I need you to look at me."

Rhett did so.

"You can't afford this."

"Afford what?"

"This anger," McNeary said. "Not toward me. Not toward Braaten. Not toward Bischoff. For one thing, it's going to make people doubt the test results."

"I don't have the mania," Rhett said.

"I know that. But do you?"

Rhett rolled his eyes again.

"I'll put it this way." McNeary lowered his voice. "After what happened with Bischoff, you're fighting an uphill battle for the minds of the crew. They don't trust you. They don't *know* you."

"Why do you care?"

McNeary gave him a long look, then turned and walked across the room to shuffle through some papers on the table near the front. "Let's say I don't. What do you think happens next? We perform decel maneuvers over the next month, enter orbit around Occassus, and then the mission starts. Let's say no one on the crew likes you. Let's say no one on the crew trusts you. What then? Can't put you back down in hypersleep, can we?"

"Afraid I'll get lonely?"

CHAPTER 2

McNeary smiled thinly. "If we land on that planet and can't trust each other, what happens to the mission? Sure, we might all do our best. We might even be the best options for our roles. But if we can't trust each other?"

Rhett gave him an unimpressed look. "All I have to do is keep you brains alive. I don't need you to like me to do that."

McNeary took a slow breath. Rhett wasn't sure he was getting to the man—from what he'd seen since waking up, the diplomat was pretty unflappable. Even so, McNeary took a few moments before responding. "Henry Bischoff. The man you killed."

Rhett stared at him.

"You served under him in the Pacific Union Insurrection, correct?"

Rhett dipped his chin.

"How well did you know him?"

"Three years his subordinate. Can't say we talked much."

McNeary didn't seem surprised. "Did you know he wrote a book? A memoir. I can't say it was the most riveting thing I ever read, but there was one bit that stuck with me. 'Do not consider odds. Consider possibilities. Otherwise, you'll be surprised at the worst of times.'"

Rhett sighed. "Meaning?"

"Suppose the Occassi mean us harm."

"Then we're fucked," Rhett said flatly. His impassive expression was well-practiced from his time in the service, his anxiety stuffed down into the toe of his boot. He flexed his foot as if to crush it.

McNeary gave him a look like he'd failed an inspection. "Suppose only *one* of them means us harm. Suppose you need to warn us about it. Or suppose that we're in a compromised position and it's up to you to get us to safety. What happens if someone hesitates because they don't trust you?"

Rhett rubbed his forehead with his thumb and forefinger.

"When it comes down to it..." McNeary adjusted another stack of papers but didn't seem to actually be looking at them. "It's my job to make sure we're successful. I can't be sure what that will take, though we've been supplied with a strong foothold for negotiating this treaty and are coming in armed with some of the brightest minds Earth had to offer. But we can't do our best work while we're worried about our safety—especially if the possibility of danger is from within our own team."

Rhett groaned. "Just tell me what you want."

"I want you to try," McNeary said, his tone making it clear he thought it was the easiest thing in the world. "It doesn't have to be Braaten, but I need you to make an effort to integrate with the team. I know you have mixed feelings about being woken when you were—about not being the ExTA's first pick for the post. You must be doubting yourself. Questioning if you really belong. Whether you're cut out for this. Believe me, the others are wondering the same thing." He let that sit for a long moment as he straightened the last stack of papers on the desk. "I don't doubt you, Rhett. I've seen your record; I know what you've been through. I know what you sacrificed to be on this mission. You'll have your chance to prove yourself to the others, but in the meantime? You need to at least convince them that you're safe."

Rhett didn't know what to say to that. His mouth hung open half an inch, but for a long time, nothing came out of it. "Sir," he finally said, regaining his trained passivity. It irked him that he'd let it slip—apparently this diplomat had enough strategic sense to stage an effective ambush.

McNeary nodded, apparently content with the response. At last he seemed to find the paper he'd been looking for, holding it up for closer inspection. "If you'd go find Galerkin and send her my way, I'd appreciate it."

Rhett stared at the wall. "Can't you ping her, sir?"

"She likes to disable it while she's working." McNeary shrugged. "I think you'll find her in her quarters—she should be almost done translating the greeting I drafted to send to the Occassi now that we're on final approach."

Rhett tried to force himself to relax, but he couldn't stop the fingernails of his right hand from biting into his palm. "Sir."

CHAPTER 2

So far as Rhett had been able to find, there wasn't a chair to be found in the entirety of the storage deck. He'd tried to simply tough it out at first—after all, he was used to standing hours at a time, given his military background—but thanks to his recent stay in hypersleep, he'd needed to make other plans. After only an hour and a half, the cramps in his legs nearly had him falling over, and he'd conceded to find a stool in the engine room and carry it through the halls and up the elevator to his post.

He wasn't the quartermaster, per se. The real quartermaster was a man by the name of Lee Chun, frozen down on E deck with many of the other auxiliary members of the crew. He wouldn't be pulled out of hypersleep until discussions with the Occassi were complete and they were ready to put the Votum down on the planet. So for now, it was Rhett's job to gather and organize the materials his team would need for their mission. It wasn't glamorous work—hardly work at all, if you listened to Braaten—but it was what needed to be done, and Rhett was available to do it.

"It's all I am," Rhett muttered to himself as he sat down on the stool and logged into the logistics station. "Passable backup."

It hadn't really bothered him—at least consciously—until McNeary brought it up. Bischoff wouldn't have been better for the job, but the fact that Rhett hadn't been the first choice...

No. Rhett didn't care. Bischoff had been a higher rank and had more experience. Of course he would be the first choice for such an important mission. And now that he'd... well. The point was that Rhett would do a perfectly good job of it, now that he was in this position.

He sighed as the logistics management database rendered across the Imageglass, instantly overwhelming him with a thousand tiny lines of text. There were filters, of course, and widgets, and a dozen other features for making the data more usable. Rhett's face twisted into a grimace. He'd been trained on all of it, at one point in time. The trouble was, that was now more than a hundred years in the past. Sure, he recognized the interface, and he could picture what some of the related screens looked like and what they were supposed to do, but how to get between them?

"Firearms," he whispered. It was probably the easiest place to start. Everyone on the team would need, at the very least, a small weapon for self-defense. The protocol for the mission allowed him to requisition up to a Phi-8, which would probably be excessive for most, but it would certainly lessen his worry. "Yeah... we'll start there."

```
PERSONAL LOG
RECORDED BY: Shamus McNeary, Captain
LOCATION: ES Votum, Outer Edge of Occassus System
TRANSCRIPT BEGINS
```

[clears throat]

This is Captain Shamus McNeary, aboard the ES Votum on approach to Occasus II. Per mission protocol, my team has been awoken from hypersleep to prepare for our diplomatic mission with the Occassi. From a technological perspective, the waking went as expected, but there was an incident involving one Lieutenant Henry Bischoff, who had been originally selected to work with my team as security officer. After exhibiting extremely erratic behavior, he took his own life, leaving us with no choice but to wake his understudy, Corporal Rhett Wethern, to fulfill his role in the mission.

Steven Caldwell, the team's medic, noted that hypersleep mania has been observed before and that more protracted stays in hypersleep—such as the 135 years the crew has endured during transit to this system—probably increase the risks associated with it. Nevertheless, the careful planning of the mission and the tenacity of my team members leave me with full confidence that the immediate danger is past. When it comes time to wake the rest of the passengers aboard the Votum, we will take every precaution to ensure the safety of every soul aboard. If the need arises, Caldwell has referred me to a list of chemical sedatives that can be used to alleviate the acute trauma of the waking process.

[pauses 1.5 seconds]

The mission, then. According to the Votum's calculations, we are approximately forty-eight days from arriving in orbit around the planet. My team is in the process of preparing a message to announce our arrival to the Occassi, which we aim to send within the next hour. Following the expected transmission delays, we hope to receive confirmation of the terms we discussed for our arrival. With any luck, the Occassi living there today will be just as friendly as the ones we made an alliance with 135 years ago. After we navigate the expected hoops of diplomacy, the Votum will land in the region the Occassi have set aside on their planet and establish the human colony-embassy that will ensure long-term peace between our species. Assuming their capacity for spaceflight mirrors our own, they will be arriving on Earth with the same intentions within the decade.

As the Votum performs gravity-braking maneuvers around the system's gas giants, my crew is busying themselves with recovery from hypersleep. As expected, we all experienced some measure of muscular atrophy, but that should be fixable before we enter orbit. Slightly more concerning are the results of our neural scans and mental aptitude testing, which are landing a few points lower than they were before they put us on ice. Caldwell assures me the decrease is likely temporary—a symptom of our disorientation and readjustment to our situation—but I can't make the assumption that he's right. Nothing good ever came just from hoping, so I'll make my plans assuming he isn't.

[pauses 3.2 seconds]

I think that's everything for now. I'll record again once we hear from the Occassi. McNeary out.

Day -46

Her tank looked just like the rest of them. A slate grey exterior, smooth and pristine, with a network of pipes, hoses, and wires sprouting from the top like a mass of unruly hair. There was technically a window, but it was tinted so dark that it appeared completely opaque from the outside. The small Imageglass panel next to it gave a simple readout about her health—although in this state, the best it could do was to report all systems as 'nominal'.

Rhett slouched against the opposite wall of the corridor, pretending to focus on the training module being spouted from the tablet lying face-down next to him.

At least Cyn was here. He kept telling himself that, kept replaying the words from her recording in his head. At least after all of this was done, he'd get to be there when she woke up. They could talk like they used to, and she could help him sort all this out.

But the mission came first. It wouldn't be that long, in the scope of things. After all, he'd spent the last 135 years sleeping. What was a few more months without her?

Rhett sighed.

"Let me guess." Sarah Galerkin—the team's translator and expert on Occassi culture—stood at the end of the corridor. "A Brief History of Occassus?"

Rhett glanced toward her. She was dressed in civilian spacer coveralls and somehow made it look remarkably professional. Her abundant black hair was pulled up against the back of her head, her make-up subtly and precisely accentuating the features of her dark face.

Rhett frowned down at the handheld beside him. He flipped it over, then nodded to her.

"Kind of makes you want to get back into the tank, doesn't it?" Galerkin smirked, leaning against the bulkhead just inside the door.

She was keeping her distance from him, wasn't she? Was it like McNeary had said?

Rhett frowned. "Is that what you want me to do?" It wasn't actually an option. The technology required to put someone into hypersleep was as enormous as it was complex. Every tank on board had been 'packed' with its passenger in a specialized facility before being loaded.

"What? No." Galerkin chuckled awkwardly. "It was a joke. I mean… I wrote it. That's my training module."

Rhett pursed his lips, glancing back at the screen in his hand. Until just then, he hadn't realized it was Galerkin's voice narrating the steady stream of images. "Huh. You don't talk the same."

Galerkin shrugged. "I know. It's something about being recorded. My voice jumps up an octave."

"McNeary's drops," Rhett said. "I think he thinks it makes him sound more official."

Galerkin laughed.

Rhett studied her for a few seconds. Up until now, the few words they'd exchanged had been terse but professional. With the initial salvo of communication needing to go out to the Occassi as they approached, she'd been pretty busy. And Rhett being what he was to the crew, it wasn't much of a surprise.

This seemed different.

"Are you doing all right?" Galerkin asked. Her tone was soft, caring. The look in her eyes…

Rhett looked away. He didn't need her pity. "He's not the first person I've killed."

Galerkin's expression went blank. She seemed to be deciding something, her lips slowly drawing thin. "You know I cried, right?"

Rhett blinked. He hadn't been expecting that. "You knew him?"

"Not for Henry." Her voice was clinical, the way it normally sounded when she talked. "When I woke up. After all that time in the quiet and the dark with only my thoughts... my brain couldn't take it. I cried for almost five straight hours when I woke up."

Rhett couldn't picture that. He looked back at Cyn's tank. Would it be like that for her? He hated seeing her cry. He hated it even more when he knew it was his fault.

"What I'm trying to say," Galerkin said, voice soft again, "is that it's traumatic at the best of times, and yours was far from the best. Caldwell says the system went through all the normal steps when waking you—an emergency protocol given the circumstances of your tank—but even so..." She shook her head. "I'm just... I'm sorry that it happened that way."

Rhett didn't know what to say, so he said nothing.

Galerkin approached slowly, glancing one by one at the names on the tanks that she passed. Her face twitched a bit as she read some of them—a hint of recognition here and there. She stopped when she reached the panel of Cyn's tank. "Your wife?"

"Girlfriend," Rhett answered.

Galerkin's eyebrows rose. "A scientist?"

"An artist. Landscapes, mostly."

"She must be quite good." Galerkin folded her arms over her chest. "The allotment for artists wasn't that large, but I can see the appeal. What could be more extraordinary than being the first to paint the landscape of an alien world?"

"I hope so."

Galerkin looked at him, her mouth opening slightly, then closing again.

Rhett's eyes narrowed. "What?"

"I was just going to say it's too bad she isn't awake right now." Galerkin shrugged. "But I imagine that's exactly what you've been thinking the whole time you've been sitting here. Just... never mind."

"Why?" It was one thing when Braaten was being obtuse; he liked that Rhett couldn't follow what he was saying. But with Galerkin, it didn't seem intentional. "What about right now?"

"*Il'ryzik karthuum*," Galerkin said. The words seemed to jump between coming from high in her nose to deep in her throat—a characteristic he'd been told to expect from the Occassi language. "The Solemn Giants."

She seemed to think that would clear up his confusion. No such luck.

"The *gas* giants," Galerkin sighed. "We're using a series of planned slingshot decelerations using their gravity wells over the next few days. For a little while here, we're going to be right up close."

Rhett blinked again. "Ah."

"Do you want to see?"

Rhett considered.

"You could take some pictures. Then Cynthia can paint them when she wakes up."

Rhett shook his head. "She never paints from photos. Says it takes the life out of the work. She has to be there... has to feel it for herself."

Galerkin chewed on the corner of her lip. "You could describe it to her. It isn't the same, but it's better than nothing. None of us will ever get this view again."

Rhett looked up at her skeptically. She offered him a wan smile and a determined gaze. "You aren't going to just let me sit here, are you?"

Galerkin exhaled sharply—almost a laugh. "If that's what you really want."

Rhett doubted that. Even so, he found himself nodding. "Sure. I'll look."

He wasn't good at describing things, but that wasn't the point. As much as Rhett hated to admit it, McNeary was right. They needed to trust each other. The better the relationship between Rhett and the others on the team, the better off the mission would be. And for what it was worth, Galerkin seemed to be trying to make it easier on him than the others.

She led him through the ship, prodding him with questions about his youth, his education, and his reason for applying to the mission. He answered curtly, but that didn't seem to annoy her like it did most people. In the time it took to reach the ship's observatory, he felt as though he'd said more than he had since waking from hypersleep.

Caldwell was seated at a table in the corner when they entered, scanning through some memo or other on the tablet in front of him. He nodded to Galerkin but gave Rhett a subtle double-take. Rhett ignored him, following Galerkin over to the broad window that separated the compartment from the darkness of space.

"How far are we?" Galerkin asked.

Rhett frowned, but when Caldwell answered it was clear enough who she'd been speaking to.

"Ten minutes?" Caldwell said. "Markus may be toying with us, though. Has us turned around so we won't see it."

Galerkin stepped up to the window, leaning almost up against it to look in the direction the ship was moving. "No, it's there. Any minute now."

They waited. Slowly, a brilliant teal curtain was pulled across the void outside. Swirling tempests of blue and yellow and black battled for dominance in Rhett's view, blotting out thoughts of grief and hope and self-pity alike. It was everything. So massive. So *impossibly* massive. The enormity of it just about flattened his mind. When it was over, he found himself slumped in a seat, his eyes feeling heavy and sunken.

"How," Rhett muttered, "could I possibly describe that?"

Chapter 3

```
MAZER BROADCAST
SOURCE: Earth
RECEIVED: January 15th, 2203
TRANSCRIPT BEGINS
```

Good morning, Captain. Director Ivanchuk checking in again.

I believe congratulations are in order! It has now been sixty years since your departure from Earth, and telemetry continues to look promising. If everything continues as expected, you'll be reaching the Occassi system in just under seventy-five years. Though the Votum has been doing the bulk of the work, given your current state, I maintain that this milestone is worth celebrating.

Speaking of milestones, it was confirmed earlier this year that another positive signal was parsed by our Receptor Buoy Matrix. Though I have not been directly involved, I understand that our initial communication with this new species—they call themselves the Xchthar—has been promising. And to think... 150 years ago, before we made contact with the Occassi, we didn't know what to expect from a first contact. Would they be friendly? Hostile? Would we be able to recognize any part of who they were or how they acted?

It just... strikes me as important. With the Occassi, there were people in the scientific community warning of the threat they might pose. Warning that we might not understand them the way we need to. That they were dangerous and should be treated as such.

But here we are, 150 years later, and we're two for two. Just makes you think... maybe the galaxy isn't so hostile after all.

As usual, I've attached an annotated history of the decade here on Earth, along with a host of entertainment options for you and the crew. There aren't as many this time—it's getting more expensive to convert the media backward into formats that the Votum will be able to process—but I think the team here has done a pretty good job of converting the most important ones from the last few years.

Here's to another seventy-five years of transit. To you, Captain, and the crew of the ES Votum: you carry the heart and good will of humanity with you. Make us proud.

Director Ivanchuk, out.

TRANSCRIPT ENDS

Day -39

"There's no mistake, sir," Braaten said, although he sounded like he couldn't quite believe it himself. "That's it. The last thing we received from Earth. There's nothing after that."

Captain McNeary rubbed at his temples, studying the display over Braaten's shoulder. They'd been called together to the observation deck to listen to the transmissions Earth had sent while they were under. It was supposed to take hours to get through them all—something Rhett had been dreading all morning. Instead, it had taken just under fifty-eight minutes.

That, Rhett thought, was decidedly worse.

"It's a mazer transmission," McNeary said. "Very precise, but very narrow. Did you check our course?"

"Obviously." Braaten scoffed. "Everything went exactly according to the original flight plan. To be honest, it's a lot cleaner than I expected. No compensation for any gamma bursts or unpredicted comet trails. As much as one can across cosmic distances, we came straight here."

McNeary stood there frowning for almost a full minute. Rhett leaned against the wall at the back of the compartment, studying the others. Caldwell was seated next to Braaten at his own terminal, desperately scrolling through log entries and periodically giving McNeary nervous glances. Galerkin sat alone at the communications console to their right, closing her eyes and listening intently for what had to be the sixth time to the recording in question.

"They could have scrapped the program," Caldwell suggested, tugging on the short white tip of his beard.

Braaten shook his head. "The broadcasts *were* expensive to send, but I find it hard to believe they would can it without notifying us at all."

McNeary stood upright. "I agree."

"And what about the other aliens?" Caldwell gestured vaguely toward his screen, "They could have mis-assessed the threat. A dark forest sort of situation."

"Smart, bringing that up." Braaten rolled his eyes. "Especially when we're just about to arrive on an alien planet. But no. They would have sent us something, *especially* in a situation like that."

To his credit, Caldwell seemed unconcerned by Braaten's utter lack of manners. He flicked his hand in the air to dismiss the response.

Captain McNeary grunted, running a hand through his slicked-back red hair. "Sarah?"

Galerkin looked up, tapping the earpiece to silence the recording. "There isn't any distress in his voice. If he had any suspicion that either the program was on the brink or that the Xchthar were a threat, I would probably be able to tell. If something happened, it happened suddenly."

McNeary nodded, glancing back toward Rhett. He paused for a moment. "What are your thoughts, Corporal?"

Rhett hesitated. "I'm... not really qualified to guess."

"Earth is twelve lightyears away, Corporal." McNeary clasped his hands behind his back. "None of us are 'qualified' to guess what happened there."

Rhett glanced toward Braaten, who eyed him in quiet warning. "I'm not a scientist."

"No." McNeary took two steps forward, expression stern as a drill sergeant's. "You're a soldier. A man who understands protocols and contingencies. And, I hope, a man who respects his commander enough to answer a question."

Rhett gritted his teeth at the use of the word 'commander', but there was nothing to be done about it. "My opinion is that it doesn't matter. Whether they missed us with the beam, scrapped the program, or started World War IV, the result for us is the same. We're on our own."

Braaten raised his eyebrows. Caldwell cleared his throat, wiping his brow and turning back to face his screen. McNeary simply nodded, face impassive.

"We should send a message." Galerkin stood, setting the earphones on the console in front of her. "If they only missed us, we can help correct their aim."

"Yeah, and we'll get the response in twenty-four years." Braaten rubbed at his forehead. "Besides, the telemetry has still been going out from our end. Since their last broadcast, they should have received at least half a dozen info packets from the Votum."

Silence hung like a choking cloud in the compartment.

"Corporal Wethern is correct," McNeary finally said. "Regardless of Earth's fate, our mission remains the same. We make contact with the Occassi, confirm our alliance with them, and we get these people safely to the planet's surface. When all that's done, we can focus our efforts on the mystery we've left behind."

Rhett dipped his chin, but it didn't feel like a victory.

"Sir," the others said, one after another.

"Now," McNeary said, turning back to Braaten. "Can you confirm the status of the message we sent to the Occassi?"

Braaten didn't even glance at his console. "It should have arrived days ago. No response yet."

CHAPTER 3

"And the planet?" McNeary returned to his side, studying the screen over his shoulder. "What do we know so far?"

Braaten gave the captain a disapproving look, but obliged him and brought up a new panel summarizing the details they'd gathered on Occassus II. "As I was telling you earlier, they don't appear to be broadcasting anything, but we're still too far away to tell much more than that."

"We're still in the midst of the gas giants." Galerkin crossed the room toward them, frowning at the readout. "The magnetic fields could easily interfere with incoming radio signals."

"Naturally, I looked only *now*, when the interference was highest." Braaten scowled. "We've been recording everything coming this way from them for *decades*. And it's been that long since they last made a sound. As of right now, I can't see any evidence of an advanced civilization living on Occassus II."

"That's enough," McNeary said. "We can't presume to know anything about the situation on the planet. For now, we await their response to our message."

The implication was clear, but unsettling.

If there is one.

The room would have been silent if not for Galerkin marching back to her station and hooking the earphones back on. "I'll look closer at the logs. We've received hundreds of communications from them. The origin was pinpointed and confirmed a dozen times over. It was definitely Occassus II."

"Yes," Braaten said, "but the last communication from their side was over seventy years ago—even before our last contact from Earth."

Caldwell paused. He'd been stroking his beard so consistently for the past few minutes that Rhett hadn't noticed until he suddenly stopped.

"No," Galerkin said, furiously tapping at her controls. "They're not gone. They can't be." She swept through the list on the screen before her, shaking her head vigorously.

"We came all this way," Caldwell muttered. "We can't be…"

Rhett stared at the others, dumbstruck. "We're alone?"

Galerkin glanced back at him, eyes growing puffy and red. "They could be underground. In hiding. Something. There's no reason to think they're all gone, even if we haven't gotten a signal in so long."

"We're not alone." McNeary's baritone cut through the rising noise, summoning their attention. "There are twelve thousand souls in hypersleep on the decks below. Regardless of the circumstances of our arrival on Occassus II, our duty to them remains the same."

He looked at his subordinates, one after another. "I understand this will take some time for you all to process. Unfortunately, we don't have any more time now than we did an hour ago. We're due to reach the planet in just over a month. When we do, we must be ready to complete our mission—which is and has always been to ensure the survival of the human race. If we can discern the nature and the cause of the Occassi's fate, we will learn from it. Whatever happens, we must all put forth our best. We rely on each other—for the good of all."

Day -35

```
PERSONAL LOG
RECORDED BY: Shamus McNeary, Captain
LOCATION: ES Votum, in gravity assisted deceleration
near Occassus IV
TRANSCRIPT BEGINS
```

[breathing for 3.4 seconds]

This is Captain Shamus McNeary, aboard the ES Votum on approach to Occassus II.

CHAPTER 3

[clears throat]

I... I suppose you must know if you're listening to this.

[coughs]

If the systems aboard the ES Votum can be believed, we have not received any contact from either Earth or the Occassi in several years... Several decades, actually.

[breathing for 1.6 seconds]

The mission... The mission has changed.

My team was selected for their intellect, their ability to think on their feet. We were selected to make contact with the Occassi and cement our alliance with them. We had all the groundwork laid for us, but we were prepared to deal with a number of issues. Technological hurdles with making their planet safe... methods of communication that we'd have to work out when contact wasn't delayed by twelve years in either direction...

But not this.

[silence for 2.3 seconds]

I'm not qualified to lead this mission. To be honest, I'm not sure who is. I've checked the passenger manifest three times over the last few days. Looking for someone... anyone... who might be better at this than me.

I found a few. Commander Tobias Black looked like a good option. Experience in leading a couple exploration missions to the outer planets of the solar system. Captain Ingrid Savasta, too. Her work in stabilizing the civil war on Ganymede was impressive, to say the least.

But I couldn't bring myself to wake them.

It's my team. My duty. My mission. I don't say that proudly. I don't say that because I think I deserve it. That I would covet this command if it were not already in my hands. The truth is...

[silence for 4.1 seconds]

I don't know what I'm saying. The burden is mine to bear. I couldn't give up my command for one reason and one reason only: if I handed it to someone else and something went wrong, that would still be on me. My legacy... my purpose...

I was put in this position. Me. I didn't ask for it, but here I am. How can I put that on someone else? How could I even sleep if I did something like that?

I guess there's always these...

[silence for 2.9 seconds]

[swallowing]

It doesn't matter. The crew depends on me. They look up to me. If I handed off the helm, it would shatter their faith. Their courage. Their strength. It doesn't matter what I think. It doesn't matter what I feel. What matters is that I have to hold them all together. Caldwell. Braaten. Wethern. Galerkin. If things are the way they look, they are the future of humanity. The fate of our entire species rests in their hands, and without me to ground them—to make them believe—they will buckle.

How could they not?

[silence for 4.3 seconds]

We'll know more in the next week. Braaten is modifying the sensor arrays on the Votum to give us a better look at the planet once we clear Occassus III's orbit. With that...

With that, we might have an idea what we'll be dealing with down there. Best case scenario, they've had some kind of event that's set them back a century or two. If we play it smart, there's a chance we can be the hand that leads them to recovery—hopefully earning our place on their world for good. Worst case scenario, the planet isn't habitable anymore. And if that's the case...

Nah. Borrowing trouble. Intel first, then we'll make a plan.

Mmm.

[breathing for 3.7 seconds]

It'll be fine.

It's going to be fine.

[exhale]

Captain McNeary, signing out.

CHAPTER 3

There were eight magnetopellets in a Phi-8 magazine. Rhett liked to count them, two at a time, four times.

One, two.

One, two.

One, two.

One, two.

Reload.

The Votum's shooting range wasn't large. Only four lanes. If everyone on the vanguard team followed his advice and came down here for some practice, there wouldn't be room for all of them. But since it was only ever him, he was starting to think of the range as excessive. What was the point of all this space if it was only used to help one man think?

Sometimes, if he was really trying to focus, he'd count rounds four at a time, but twice.

One, two, three, four.

One, two, three, four.

Reload.

The charge on the sidearm's battery would only go for a dozen or so magazines before he'd have to swap it for one off the charger. The product labeling said fourteen, but that was bullshit.

He'd been trying to count for the better part of an hour now, but with everything going on, he kept finding himself lost on the count after seven or eight magazines. He knew what Braaten would say, of course. *Meathead can't even count to ten.* It would be a stupid thing for him to actually *say*, of course, because using a weapon with the stopping power of a Phi-8, a trained soldier usually only had to count to one.

Rhett felt a breath of air from his left and glanced that way. The door slid closed as Galerkin stepped into the range.

Rhett nodded to her, setting his firearm on the bench and removing his earplugs. She was wearing something like her usual expression—stern and calculating, deliberately obscure and professional. But there were differences. A tightness to the cheeks, a sunkenness to the eyes. He'd seen it before, dozens of times. It was the face people made when they were trying not to show how much they were shitting themselves over what was going on around them.

"You here to shoot?" Rhett asked.

She met his gaze. Nodded.

"Ever handled a weapon before?"

She paused. Shook her head, bracing as if for some critique. But she wasn't talking to Braaten. She was talking to Rhett.

"I'll show you."

He'd been trying to convince everyone to come down here and get some practice in for days. Now that their mission was looking increasingly complicated, it seemed more important than ever. Galerkin was the first person to take him up on it.

He explained the parts of the gun to her first, trying to mimic the clerical, teaching tone she used when talking about the Occassi. He wasn't sure how successful he was, but she nodded along and asked a question here and there. He helped her position her hands, take a proper stance, and line up the sights on the unused target down-range. After a few missed shots, she managed to score a couple hits near the edge.

"Not bad." Rhett loaded a second pistol so he could resume shooting next to her. "You can use that once we're down on the planet. Get used to it now, and you'll be more comfortable with it when the time comes."

"I don't want it." Galerkin fired a few more shots, emptying her magazine, then pulled the trigger twice more, looking confused as it made its characteristic buzz—the electronic equivalent of a click.

CHAPTER 3

Rhett held out another magazine toward her. "Pull back on the button on the left side."

She did so, sliding the spent magazine free and trading Rhett for it. She loaded the new one, lined herself back up the way he'd showed her, and pulled the trigger a few more times. These shots were a bit wild—she wasn't squeezing the trigger like he'd told her—and she lowered the gun, releasing a sigh.

"Things usually come easier for you?" Rhett asked. He took a couple shots himself, landing all of them within a few centimeters of the center of the target.

"Is that what you think?" she asked. "That everything is easy for the rest of us? That you're the only one that earned your way here?"

Rhett frowned. "I'm the one who didn't. Remember?"

Galerkin hung her head, a single obsidian curl escaping from the knot at the back of her head. "I'm sorry. You didn't deserve that."

Rhett turned back to the target, trying to remember how many mags he'd gone through since he last swapped the battery. It was no use, though. He had lost count again. "Why don't you want the gun?"

She lined up again, took a deep breath, and fired twice more. Closer, but still missing the target.

Rhett flicked the switch on the wall to bring her target ten feet closer. "Don't hold your breath. Just breathe smoothly."

"As if I'll be breathing smoothly if I need to use this thing."

"No. You won't."

She glanced at him.

"You taught at a university, right?"

"Selkford, yes."

"Do you practice your lectures?"

"Sometimes." She lowered the gun. "Depends on who I'm giving them to."

"What good does that do for you?"

She shrugged, returning the firearm to the bench. Rhett flicked the safety on his, setting it beside hers, then did the same for hers.

"It just goes smoother. Don't have to look at my notes as often."

"Same thing here," Rhett said. "Practice until you don't have to think about it anymore. Until you don't need to focus on it to get it right. Because when you actually need it? You'll be focusing on something else."

She chewed her lip, nodding contemplatively. Her eyes stood fixed on the pistol for a little while, then shifted to her target down the range. "I don't want to need it."

"That doesn't mean you won't," Rhett said. "That's what I've been trying to tell everyone."

"I don't have enough time to get good at this. There are too many other things that need done."

"By you?"

She fixed her dark eyes on him, an angry stare that told him he was right.

"However much time you have," Rhett said, "it's better than no time at all."

Galerkin turned her resentment on the gun, then picked it up, switched the safety back off, and lined up on the target.

Day -28

"Well, it's good to see the swelling going down," Caldwell said, inspecting Rhett's arm. "It could have been a lot worse, you know. Considering how it happened."

"As I said." Rhett shrugged.

The medic clicked his tongue, opening and closing three different cabinets before finding what he was looking for. Given the number of passengers on board the Votum, it made sense that its medical bay was so large—sixty beds, lined up in complex rows and separated by plexishield projectors—but with only the five members of the vanguard team awake, it seemed rather excessive.

CHAPTER 3

"Yes, well..." Caldwell chuckled nervously, adjusting the nozzle of a propellant can and dispensing a thin layer of anti-inflammatory over Rhett's arm. "I can understand that." The sharp, rhythmic exhale sounded less like a laugh with each repetition. "And you're sure you don't have anything to report? No... extraneous emotional repercussions?"

Rhett gave him a look.

The man studied him for a long moment, the age of his face seeming a fragile veneer covering a bright and insightful soul beneath. He was probably almost sixty, but between his manner and his sense of humor, it was hard to think of him as 'old'. "I know you said you're fine, but if you aren't... it wouldn't be shameful to say so. There are a variety of options available for calming the nerves—several that are routinely prescribed for victims of trauma and for the management of hypersleep mania symptoms."

"Do I look manic to you?"

Caldwell narrowed his eyes at him, giving appraising glances to the veins in his temples and neck. "I'll admit that you're not showing most of the classic symptoms."

"Aside from the homicide."

Caldwell choked for a second, then coughed for several more.

"Come on." Rhett shook his head. "It's been weeks since I was brought out. You can't still be worried about the mania."

Caldwell regained his composure with a long breath. "It varies. Some people show no symptoms at all; for others, it can take up to a year for them to fully subside."

"A year." Rhett raised his eyebrows. "Can't say they mentioned that in the training."

"It's very rare," Caldwell said, returning the dispenser to the cabinet. "If the clinical numbers can be trusted, there will only be one or two among the whole twelve-thousand colonists who struggle for that long. And again, there are effective treatments, so long as we can identify the problem before..."

"Someone dies."

"Well." Caldwell hesitated. "Yes."

Rhett stood, rolling down the sleeve of his uniform and wincing as he refastened the cuff at his wrist. He glanced toward the medic, who appeared to be waiting for an answer. "I'll let you know."

Caldwell's expression didn't change.

Rhett frowned. "What?"

"You seem..." Caldwell scratched at his scalp. "Never mind."

Rhett's frown deepened. "What do you want, Caldwell?"

"What? Nothing. That wasn't what I—"

A pair of low electric tones announced an overhead communication. "Attention, crew," McNeary's voice said. "Your immediate attendance is required in the observatory."

Caldwell and Rhett looked at the speaker overhead, then at each other.

"That doesn't sound good," Caldwell muttered.

"Name one thing that has since we woke up."

Caldwell pursed his lips. "Some of the options in the mess hall are okay."

Rhett didn't know how to respond to that.

When they reached the observatory, Braaten and the captain were arguing over what they saw on the display table. They looked up as Caldwell and Rhett entered but resumed where they'd left off without further greeting.

"It can't be a natural phenomenon," Braaten insisted. "It defies too many natural laws."

"But there's no active energy usage on the surface." McNeary jabbed a finger at the display.

"Not from a technological standpoint. Not as far as we can detect."

"So there isn't anything maintaining it," McNeary said. "Nothing technological to explain its existence. So it must be natural."

"Not *necessarily*." Braaten huffed, giving Caldwell a nod as he approached the table. "Take a look at this. You probably have a—"

"What in God's name?" Caldwell stared at the screen on the table's surface. "Is that... is that where we're going?"

CHAPTER 3

Rhett approached more cautiously, glancing in the space between bodies until he made it around to an empty side. "What? A hurricane?"

"Meathead." Braaten barked a joyless laugh. "If only."

"Take a look at the size." McNeary gestured toward the scale at the side of the screen.

Caldwell gaped. "It's over a thousand miles across."

"Sounds big," Rhett said.

"Twelve hundred," Braaten corrected. "And yes, that's 'big'. Four times the size of a typical hurricane, although not quite as large as the record on Earth. But look at its location."

"It's over land," Caldwell said. "Hundreds of *miles* inland. It should have lost a ton of strength that far from the ocean."

"It has," Braaten said. "And look at this." He tapped a series of buttons on the display, remapping its colors from photographic to infrared.

Caldwell's eyes narrowed. "1800 degrees Fahrenheit?"

Rhett leaned closer. "Just in the eye, though."

Braaten sighed. "That's hot enough to melt glass, meathead. And that eye is nearly twenty miles across."

"Huh," Rhett muttered. "No wonder they're gone."

"We still don't know that," Galerkin said.

The other four looked up with a start. Apparently, Rhett wasn't the only one who hadn't heard her come in.

"There's no signal," Braaten said. "No sign of artificial electromagnetic fields. No lights on at night. I think it's safe to say we'll never meet them." With a smirk, he added, "Guess you got woken up for nothing."

The captain gave Braaten a warning look. "We still don't know the extent of the damage. Remember: possibilities, not odds. When we enter orbit, we will be able to make more accurate assessments. For now, I need Braaten and Caldwell working on a solution."

"Solution?" Caldwell raised an eyebrow. "A solution to…"

"The storm."

"It's not just a seasonal thing," Braaten said. "Before we got close enough to discern the planet's actual rotation speed, we were accidentally measuring it based on the speed of the storm. It's circled the planet four times since we've had eyes on it, and projections suggest it's been doing that for decades."

"And you want us to find a *solution*?" Caldwell shook his head. "What does that even mean?"

"It means," McNeary said, "that if Braaten is right and it isn't natural, you need to find out what's causing it so we can stop it. And if it *is* natural, we need to scour through the personnel logs to find a meteorologist to wake up so they can help you invent the science of manipulating weather."

Caldwell nodded slowly, glancing between the captain and Braaten.

"We have twenty-six days until we establish our orbit," McNeary said. "I think it would be best if we had a plan by then. Understood?"

"Come on, old man," Braaten griped. "What are we supposed to—"

"I don't know," McNeary snapped, eyes wild. He regained control in an instant, returning to the same placid expression he usually wore. "You're the scientists. I know you didn't sign up for this challenge, but it has been placed before us. Given the information we have, there's a good chance the entire human race is relying on what we do right here, right now." He looked at his crew, one after another. "We're a team. We're *the* team. We can't flinch. Can't waver. Can't back down. It's forward or nowhere at all. We find a way. All right?"

"Right," Galerkin said, stepping forward. "We find a way."

Braaten rolled his eyes. "Sure. The *doctor* and *I* will find a way."

"Yes," Caldwell agreed, discretely brushing something from his cheek. "We will."

Rhett gritted his teeth. As he glanced around the group, he was reminded how much he didn't belong. He hadn't been chosen for this. He wasn't as smart as they were. And even now, not one of them trusted him.

"Corporal?" McNeary turned his eyes on him, followed by the other three.

Rhett hesitated. "Sure. It's not like there's somewhere else to go."

The others nodded slowly, as if what he'd said was somehow meaningful or wise.

"All right," McNeary said. "Let's figure this out."

Chapter 4

Day -19

PERSONAL LOG
RECORDED BY: Shamus McNeary, Captain
LOCATION: ES Votum, on final approach to Occassus II
TRANSCRIPT BEGINS

[clears throat]

This is Captain Shamus McNeary.

[breathing for 4.1 seconds]

Things are worse than we realized. I had hoped that whatever destroyed the Occassi would be long gone by now. Given that it has been 74 years since our last communication from them, events like a nuclear war would have had most of their side-effects settle by now. At least enough to work around.

But the Occassi... well, they got creative about how to end their civilization. The brains on the team are pretty sure the storm was created, although they haven't been able to tell me how yet. All I can say is that it makes no goddamn sense.

[sigh]

I've been watching it as we get closer. It's all I can do sometimes. When I can't sleep, I pull up the latest telemetry and just stare at it. Swirling... slowly swirling... swelling and shrinking... consuming and destroying everything it passes. I stare into

CHAPTER 4

its eye, which is starting to visibly glow with the heat. I sometimes feel like it's staring back at me. Sucking me in. Growing larger and larger...

I need to sleep more.

If only I could.

[silence for 4.3 seconds]

[swallowing]

[breathing for 2.9 seconds]

I've asked the crew to make recordings of their own. This mission... if we get through it, it will be one of the most important turning points in human history. In the next couple months, we will either save humanity or doom it forever.

Heh... no pressure.

[breathing for 5.3 seconds]

I can't be the only one recording. I can't be the only voice the history books show. Not me.

Not me.

If you're listening to this, it means we made it through. We figured it out. We saved everyone.

I guess... I guess I can pretend that's what's going to happen. For them, at least. I have to be strong... have to be confident... have to...

[swallows]

[silence for 8.1 seconds]

Yes. For posterity, I have ordered the rest of the team to make recordings in advance of our arrival on Occassus II. Differences in perspective, predictions, etcetera, will be important markers in understanding who we were and what we did here. If we succeed, history shows that we will be idolized. Elevated to the status of heroes. A myth in our own right.

But we don't deserve that.

Let these recordings show that we are human. Let them show that we are fallible. Let them show that we lack, that we fear, that we hope and that we despair. Let them show that being so—that doing so—did not stop us from succeeding in our mission.

That our imperfection was not enough to keep us from the salvation of the entirety of humanity.

Or, if nobody ever hears this...

[sigh]

...that it was.

McNeary out.

TRANSCRIPT ENDS

PERSONAL LOG
RECORDED BY: Steven Caldwell, PhD, Astrobiology (with Markus Braaten, PhD, Physics and Mechanical Engineering)
TRANSCRIPT BEGINS

[Braaten, distantly] For the record, old man, this is fucking stupid.

[Caldwell] Oh, Mark. It makes perfect sense if you think about it. This is a historic mission. Naturally, we should be recording our thoughts for posterity.

[Braaten] It already was *a historic mission, Chops. He didn't care what we thought until he realized the fate of the whole human race might be hanging in the balance.*

[Caldwell] And... that's not a good enough reason?

[distant sigh]

[Caldwell] Well, I think it's valid. And as I said, you don't have to do your own. Since we're working together, we may as well do it this way to save time.

CHAPTER 4

[Braaten] It's too bad they're being encrypted on the way in. Would have liked to hear the meathead's "thoughts". Do you think they'd be in cohesive sentences?

[Caldwell] I think we should probably focus on the task at hand.

[Braaten] And what, you can only do one thing at a time? Personally, I'm fully capable of parsing these materials lists and *throwing shit at our least productive teammate at the same time.*

[sigh]

[Caldwell, louder] All right. Log of Steven Caldwell and Markus Braaten, concerning our progress in solving the problem of the Hellstorm on Occassus II.

[Braaten] Really? Come on. "Hellstorm"?

[Caldwell] It's hot, isn't it? Killed an entire planet, so I'd say it came from hell.

[Braaten] No, no, no. It's a terrible name. Even ignoring the completely unscientific nature of the reference, it has absolutely no subtlety. Shit, it's good they didn't let you name the Votum. You would have called it the "ES Goes Far Away".

[Caldwell] I prefer "Heaven's Chariot".

[Braaten] Meaning what? We're all dead?

[Caldwell] What? No. I... never mind.

[clears throat]

[Caldwell] We've determined—

[Braaten] Think *we've determined.*

[sigh]

[Caldwell] I am in agreement with Mark that the storm isn't being maintained by any detectable macroscopic machinery. I also agree that it seems unlikely that it was active on the planet while the Occassi were thriving there, implying at the very least that it is new and more than likely unnatural in origin.

Although my expertise is not in astrobiology specifically, I was selected for this post in part due to my interest in xenobiology and extrasolar ecosystems. In my professional opinion, it seems plausible that the Hellphoon—

[Braaten] Nope. Shit, too.

[Caldwell] —has a biological cause. Given that, we are currently exploring material lists of what is in storage in the Votum's cargo bays in the hopes that we have what we need to target it from that angle.

[Braaten] Formaldehyde?

[Caldwell] Dangerous for us, too.

[Braaten] Mm.

[Caldwell] As of yet... there isn't much to report. But as we progress, I'll be sure to record a bit more.

[Braaten] Waste of time.

[Caldwell] Steven Caldwell, out.

TRANSCRIPT ENDS

Day -16

```
PERSONAL LOG
RECORDED BY: Sarah Galerkin, PhD, Xenolinguistics
TRANSCRIPT BEGINS
```

This is Sarah Galerkin, recording on April the 23rd, 2272. Report requested by Captain Shamus McNeary and inputted directly into the systems of the ES Votum, on approach to Occassus.

Tensions run high amongst the crew. It's hard to walk down a hall without feeling the weight of stress emanating from my crewmates. They have plenty of reason—our mission is taking us in an unexpected direction. But I believe that, when we touch down on the planet, things will be better than they look from up here. In space, only the largest objects are visible. Energy can only be recorded in massive quantities, and with a meteorological system like that moving around the planet, it isn't surprising that nothing else can be detected.

We've decided to send a distress signal back to Earth, regardless of the likelihood of it being answered in our lifetime. Though the situation appears dire, we must continue to plan for every eventuality. Nothing is ever as bad as it seems.

Regardless of the state of the Occassi's habitation of the surface, it is unlikely that whatever befell them managed to wipe them out completely. What my crewmates fail to understand is the resilience of intelligence. Humanity has, in the last three hundred years alone, evaded five different potential extinction events. Six, if you count this one—and once again, I'm not convinced that we should. The course that technology takes—especially when it comes to high output energy sources—has a tendency to be volatile in its early years until a species' social virtues catch up to their newfound technological abilities. It is my theory that we have arrived at just such a time in Occassi history—a time of tumult, loss, and destruction, surely—but one that will not overcome them. In a hundred years' time, they will be thriving once again, in a new position of respect for the dangers of the advanced tools they gave birth to, and we will be there at their side.

But regardless of my predictions for the mission, my role will remain integral even if we do—by some stroke of insidious misfortune—land on a truly dead world. Even if the storm managed to kill the Occassi, it cannot have eliminated everything they built. Certainly not so quickly. Tragic as it might be, there will be something to learn from what they left behind—if only for the satisfaction of the mystery. Though my crewmates have some measure of talents in their respective fields, only I am qualified to decipher the written and spoken language of the Occassi in whatever form we encounter it.

[silence for 2.8 seconds]

At this time, I do not believe I have anything more to add. To whoever listens to this, I wish you well.

TRANSCRIPT ENDS

Day -13

Excerpt from PERSONAL LOG
RECORDED BY: Steven Caldwell, PhD, Astrobiology
(with Markus Braaten, PhD, Physics and Mechanical Engineering)
TRANSCRIPT BEGINS

...

[Caldwell] Further study of the storm would seem to confirm my suspicions that its energy is at least partially biological. Spectral analysis of the air in front of and behind the storm indicate some very distinctive chemical shifts that indicate active catabolism near its eye. The logical conclusion is that the organisms—probably something like a bacteria—are either creating or directly benefiting from the extreme temperatures there. It's really quite remarkable, we—

[Braaten] What, you didn't record your rant about them the first time?

[Caldwell] No. I wasn't ready at the time.

[Braaten] So I have to listen to it all *again*?

[Caldwell] You can go if you'd like. But it was partly your discovery. I couldn't have calibrated the Votum's astromeric spectrometers by myself.

[silence for 2.2 seconds]

[Braaten] Fine. You can go over it again.

[Caldwell] Thank you. Now, as I was saying—

...

CHAPTER 4

TRANSCRIPT ENDS

Day -10

PERSONAL LOG
RECORDED BY: Corporal Rhett Wethern, Security Officer
TRANSCRIPT BEGINS

[silence for 12.1 seconds]

McNeary said I had to do this.

[silence for 2.9 seconds]

Like I'd know what to say.

Like anything I have to say is important.

[sigh]

It is what it is. I wasn't the one chosen for the mission. The mission isn't the one we came here to do.

[silence for 4.3 seconds]

Honestly not sure I'm that broken up about it. Don't hate me for it—meeting aliens was probably going to be... something. But what was I supposed to do during that?

This, though. Exploring a dead planet? Traveling long distances? Keeping an eye out for unknown threats?

At least I'll have something to do.

[silence for 2.7 seconds]
Not sure what else to say.
Guess that's that.

TRANSCRIPT ENDS

Day -6

PERSONAL LOG
RECORDED BY: Steven Caldwell, PhD, Astrobiology (with Markus Braaten, PhD, Physics and Mechanical Engineering)
TRANSCRIPT BEGINS

[Caldwell] This is Steven Caldwell, recording alongside Markus Braaten concerning the completion of the...

[Braaten] Stormpunchers.

[whistling]

[Caldwell] And you say I'm bad at names.

[Braaten] Well, I couldn't let you call them "God's Fists" or something.

[Caldwell] I don't think God has any need to fight with His fists.

[Braaten] Mm. Well, the stormpunchers. I won't get into all the technical details—although if you're interested, feel free to look at Engineering File 2272-0106, which includes the complete specifications. Hopefully all it will be needed for is the museum exhibit about me, but if we need them again, it's all right there.

[Caldwell] *Assuming they work.*

[Braaten] *You're still doubting?*

[Caldwell] *All I'm saying is that the design is running on a few more assumptions than might be practical.*

[Braaten] *Bah. We're out of time. The old man wanted it done, and now it is. If it can't do the job, we'll just have to work another miracle for him in record time.*

[Caldwell] *And every time I think I've understood the size of your ego...*

[Braaten] *The stormpunchers. In essence, they use a specialized electromagnetic dispersion technique to interact with the high-energy ions we are observing to be a hallmark of whatever is maintaining the storm's power. We had to build them compact enough to carry, so they don't have as much power as I would have liked, but given enough exposures between them and the storm, its power should steadily be reduced until it falls below the critical value of self-sustaining.*

[Caldwell] *I thought you said you wouldn't get technical.*

[Braaten] *You think* that *was technical?*

[Caldwell] *Have you ever even* talked *to a normal person?*

[Braaten] *Fine! Fine. We set up the punchers, the storm gets weaker. Happy?*

[Caldwell] *Better.*

[Braaten] *We've got five, one for each of us to carry, and I've charted the ideal deployment locations to optimize the diminishment of the storm. Fortunately, they're all on the same landmass—a supercontinent our translator is calling 'Miar'. Unfortunately, it's still going to involve a bit of travel on our part. But Chops has bothered to be useful long enough to locate a means of transportation that should make things a little easier.*

[Caldwell] *It's not much—the Votum wasn't designed with an exploration mission in mind—but it did come with a handful of deployable rovers. They're designed to fit three people each, plus supplies, so I've put in a request for the system to prepare two of them for launch alongside our own lander. So long as it works properly, we shouldn't have to travel far to get to them, and then we'll be able to move around the terrain fairly easily.*

[Braaten] So that's it. That's the plan. Chops and me, doing all the work. Figuring it out. Making it all possible. Happy now, old man?

TRANSCRIPT ENDS

Chapter 5

Day 1

Re-entry started with the shake. The whole compartment vibrated, the glow of the heat shield casting their narrow porthole windows in an angry light. It ascended to a sort of brain-rattling tremor, knocking around Rhett's grey matter after it had already been wrung loose by the recent hypersleep. His only salvation was that it would only last a minute or two. Once they were low enough, the deceleration thrusters would—

He felt a series of pops travel the entire length of his spine in a fraction of a second. While part of him was amused that the lander had been the most successful chiropractor he'd ever had, the other part was busy twisting his face up from the sudden burst of pain. That was from the hypersleep, too. It took the joints a bit to remember they could move after you woke up, despite the PT they'd been doing in the time since.

135 years was a long time in hypersleep.

The pressure against the bottom of his boots slowly lessened as their descent stabilized. A minute later, the only weight that pressed up against him was the gravity of Occassus itself.

He glanced to his left, assessing his comrades where they sat strapped into a row. Caldwell was the only one in obvious pain—unsurprising, considering his age. Braaten wore a rueful grin, but the set of his jaw, the gap between his teeth... there was an anxiety to the expression that he looked to be trying to hide. Galerkin's face was all relief. She'd been intensely silent all morning as they prepared for the drop, and now that they were on the ground, she looked like she would seriously consider kissing it. McNeary wore a mask as impassive as the dead space between stars—as if nothing were going on and there was never a need to worry.

How does he do that?

"Everyone all right?" McNeary asked.

"Think I chipped a tooth," Caldwell answered.

Galerkin grimaced while Braaten only narrowly contained a nervous laugh.

"Well, so long as that's the only broken bone we've got to deal with." McNeary unclipped his harness, stretching as he stood. "I'd say that our first time landing on an alien planet went remarkably well."

The others stood too, each migrating to their various stations on the lander to check systems and prepare to disembark. Their supply packs, including each of their stormpunchers, had already been prepared before they landed. Rhett punched the code into his locker and hauled out his pack, snapping the belt around his waist. He sighed at the underwhelming standard issue Phi-8 sidearm but strapped it to this thigh and slipped his extra magazines and batteries into his suit's utility pockets.

"The ship is sending confirmation of our landing location," Caldwell announced from his station. "We're about a week in the shadow of the storm. Shouldn't have to deal with it again for... 214 days, according to this calculation."

Rhett frowned. "I thought you said it was circling the planet every few days."

"It wobbles, meathead," Braaten said tersely. "Doesn't pass the same spot with its eye except for once every several dozen revolutions."

"Handy."

"It isn't, actually," Braaten said, rubbing his forehead as if he were having trouble explaining something to an idiot child. "It means there isn't a safe place on the planet. Maybe it doesn't hit a certain spot too often, but you can't settle down anywhere knowing it will be at most a year from being melted into glass."

Rhett pursed his lips. "Ah."

McNeary cleared his throat. "Do we have confirmation on the SLOOPs' landing positions?"

Caldwell nodded. "Importing to our navbraces now."

With a too-cheerful beep, everyone's left wrist synced up with the Votum's latest telemetry.

"Should be good to go," he said, shining the visor on his helmet before putting it on—as if it wouldn't get dirty immediately with all the dust the storm had kicked up.

Rhett resisted the urge to face palm, then checked the systems of his own suit. Everything was in the green—so far so good.

"Anything we should be looking out for, Sarah?" McNeary asked. "You've studied the ecological records the Occassi sent us."

"Come on, old man," Braaten groaned. "You saw the storm. 1800 degrees, remember? Nothing's going to have survived that."

McNeary gave him a look of admonishment. "I should think a scientist would know it's dangerous to be too certain about anything. You said yourself there will be pockets the heat will have missed."

"And *those* will have experienced nearly three-hundred mile-an-hour winds. I'm just saying—"

"We might be among the last humans alive in the galaxy." McNeary leveled a stare on him. "And while we were napping, we missed the door closing on the only two civilizations we knew to be friendly. If our mission fails, I will not have it be because of *your ego*. Is that understood?"

Braaten blanched. His mouth moved as he stared at McNeary, then toward the others. Heat rose to his cheeks, and for once he had nothing to say.

Maybe McNeary was a captain after all.

McNeary moved on. "Everyone showing the locations on their navbraces? SLOOPs and deployment sites?"

"Sir." The answer bounced around the confines of the lander.

"Good," the captain said. "Final checks, then, everybody. Sidearms. Bags. Stormpunchers. Suit systems. Make sure everything's in the green. We're not going to waste any time."

Rhett and the others nodded. "Yes sir."

The last two helmets clicked into place, sending the manufacturing company's hallmark jingle through each of their earpieces. Braaten punched his access code into the door control, following the others as they stepped into the airlock.

McNeary glanced at Caldwell. "Remind me what their atmosphere is like again?"

"Almost breathable, sir," Caldwell answered. "Chemically, its ratios are very similar to Earth's. But with that storm..." He nodded, as if his meaning was clear.

The captain turned his whole head toward him, presumably revealing a raised eyebrow.

"It kicks up a lot of shit," Braaten filled in, not even sparing Caldwell a glance. "Dust. Sulphur. A handful of other novel chemicals the ship's computer predicts to be noxious."

"*But*," Caldwell added, "the filtration units on the suit can handle it. The main thing we're left to wonder is how often we'll be replacing the filter modules. Best guess is once every month."

The captain, seeming satisfied, nodded to Caldwell at the airlock cycler. With a few more key presses, the door closed behind them, and a mechanical whir heralded the start of their mission. But when the outer hatch folded open, blasting them all with a wave of warm air, the entire crew held their breath.

They had expected it to be barren. They'd expected destruction and emptiness as far as the eye could see. What they had not expected was the shining, glittering *brilliance* of the wasteland. The very ground glistened, rolling like honey into the distance in rivulets and bulges.

"Glare shields, everyone," McNeary ordered.

At the press of a button, a twelve-nanometer-thick screen swooped down over each of their visors.

Caldwell stooped, brushing a gloved finger over the smooth surface below them. "It really is." He shook his head. "It's glass. This must have been a desert, and the storm melted it."

Rhett shrugged. "Could have been nukes."

"Negligible chance," Braaten grunted. "Not enough radiation."

"Even if it didn't happen recently?" Rhett blinked at the landscape, trying to get a sense of scale. With no relatable features like trees or grass, it was difficult to judge distances more than a few dozen feet away.

"Meathead." Braaten rolled his eyes. "So they survived their own nuclear apocalypse, only to wipe themselves out hundreds of years later in some other way? Do you know the odds of—"

"Possibilities, Markus," McNeary reminded him.

"Doctor Braaten," the scientist snapped. "I have a PhD. Two, in fact."

"Certainly not in social skills," Caldwell quipped.

"Enough." The captain raised a hand—not as if to strike, but as if to offer surrender. Oddly, this seemed to be enough to silence them. He turned to Galerkin. "How much do we know about their history? Is it possible this... geological feature—"

"I'd hardly call it *that*."

"—was not caused by the storm?"

The translator looked pensive for a long moment, her fingers idly fiddling with the thumb break on her thigh holster. She was the only one Rhett had managed to convince to carry a weapon. "As much as I hate to admit it, we don't know much about their society or history. Just because we haven't gone to the brink and come back doesn't mean they never did. We don't know how common that is for intelligent life."

"Well, this is the brink." McNeary gestured around them, then to their lander. "We don't need common. Just possible. That's why we're here."

Most of them nodded, but Rhett simply checked his navbrace, trying to orient himself with the distant mountains it indicated to the northeast. They should be no more than forty miles away, visible based upon the curvature of the planet, but they eluded him in the haze of distance. He didn't like that, tactically, but he reminded himself they weren't here to fight a war.

At a gesture from the captain, they began their trek across the glass dunes. Little bits of small talk were exchanged as they walked. Comments about the cloud shapes—not unlike Earth's, if a little browner. About the temperature—warm for wearing so much suit, but they'd trained in worse. About the gravity—perhaps a fraction more than Earth, or was that the comparison to the artificiality of the Votum's?

After an hour, the glass beneath them began to show patches of more recognizable stone and was eventually overtaken by dirt and gravel.

"It must have been beautiful," Galerkin said.

A few of them looked at her, but none of them answered. They were all thinking the same thing. This burned-out husk of a planet must have looked very much like Earth had. And now it might still look very much like Earth *did*.

"It may be again," McNeary offered. It felt flimsy, even for his optimism.

After another hour, the silence of the planet began to weigh on them. Oppressive in its omnipresence, the stillness seemed to reach through their suits with a chilling hand. Their presence—their noise—was an unnatural thing in this place. An *unwelcome* thing.

Cyn wasn't going to like this.

"Is there no green at all?" Rhett asked.

"From what we gathered based on their communications with us," Galerkin said, "their biosphere isn't based around photosynthetic autotrophs."

Rhett blinked at her.

"There's no plants, meathead," Braaten said. "Never was."

"But there *are* autotrophs," Galerkin added. "If we're translating correctly, they sound like chemotrophs, although I am sure we'll know more once we get to see an actual specimen."

Rhett nodded, pretending he knew exactly what she meant. "And those? Any of... those around?"

"Depends on the latitude," Caldwell answered, tapping his fingers on his navbrace. "Above forty-two degrees both north and south, you start to see some signs, even from orbit. Not much between, though. Nothing nearby."

"Path of the storm is the best place to stop the storm," Braaten said. "Doesn't need to be pretty."

CHAPTER 5

"And we're sure there's no trace of advanced life above those latitudes?" Galerkin asked, studying an image on the navbrace on her wrist.

Caldwell shook his head. "Nothing detectable. The Votum did a full sweep, and not just for radio spectrums. It checked infrared. Chemical signatures. Signs of energy use. Didn't come up with a single thing from pole to pole."

Galerkin nodded, lowering her navbrace, but her expression remained pensive.

"How long did you say the days were again?" McNeary asked as the sun began to descend before them.

"Twenty-five and a half hours." Braaten shrugged. "Minus a few minutes."

The captain nodded. "We should pitch camp long before night comes. I want us safely inside our prefabs before dark."

"But I just said, there's nothing out h—" Braaten began to protest.

"On a mission with the whole of the human race at stake," McNeary snapped, "it pays to be cautious."

Braaten pursed his lips. "A little on-edge there, old man?"

McNeary leveled a stare at him that said all it needed to. He would act the diplomat when he could, but he would be captain when he had to.

"How long will it take before we can take these masks off?" Caldwell broke the silence. "I've got sweat pooling up to my ankles in this suit."

"The models diverge depending on where the storm is on its cycle when we get the last stormpuncher up," Braaten answered, his voice now lacking its usual abrasive levity. "But once they are all in place, most models predict it will be a handful of months."

"*Months.*" Caldwell spat the word out like an insect that had crawled into his mouth. For a moment, he actually looked his age. "I won't make it days."

"The prefabs filter air, too," McNeary said. "You'll be able to take it off any time we've sheltered for the night."

Caldwell tried to scratch his head but found the back of his helmet in the way. He swore under his breath.

"I still don't understand why we didn't leave a couple people awake up there," Rhett said. "Just in case we need backup."

"Backup?" Braaten sneered. "How could they back us up? There was only one lander on the Votum."

"Seems like poor planning." Rhett had been wondering about that.

"Do you have *any* idea how large interstellar distances are? They couldn't just send everything along with us. Same reason we couldn't haul a hypersleep packer all the way out here."

Rhett shrugged.

"And what about food?" Braaten kept pressing. "It's a limited resource on board. Want them to starve if things take longer than expected down here?"

What an asshole. Rhett narrowed his eyes at him. "Longer than months?"

Braaten laughed. "I'm sure you have a better plan."

"We could split up," Rhett suggested. "We're each carrying a stormpuncher. Each of us has food and water and a prefab. We could each hit our destination in, what, a matter of weeks?"

Though he'd aimed the comment at Braaten, it was Galerkin that answered first.

"You want to walk out there alone?" She stopped walking, prompting the others to do the same. "By yourself?"

"It would only be weeks," Rhett recovered sluggishly, surprised by the sudden addition of a second front to his battle. "A month, tops. A quick sprint and this is all over, rather than a marathon together."

Braaten shook his head. "That is about the stupidest thing I've ever heard. Guess it's no surprise, coming from you."

"You think I *want* to be out here alone?" Rhett scowled. "I just want to get this over with."

"Enough!" The captain slashed his arm through the air. "Corporal, you know exactly why we can't do any such thing. It might look like an empty planet, but it doesn't take something alive to kill you. And if none of us are there to help each other when something happens? Little mistakes have fatal consequences. Weren't you the one just talking about backup?"

Rhett knew he was right. Obviously he was. But McNeary's placid exterior had slipped for a moment, revealing a side Rhett had not seen before. A side the captain might not have wanted seen.

Fear.

But who wouldn't be afraid? In such a strange place? With such great stakes? They knew almost nothing about this world, and yet they walked its surface as if nothing could touch them, living or dead. They thought to change the shape of a *world*, and yet they'd only been here for a handful of hours. The audacity.

"We could have landed nearer to the first deployment site, don't you think?" Galerkin scowled as she once again studied her navbrace. Her breath sounded faintly labored over the microphone.

"Not according to projections," Caldwell replied. "Our current landing zone will be out of the way for the next several cycles of the Hellstorm, based on its Coriolis wobble."

"I told you we're not calling it that," Braaten said.

"Then what *do* you want to call it, smart guy?"

"We could call it the Eye," Braaten suggested.

"The Eye of Occassus?" McNeary expounded.

"How about the Glass Storm?" Rhett offered.

"Eye is good." Galerkin nodded. "In Occassi, though. 'Nuhalriu'."

A few grunts answered her, and they moved on.

The dirt and gravel field transitioned steadily into rolling hills, bare and crumbling from the wind. Before long, they found themselves on the bank of a river. It flowed slowly, but its depth suggested its current might be deceptively strong.

"You saw this on the map?" McNeary eyed Caldwell, who had been assigned navigation duties to ensure Rhett could focus on their 'moment-to-moment tactical situation'.

Caldwell nodded, taking deep enough breaths to be heard through the microphone. "Walking its bank looked to be the smoothest topography. The SLOOPs won't be far once we cross it."

"Where will we do that?"

"An old bridge."

Most of the others frowned as the captain spoke for them. "An *Occassi* bridge?"

"We'll have to judge its stability, of course," Caldwell said, "but all indications are that it's made of a sort of granite local to this region. It would be difficult to knock down even if you wanted to."

They came upon the bridge less than an hour later. True to his word, it had been built broad and thick. Its arches swept wide over the water, hinting at a complex set of details that might have once been engraved into its various faces. Now, the entire thing had been worn almost smooth save for the grossest architectural motifs.

"Can you believe it?" Galerkin's whisper came through volume-adjusted by their comms. "The first time we've seen actual *alien* architecture. It's almost... almost a fusion between Greco-Roman and Indonesian designs. But not quite..."

"Looks strong enough," Braaten said. "We maybe could have landed on it."

It might have even been true. It stood almost forty feet wide, with twenty feet from its top to the water. A simple marvel, but one that had survived the test of time. It was no wonder it had been detected from space.

They crossed in the planet's continued silence and spotted the oblong re-entry crate a few minutes later. Following the Votum's calculations, it had set down in a slight bowl in the landscape, where it wouldn't easily be seen from longer distances. Rhett and Braaten pulled the release levers on either side of the hatch, watching as the side wall of the container folded open like a ramp. Inside were the two SLOOPs, light-duty traversal vehicles that could each seat three with a little cargo. Although the large hoop-style wheel that surrounded the cab made them look futuristic, Rhett reminded himself they were designed to do essentially the same thing as a golf cart—if a little faster.

"Didn't realize I was joining a monocycle gang." Caldwell chortled, stepping up to one of the machines. A ladder hung from the side of the cab, its bottom rung a couple feet from the ground. It looked like it should topple when the man put his weight on it—tipping the wheel toward him—but it only leaned about an inch his direction as he began to climb.

"Gyroscopic stabilizers," Braaten said. "Keeps them from wobbling."

Rhett glanced toward him.

"Your mouth was hanging open."

It hadn't been. Rhett had seen vehicles like this in the service, and they were surprisingly common in the outer colonies. From what he understood, their design worked better in the combination of rough terrain and reduced gravity.

"Let's minimize the chatter." McNeary approached the second SLOOP. "We still have a long way to go today."

Nightfall came slowly, but the crew kept a steady eye on the sun as it made its descent. At the captain's orders, they began to pitch camp a few miles from the riverbank, poised on a small rise that gave them a clear vantage for several miles in each direction. The ground was suitably flat, even soft, making deployment of their Personafab™ prefab shelters a simple matter. They huddled around a small deuterocine stove while Rhett did the honors of heating up a rack of five nutrient plaster cylinders.

"I'm going to miss the ship's food," Caldwell admitted. "After a hundred thirty-five years of that, this hyperfood stuff... it just isn't the same."

"You ate the ship's food a total of what, two-hundred times?" Braaten narrowed his eyes at him. "You can't count all the years in cryo."

"You've got it wrong, smart guy." Caldwell grinned ruefully. "I'm not an old flat yet. Still have my metabolism. I've been eating the ship's food at least four times a day."

"What?" Braaten scowled at him. "I haven't had my metabolism since I was thirty. How could you..."

Caldwell shrugged. "Not enough to do while we waited to enter orbit."

"No wonder you were always late while I was working on the punchers," Braaten said. "Damn it, you're almost as bad as the—"

"Plaster's up," Rhett announced, cutting him off. Protected by their gloves, they each pried a cylinder from its snap-enclosure on the heating rack. After a moment of struggle for a few of them, they found their suit's nutrient aperture on the left side of their abdomen and slid it open. Once the cylinder clicked into place, the suit performed its function of mixing the plaster with the correct dose of water and feeding the slurry up through the mouth hose in their helmet.

"Ack." It was McNeary complaining this time, but he kept it simple.

"Chocolate flavored?" Caldwell saw his opportunity and took his turn. "They had to ruin a perfectly good flavor by making it taste like... like..."

"Ass?" Braaten supplied.

"Ass can be better," Caldwell said. "It's a matter of hygiene."

"Please." Rhett grimaced. "Let me enjoy my terrible food in peace."

They grumbled their assent, watching together as the orange sun of Occassus touched the eastern horizon. The sky, which had been a dull shade of grey-brown for most of the day, blossomed into a vast array of colors that seemed all too familiar. It shouldn't have surprised Rhett that a planet with such a similar atmosphere would have similar sunsets, and yet he might have been able to forget, if for a moment, that he was almost twelve lightyears from his birth planet.

"They have a name for that?" Rhett wondered.

"The sunset?" Galerkin asked.

"The sun."

"Baitahili." After a moment's pause, she expounded. "It was actually one of the first words we exchanged with them. A sort of universal symbol of common ground. We were two peoples, so far apart, yet we both had experienced life beneath a sun."

"It's remarkably similar, too," Braaten offered. "Main sequence, similar surface temp. Main difference is the K vs G spectral type."

"And it's orange."

Rhett smirked as the scientist took the bait, glowering at him like he was a moron. "Yeah... that's what having a K spectral type means..."

McNeary grunted, flicking his wrist as if to dismiss a bad smell. "Shouldn't objectify her like that. The old one's gone. Left behind. This one... Baitalia? She's the only one we've got now."

"Baitahili." Galerkin repeated the word, but no one was listening. They were still staring out at the sun as its last edge began to sink below the distant hills.

Caldwell nodded, pondering. "I guess I could get used to this one."

They retreated into their prefabs a few minutes later. They weren't much, in terms of shelter—just an automated aluminum frame sheathed in a neofiber mesh. The air quality and temperature regulation was handled by a boxy console near the foot, which also served as the face of the device when it was folded up for transport. Rhett had set up a few sensors, which came online with a series of beeps and jingles. If anything approached their camp, they'd know about it. Just in case.

Rhett sat quietly on the bed-floor of the tiny room. The ceiling hung low above him, illuminated only by a strip of red holoescent tubing. He'd paused halfway through stripping his suit, letting the upper body of it hang about his waist in the disorderly clumps of its in-borne technology. His helmet hung on the far wall, staring back at him through its horizontal cyclopean eye.

Through the thinness of the prefab walls, he could hear the captain's voice, no doubt recording another one of those messages. History in the making, he kept saying. He was obviously right, assuming they succeeded, but Rhett couldn't bring himself to like it. To be at a crux of history—or in this case, *the* crux of history, if there was to be any more of it—was a place of unimaginable pressure. Anything they did would be recorded. Remembered. Judged. History would always remember that Caldwell was eccentric, Galerkin was an intellectual, Braaten was an asshole, McNeary was a wise and cautious leader, and that Rhett... what would they remember about him? That he was impatient, maybe. He already regretted his suggestion to split up. It was stupid. Reckless. His crewmates would remember that.

Why was he so worried now? He'd known he'd be in the limelight when he signed on for the original mission. Meeting an alien race? Forging a treaty of asylum? Setting the groundwork for a colony of humans on their planet? None of that was inconsequential. None of that would have been forgotten, at least by anyone who would live on Occassus. They would have been heroes.

Wouldn't they still?

He stripped the rest of his suit, plugging its four data and power cables into the wall of the prefab at the foot of his bed. After a moment of fiddling, the navbrace came free from the rest of the suit. He strapped it to his bare arm before lying back against his pillow.

They weren't supposed to have any personal data on their navbraces. ExTA policy. But like most soldiers who'd served more than a few years, he'd found himself a navbreaker back on Earth to sneak a small cache onto the device. He flipped through a handful of images from his hometown. His mother was in one of them. His childhood dog. His girlfriend, Cyn.

His eyes wandered as his mind did, staring as if through the roof of his prefab. Somewhere in orbit, she was asleep on the ship, waiting for him and his crew to send the ready signal. When the talks with the aliens were finished, the captain was supposed to input landing coordinates for the whole of the Votum to touch down on the surface. They were supposed to begin a new life here. As much as the situation had changed, the plan in that regard was remarkably the same.

Rhett just wanted them to hurry up so he could see her again. He studied her picture on his wrist. They'd gone on a hiking trip together when he'd been on planet-leave. There were still a few wild places left on Earth. This one had been in Montana. She'd wanted to see mountains. Trees. Rivers. Lakes. Wild animals. Things she couldn't find in the city. They'd seen them all.

His smile slowly waned. What about this planet? What was here for her? There were mountains and rivers, yes. But trees? Wild animals? There weren't even any cities—at least not living ones. He sighed.

She hadn't even wanted to leave. Earth was her home, she'd told him. She didn't belong in space. Didn't like how big it was. And another planet? She'd practically broken down when he received his appointment for this mission. An appointment he'd never told her he'd requested.

CHAPTER 5

Rhett closed the album and returned the navbrace to its place on his suit.

"She's really going to kill me this time," he muttered. "If Occassus doesn't get me first."

Chapter 6

Day 3

PERSONAL LOG
RECORDED BY: Shamus McNeary, Captain
LOCATION: The Stormshadow Hinterlands, Occassus II
TRANSCRIPT BEGINS

This is Captain Shamus McNeary, transmitting on the third day of the Occassus mission. It's early morning now. My crew has yet to rouse, so I'm taking the opportunity to send this. The first few days of the mission have been...

[sigh]

As good as can be expected. My team is holding up better than anticipated, under the circumstances. Their spirits are being held aloft by humor for now, but I suspect that will pass in the next few days. There's a lot of work for us to do here, and none of us were explicitly prepared for any of it.

I... I trust them. I believe in them. I hope they believe in me. From what I can tell, I've made progress in uniting them and conjuring their loyalty. All I have to do is hold on, whatever it takes. I...

[breathing for 6.3 seconds]

It's getting harder. I don't like hiding it, but it's...

Would they even listen to me if they knew?

[sighs]

CHAPTER 6

But the... supplements... are working. That's what matters. That is what matters. It will pass with time, and these are helping me keep control. I don't have to do this forever. Not forever. Just for long enough... long enough to get them through...

[breathing for 9.8 seconds]

We can do this. We were chosen for a reason. We've trained to adapt and to problem solve. I have no doubt that we can succeed in our mission, so long as we can remain focused. The people aboard the Votum can rest assured that their fate is in good, capable hands.

But there are things to consider. The empty planet that we now walk leaves many questions and has supplied few answers. If we are to succeed—

[distantly] *Don't you think they know what we're up against?*

[grunt]

Good morning to you, too, Rhett. How long have you been there?

[silence for 1.3 seconds]

Never mind. If you'll allow me, I'm simply explaining our situation for historical purposes.

[distantly] *I understand what you're doing. I'm just saying, by the time they're listening to that, they'll already know all of what you're going to say.*

Firstly, it's a matter of procedure, Corporal. Secondly, it helps some of us to think certain things through out loud. With the stakes being what they are, I need to be my sharpest.

[distant chuckle]

[distantly] *Sharpen all you want, Captain. I'm going to wake the others.*

[sigh]

Fine. You're right. We should get moving.

I'll transmit again later.

McNeary out.

TRANSCRIPT ENDS

Day 4

"There's definitely a rumbling," Braaten agreed. "When did you say you first heard it?"

"I felt it." Galerkin pursed her lips, still breathing hard. "Three hours before dawn?"

"Anything obvious from the ship?" McNeary turned an eye toward Caldwell, who was feverishly flipping through orbital images.

"The Votum's last circuit was around that time, but her sensors aren't good at detecting seismic activity on such a small scale." The sweat on his brow was clear even through the visor of his helmet. "When she comes around again in forty-two min—"

"Too long." The captain rapped his knuckles against his forehead. "I thought you said it was dormant."

"It was!" Caldwell cleared his throat. "Is."

As if holding their breath could help them verify, the five crewmates stood still and watchful on the rocky slope. They'd left the SLOOPs behind an hour before to reach the deployment site of the first stormpuncher, and it was still more than two miles and 5000 feet of elevation gain to the top. Rhett, though a bit worse for the hypersleep, had been conditioned for the task by his hiking back on Earth and his military service. But some of the others, mostly Caldwell and Galerkin, were struggling.

"And if we place the puncher and then it erupts a few weeks later, then what?" Rhett pointed out. "Whether we're here or not when it happens, the mission's fucked."

"It *could* still work with four," Braaten said. "The timetable is a lot worse, though."

"How much worse?" McNeary eyed the slope above. It wouldn't matter what the answer was, Rhett knew, but the information would interest his obsession with 'possibilities'.

"Years instead of months." Braaten shrugged. "Maybe even decades."

Sounds like a winning option.

The captain only paused for a moment. "Can you calculate an alternative fifth location to this one?"

"I..." Braaten's brow furrowed. "It would take a few hours, but—"

"You'll do it when we pitch camp tonight." McNeary paused as another wave of rumbling shook the ground beneath their feet for a few seconds. They were getting stronger. "For now, we need to get off this mountain. This deployment zone is too dangerous."

For once, no one argued. They turned carefully, doing their best to mind loose stones that could easily roll ankles now that they were travelling downhill with their heavy packs.

While on the occasional stretch of relatively level ground, Rhett took a moment to appreciate the view. Though it certainly couldn't match any of the vistas he'd explored on Earth, this planet did have a sort of beauty in its dire serenity. They'd left the swath of glassed terrain behind them, trading it for a rocky and dust-strewn landscape that had been battered more by the wind than the heat. But ever since they'd reached the foot of this chain of mountains, little patches of almost-plant life had begun cropping up. Shrubs and grasses mostly, which the brains assured him were closer to fungi than plants, but their effect in transforming the feeling of the countryside had been immense and immediate. This wasn't an altogether dead place. This planet was still alive, just a little... empty.

Plus, according to Caldwell, they were good for the erosion.

Rhett rolled his eyes with a smirk, wobbling slightly as his foot shifted a bit under him.

Concentrate. You can mock your crewmates when you're not hiking down a maybe-not-so-dormant volcano on an alien planet.

Rhett scowled, scanning the hills below for what must have been the fortieth time that day. Perhaps the others had realized what the not-plant life implied, but perhaps they were still too gleeful in their honeymoon with something natural and alive. It seemed simple to him, though: if there was some life, there was probably more life. If there were not-plants to eat, there was probably something that ate them. If something ate the plants, then something probably ate the thing that ate the plants. It didn't take many steps like that before they had to be concerned about things that might be willing and able to eat *them* as well.

This apparently empty planet might be little more than a hiding place for something that could already know they were here.

At the time of that realization, his experience as a hunter in his youth churned to the surface of his mind. He began studying the ground, looking for spoor. Tracks would be hard to discern, he imagined, without knowing exactly how the creatures of this planet traveled. Did they have legs? Tentacles? Did they slither like snakes? It could be something altogether stranger than that, he realized. Would he even recognize scat if he saw it? Many terrestrial creatures on Earth had fairly similar scat, in terms appearance, and those that ate plants had a degree of similarity in their consistency, but once again he realized he was grappling with something beyond his ken.

His face resolved into a rueful grin as he realized he was actively wondering what alien shit looked like.

Yep. That was what you signed up for. Definitely.

The others didn't need to know yet. Or at least, they didn't need it spelled out for them right now. They were the brains anyway—they probably already knew. And there were enough risks in their current task that he doubted they needed yet another concern to grapple with. He'd tell them tonight, when they were relatively safe and had access to sturdy prefab walls behind which to ponder the possible threat.

"Are you sure this is the way we came?" McNeary asked.

CHAPTER 6

Caldwell shook his head. "It's a shorter way down. I figured we should probably get clear of the—"

A whooshing gunshot of a sound stabbed into Rhett's mind through his earpiece. It took a few seconds for him to gather himself, and a sharp ringing remained even as he blinked himself into a semblance of clarity. He was bent over, clutching his helmet. His memory rewound the moments that had brought him here—the earth shaking suddenly, a burst of hot air rushing across him, a voice suddenly cut short. Whose voice? He tried to remember.

He glanced around warily, finding three people crouched around him, shielding their heads as he was. Their suit colors revealed their identities. McNeary in his captain's red. Braaten in blue. Galerkin was behind him, her suit a rugged brown. Which left...

Rhett's eye tracked a crumbled mass as it plummeted twenty feet from him on his left. It struck the ground with a muffled thump, the sound muted by his helmet. The tactical part of him noted how much of a vulnerability that was. If something—the life on this planet that might be hunting them—was approaching, would they even hear it through their helmets?

McNeary's arms signaled them to hold. Once. Twice. Rhett realized the man's mouth was moving, but he wasn't hearing anything through his earpiece. Was it broken? But there was that damn ringing. It still hadn't gone away. Could it be his ear that was broken? He followed the captain's eyes back to Galerkin, who was staring at the object that had fallen from above them. It looked like she might try to crawl to it, knees down, one hand touching the ground beneath her, the other outstretched. She withdrew her hand, holding it over where her mouth was beneath the mask.

It finally clicked in Rhett's mind. Caldwell. The man had just been talking, and then...

Rhett tried to remember where the medic had been walking. His eyes found the spot, but there was only a crater there, inverted as if something had blown out of it, rather than into it. Dust and steam rose from it, and he could discern the stench of sulphur even through his mask's filters.

It must have been some kind of volcanic geyser. Caldwell had stepped in just the wrong spot and buckled the stones, allowing it to release its pressure in a stream of white-hot steam. For him to have fallen after so much time... how long had it been? Four seconds? Five? It didn't matter. They were standing in a minefield, and they'd only just realized it. Where it began and where it ended... how could they even guess?

McNeary had already figured all that out, of course. That was why he'd given the hold order. It was the only sensible thing for them to do, unless they could figure a safe way out.

McNeary's mouth was moving again. Still, there was nothing. The captain turned to Braaten, no doubt continuing to speak. From Braaten's expression of growing terror, Rhett suspected he couldn't hear anything either.

So they were either all deaf, or their mics were out.

They turned again to the crumpled form of Caldwell, lying in the dust a short distance down the hill. He had been wearing a green suit, but it was difficult to tell from here. Most of what Rhett could see was pink and red and brown. His suit must have ruptured, the force of either being launched or landing ripping through suit and flesh alike. There was no way he could have survived.

The crewmates looked at each other again, fear possessing most of their features. They might be able to find a way out of this, but if they couldn't even communicate without looking directly at each other? There was no way to warn each other of anything.

Rhett took a deep breath. He already knew what he had to do, but the others wouldn't like it. Still, it was his place on the crew to be reckless. It might be a flaw most of the time, but every once in a while, he could do something none of the others would even consider. He blinked slowly, confirming the utility knife he carried was still strapped to the thigh of his suit. Then he took another deep breath, held it, and clicked his helmet off and pulled it over his head.

The sound and feeling of a cool breeze joined the ever-present tinnitic whine. So he at least had *some* hearing left. If he succeeded, it would at least be worth something.

CHAPTER 6

He looked down at the helmet in his hands, studying the line between the breathing apparatus and the protective visor unit. They were manufactured by separate companies, joined together to suit both purposes. But that joining was a vulnerability. He slipped the knife from its sheath and touched the tip to the bridge of the mask's nose.

In his periphery, he could see at least one pair of arms flapping in alarm. He smirked at that as his blade finally bit through the welding plastic at the joint. His lungs burned as he continued to cut—one side, then the other—before finally he ripped the visor-helmet module free from the mask and filtration unit. With hands that had begun to shake, he slipped that part back over his head, engaging the seal once again, this time without any annoying jingle in his ear.

Air! He gasped a breath, gulping at it like a man dying of thirst. He looked up at his crewmates, whose eyes were filled with a mixture of awe and horror. His helmet was less than half of what it had been only a minute before. Now, it covered mouth and nose, much of his cheeks, and met its junction with the suit at his neck. The mouth hose and all the filtration systems were intact, but the eye, head, and ear protection it had offered were gone.

Rhett gestured to his empty ear, giving a thumbs-up. He could hear. He glanced back at Galerkin, making sure she'd seen it. She just shook her head, uneasy acceptance furrowing her brow. She motioned him toward her.

He focused on the ground, finding the marks his boots had made as he'd come to where he stood. Those same places should be safe again. He stepped carefully but soon found his way back to her. He signaled with his fingers to give her time to store her breath. Three. Two. One.

The helmet clicked off, snagging for only a moment where her tightly bound hair had been jostled by the explosion. He set to work on it quickly, this time knowing better where to cut and how. He handed it back to her with a nod, helping to guide the mask back into its slots at the neck of her suit. She waited for the seals to engage, then took a few breaths—deep and ragged from the trauma they'd just experienced.

She looked at him. "You know you're insane, right?"

"Just insane enough." Rhett nodded, tugging his earpiece out and tucking it into one of the pouches on his suit. The ringing continued. "Stay right there."

She grimaced but nodded. He turned and advanced toward McNeary next, who met him halfway with a similar care for where their footprints had landed. Surgery on his mask went even quicker than the last, and Rhett nodded his approval as he slipped the thing back over the captain's head. He looked different without the upper half of his helmet. It had only been a few days since they'd landed, but Rhett realized he'd already gotten used to the look of the captain through the visor. Now, with his eyes unguarded and his thinning red hair exposed to the brisk wind, he seemed somehow more vulnerable.

"We'll have to get back on the path we took here," McNeary muttered, turning again to the body down the hill. "Shortcuts…"

He shook his head, and Rhett became acutely aware that he was also referring to Rhett's own plan of splitting up from a few days before.

"We'll be more careful," Rhett said, glancing toward Braaten, who hadn't yet dared to move.

"I hope that will be enough."

Chapter 7

Day 7

```
PERSONAL LOG
RECORDED BY: Shamus McNeary, Captain
LOCATION: The Maroon Steppe, Occassus II
TRANSCRIPT BEGINS
```

I...

[breathing for 3.2 seconds]

I should have recorded this sooner. I just... I didn't know what to say. I didn't know how to say it.

[sigh]

I still don't.

[breathing for 1.7 seconds]

Three days ago, on the fourth day of our mission, Steven Caldwell... died.

We were on our way up the slope of a dormant volcano to place the first of the so-called stormpunchers. It was sudden. Unexpected. None of us were ready for it.

I don't know... I don't know why this one is so much harder for me. He isn't the first person to have died since we woke from hypersleep. Bischoff...

If I chose to think of it this way, I could even say all of humanity died since I woke up, save the passengers of the Votum.

But Steven... He was a good man. He deserved so much better. If it weren't for him, we probably wouldn't even have a plan for how to deal with the storm. Nuhalriu, the crew is calling it. Markus is brilliant, of course, but his gifts with technology would not be complete without an understanding of what he was designing the punchers to do. If we make it through this... if humanity is saved...

We owe a lot to Steven Caldwell.

You'll be remembered, friend. We will continue on, remembering you, thanking you... owing you...

Rest well, my friend.

[breathing for 5.2 seconds]

McNeary out.

TRANSCRIPT ENDS

Day 9

"What is it?" McNeary pointed.

Rhett clicked the sideguard of the SLOOP closed behind him and bounded up the rocky outcropping, stopping suddenly as he looked out over the top of it. The captain's question hung in the air like a slowly stretching strand of tar. Everything that went through their minds stuck to it, and yet they could make no movements toward fluid understanding.

Braaten tapped feverishly at his navbrace. "Orbital imagery indicates it has at least nine square miles of surface area. Amorphous in shape. Comparing this spot over the last two weeks shows signs that it's moving, if slowly." He shook his head, grumbling about bogus readings. "I'm not sure if I believe this, but between the

CHAPTER 7

chemical spectrograph and the above-ambient temperatures its maintaining, the ship is wanting to categorize it as undergoing catabolism."

"Okay." McNeary waved his hand at the jargon. "But what *is* it?"

Rhett stepped to the precipice beside them, looking up from his own navbrace to stare out over the wide stretch of glossy blackness. "Some kind of living ooze."

"It looks like crude oil," Galerkin said. "You know, the fossil fuel they used before the 22nd century?"

Rhett echoed the others in shaking his head. He wasn't alone in not being familiar with centuries-old technology. But whatever this thing was, it was enormous, and it was *ugly*. Across its surface, yellow liver spots sprung up in patches, like they'd been sun-bleached. What purpose might they serve for this enormous... creature?

Rhett eyed the captain. "Think it's dangerous?"

"No sense risking it," McNeary answered. "We won't lose more than a day if we go around, so long as it doesn't change its speed or direction. Braaten, take a look at the path ahead of us. If there are more of these, I don't want to come this close to them. If we'd known two hours ago, there would have been a more direct path around."

Braaten nodded. "Yes sir."

Rhett studied him. Braaten would certainly deny it if it were brought up in conversation, but Caldwell's death had changed him. He'd stopped calling everyone by their nicknames—even Rhett. It was like he'd lost some of his fire. Perhaps it was simply the brother-vs-brother relationship the two had nurtured, mutually tormenting each other at every opportunity. Without Caldwell, there was no one who would both take and reciprocate mockery. But other things had changed as well. The group needed someone to head up navigation. Without announcing himself for the task, nor being explicitly assigned it by the captain, so far as Rhett knew, Braaten had taken on the duty. Probably to avoid letting Rhett get any ideas.

"So it's an alien," Braaten said as they descended the far side of the hill. "How can we be sure it isn't an Occassi? What do we know about what they looked like?"

"Come on, Braaten." Rhett tried his part to be the brother. "Don't you think if they were sentient pools of sludge, they would have said so?"

Galerkin cleared her throat, wearing her thoughtful lecturing face, "It's incredibly difficult to describe oneself in a language in which you have no basis. We tried for a long time to express to them our shape, and to understand when they tried to express theirs. It all comes down to points of similarity. Things we have in common."

Braaten and Rhett shared a look, realizing they'd gotten her on one of her tangents.

"So, things we are fairly certain about," she went on. "They have hands, or at least something that can be used to manipulate things in their surroundings. They have sight, in that they can detect electromagnetic radiation, but eyes specifically are a more abstract concept. It's really rather interesting to see what traits come about to be convergent even across such astronomical distances…"

Rhett kept listening, hoping to gain insight into the aliens who'd once walked this world. Her monologue went many places, but describing anything useful wasn't exactly one of them. She got like that sometimes. Acting like the others could understand her. Maybe Braaten actually could. In any case, it wasn't his conversation to participate in.

A few hours later, it was Braaten's turn to be contemplative. "Ten years is a long time, guys. What are we going to do while we wait for the punchers to work?"

It was the elephant in the room, and none of them had yet to speak of it. It was a simple truth, though. They'd left Caldwell's stormpuncher where they'd left his body. Surrounded by such unstable ground, they'd been forced to make a terrible decision: to take the long path to defeating the storm. Even if they got all four remaining devices in place, they would have a long wait in store for them.

"I think I'm comfortable admitting," Rhett said after a few minutes of silence, "that I'm starting to feel the doom setting in."

CHAPTER 7

"And that's if we *win*," Braaten said. "I mean, unless we can somehow get back to the one Caldwell—"

"Out of the question," McNeary said flatly. "We take the long way. The only way we can be certain."

"We haven't even placed our first puncher yet." Braaten rubbed his temples with his thumbs. "We're just... so far away."

"I don't suppose any of you ever ran a marathon back on Earth?" McNeary asked.

"Track in high school," Rhett said. "That was a while ago, though. Almost... 145 years?"

The two behind him snickered joylessly, but the captain remained stoic.

"It's different with a marathon," McNeary said. "It's different when you can't see the finish line. When you know that, in theory, it has to be there, somewhere far down the trail. When you start, you know it will be there, but once you've been running for miles..." He scratched his head. "There comes a point where you wonder if it will ever come. You feel tired and sore already, but you still have so far to go. You look behind you and know that you fought for every brutal mile, but the worst is still ahead of you. You come to the brink of yourself, to the brink of what you think you can do, to the edge of what your body will even accept as possible. And then?"

He looked at them, as if expecting an answer.

No one spoke.

"You keep running," McNeary said. "Now come on. Let's get back to the SLOOPs."

Day 10

Rhett grew so used to the whirring of the SLOOPs' orbital motors during the day that he always felt a bizarre lack when they stopped for the evening. The air here was too still, although he couldn't say if it was different from Earth. After an afternoon of the air being blasted into his face through the open sides of the vehicle, the stillness made the skin of his cheeks and forehead tingle.

Rhett leaned backward in his seat, breathing slow and long, before reaching for the seatbelt buckle at his hip.

"Are you all right?" Sarah asked.

Rhett had been thinking about her that way—as 'Sarah', rather than 'Galerkin'—ever since Caldwell's death. He glanced at her, seated just behind him and to his right. The SLOOPs had three seats—one for the driver in the front, the other two just behind. It had a meager space for cargo below the seating area, but it was large enough for their packs, so they'd made it work.

"I'm fine," Rhett said. He kicked the ladder's release as he stood and turned, listening for the clank of it reaching the ground below. It was always a little awkward climbing down—the vehicles' gyroscopic stabilization didn't completely negate the sensation that the massive wheel that encircled the cab might simply topple over when an improper weight was applied to one side.

Rhett suppressed a sigh of relief as he touched the ground, glancing up to make sure Sarah was climbing down okay.

"You have a girlfriend, Rhett," Sarah said, amused.

Rhett sputtered as he met her eyes. "What? I wasn't—"

"Then look somewhere else."

Rhett furrowed his brows, grateful for the mask covering the flush of his cheeks as he threw a glance toward McNeary and Braaten at the other SLOOP. They showed no signs of having heard the exchange, which was the most he could hope for.

"I'm sorry," Rhett said as she reached the ground. "I wasn't—"

"Sure," Sarah said. "It's fine."

He couldn't be sure, but he almost thought she looked disappointed.

"So..." Rhett hesitated. "We've been here for a little while now and I haven't heard you mention it again..."

Sarah frowned at him.

"Do you still think they're around? The Occassi, I mean."

She relaxed a degree. "Haven't seen much to indicate one way or the other."

"Hmm."

"On the one hand, we have yet to see anything that could be considered an equivalent for animal life. On the other, we *have* seen at least two dozen unique species of non-mobile life. Probably more, except that we don't have the tools or knowledge to differentiate them yet. Then there was that ooze field yesterday..." She pursed her lips, considering further as they approached Braaten and McNeary. "I don't know. I still think it's too early to rule out."

"Rule out what?" Braaten asked. "The existence of the meathead's brain?"

Rhett rolled his eyes. How Braaten had found his way back to that again, Rhett would never guess.

"Braaten," McNeary scolded. "How's that mask fitting?"

Braaten made a face. "He *removed* part of it. He didn't *invent* the damn thing."

"Just shut up," Sarah said. "You're starting to sound as dumb as you look."

Braaten gave her a look halfway between impressed and offended but said nothing.

As had become their tradition, dinner was a nearly wordless and completely joyless affair. The empty slot on the nutrient plaster rack glared at them even now, reminding them of the one they had lost. They had said words for Caldwell's passing a few days before, but it hadn't made things any easier. There were simply too few of them, and his personality had been too important to the group's chemistry. No matter how the others tried, they could not fill the hole he had left behind.

There was a knock on the side of Rhett's prefab sometime after sundown. For a moment, his mind raced. It was late; there shouldn't be anyone still up in their camp. Was it something else, then? A creature? He reached for his sidearm, but then—

"Can I talk to you for a minute?"

It was Sarah's voice.

Rhett blinked. Of course it wasn't an alien creature coming to kill them. What sort of creature would *knock* first? Maybe he'd hurt his head more than he'd thought on the side of that volcano. He rapped his knuckles on his temple, cursing the ringing in his ears once again.

"Uh, yeah." He snatched his mask from its place on his wall. "Just a second."

Rhett unsealed the door, raising an eyebrow at her form standing over the squat structure, staring out into the wilderness. He stood up, wobbling as his weight settled back into his boots. Part of him resented having to put them back on thirty seconds after he had taken them off, but Sarah rarely did anything without reason.

He rolled his shoulders. "Something on your mind?"

She wandered a few steps from the other prefabs, prompting him to click on the holoescent lamp on the front of his suit and direct it down toward their feet.

Once out of earshot, she paused, sighing as a brisk wind whipped a few hairs loose from her tight braid. "Rhett," She looked down for a moment, then warily back out into the darkness. "I think I am going to die here."

"We live here now, Sarah. We're all going to die here."

She turned to him, a sad certainty hovering behind her eyes. "I mean soon. I'm not... I'm not built for this place."

"Sarah, you're being ridic—"

"Listen to me!"

Rhett's eyebrows furrowed. This wasn't like her. Where was her objective perspective? Her scientific demeanor?

"When it happens, I want you to bury me, okay?" She was deadly serious. "*Actually* bury me. Not like... not like what happened to Steven."

Rhett hesitated at her calling Caldwell by his first name. She really was a relational creature, wasn't she? She built bonds in no time and could talk to anyone. It made sense that she had ended up in a profession dedicated to not only language, but to communication at its deepest level. She'd come here to meet new beings, to find common ground with them, to form bonds and to share experiences. Instead, they'd arrived to find this broken wasteland on an empty planet. The only people she'd been able to speak to for the last several weeks were the crewmates she'd awoken with, and in that time, two of them had already been killed.

Rhett wanted to argue with her. To tell her he could protect her. That their success was certain, so long as they were smart and careful. That no one else had to die. But the words wouldn't come out. As their eyes remained locked, soul mingling with soul through such distant windows, the lies refused to take up residence on his tongue. He wasn't sure the odds were on their side anymore. He wasn't even sure if what they were trying to do was possible.

"I'll do it," he muttered. "Even if I have to use my bare hands."

She looked away.

Suddenly, Rhett felt alone in the darkness of the alien steppe. This place he would be forced to call home... it didn't want him here. It didn't want any of them. Perhaps that was what Sarah felt. There was a distance here—between their bodies and the planet. Earth had not carried them with such disregard. Her embrace had been certain, as a mother to her own children, but this new mother... Occassus had turned cold when she'd lost her own young.

Rhett stared upward, the clear night sky giving clear view to a host of constellations no human had ever known. Somewhere up there, an impossibly small speck swung about this world carrying the last vestige of his species. Cyn was up there, sleeping like the rest of them. What if the all-clear was never sent? Would the ship wake them eventually, allowing them to make an attempt at survival there in orbit? Would there be another team sent if Rhett and the others failed?

No. The protocols had been designed with their mission in mind. He supposed it was possible there had been someone far-sighted enough to program fail-safes into the machine mind of the Votum, but he couldn't imagine what the terms might be. How long could the ship keep them in hypersleep before risking their safety? Would it wake them just before it ran out of power? After double the expected duration of sleep had elapsed? What if that last clump of humanity remained there, technically alive but inanimate in orbit? Could it be hundreds of years? A thousand? When would you even call them extinct?

"Do you think he had family up there?" Sarah nudged his shoulder with her own.

"He never mentioned anyone." Rhett pursed his lips. "But he wasn't a young man. He might have wanted to keep it to himself."

She shook her head. "I think we'd have heard. He would have told us about their cooking or something."

"He did have a thing about food."

She laughed, but it faded quickly. "That's bad, isn't it? We shouldn't make fun of him."

"He's gone." Rhett shrugged. "I think it matters more that we remember him, rather than *how* we remember him."

Her eyes relaxed a bit at that, but he couldn't quite tell what her expression said with the mask covering more than half of it. She looked back up into the deepening black of the night sky.

"What about you?" he finally asked. "Do you have family up there?"

She sighed. "A brother. An engineer."

"Older?"

"Younger." She shook her head. "He's going to miss me."

"Sarah, you can't talk that way."

She sniffed, and he realized there were tears in her eyes. "Why not?"

CHAPTER 7

"It's Braaten." Rhett threw a mockingly wary glance back at the prefabs. "He has very sensitive feelings."

Sarah laughed, the suddenness of it forcing a pair of tears to escape. She wiped them with the sleeve of her suit. "I would have liked to meet your girlfriend. The way you talk about her... she seems nice."

"You're going to like her," Rhett said. "*When* you meet her."

For once, Sarah wasn't listening. "I know what I said earlier about her painting the landscapes here." She looked back out over the steppe. "I guess I didn't expect things to be so... stark."

Rhett chuckled. "I keep telling myself that if I survive all this, she'll be the one that kills me."

She shook her head, reaching her hands up to gather the wandering strands of her hair. "It's hard to imagine... but if any more children are born to the human race, they will be born on this planet."

"I'm not with McNeary on that one. I haven't given up hope on Earth."

"You don't seem to think they'll be coming to our rescue either."

"I'm a pragmatist," Rhett said. "Even if they made it, we'll probably never hear from them."

"Society takes time to rebuild," she agreed. "Maybe our great-grandchildren."

"Now *there's* some optimism."

She didn't laugh this time. "The Occassi... if they're still here, and just hiding somewhere, trying to rebuild... What if they don't know *we're* here? If their society has collapsed, then what use will our negotiations from over a century ago be? What if we can't find the peace we came to secure?"

"That's exactly why you have to survive. Humanity still needs you."

Sarah nodded and turned back to the prefabs, a distant expression on her face. After a few steps, she stopped, turning toward him without meeting his eyes. A string of words escaped her lips, but until she ducked through her door and closed it behind her, his mind couldn't make sense of them.

"Only if it survives."

Chapter 8

Day 12

PERSONAL LOG
RECORDED BY: Shamus McNeary, Captain
LOCATION: Mihaar Lowlands, Occassus II
TRANSCRIPT BEGINS

This is Captain Shamus McNeary, reporting again on the exploration and restoration mission on Occassus II.

Over the last day and half, we have been making our way across a wide dried-up lakebed that must have once supported a thriving agricultural community. Though Sarah jumps at every opportunity to study the Occassi's architecture, this region hasn't supplied her with much besides a repeating cycle of excitement and disappointment.

There are structures—or what remains of them—in and around the lakebed, but there isn't much to be gleaned from them. They're up on stilts, suggesting that either space on the nearby land was at a premium or that there was something valuable in the water that once filled this space, but nothing by way of markings remains. Rhett did manage to convince me that he could climb up the side of one of the shorter and more stable looking structures, but from the pictures he took and what he described, everything inside is encased in that same semi-transparent glass that the storm—Nuhalriu, we're calling it—has a habit of leaving behind.

CHAPTER 8

The good news is that we're getting close to the first deployment zone. Assuming the topography is true to orbital images, it should only be a few more days before we reach it. I think once we have that set up, everyone will feel a little bit lighter.

[breathing for 2.4 seconds]

At least I hope so.

The acute grief has come and gone for most of them. They don't talk about Caldwell much anymore, but it's hard to blame them. The more we think about his death, the more certain we become of our own. I've been careful to leave this one be—the best thing I can do for the crew is to keep them on task, keep them focused. We just have to keep going. Keep moving. Keep making progress.

[breathing for 4.1 seconds]

I think it's getting to them, though. I know it's getting to me. We saw some creatures fly by yesterday morning. They might have been birds, but we didn't get a good look at them. Galerkin assures me that feathers are a rather unique mutation and that none of our communications with the Occassi suggest that morphology emerged on this planet. You know what? Never mind. The point is that I saw them and said to the others, "Look. It's just like home."

And they just... looked at me. Braaten gave me one of those looks he usually uses on Corporal Wethern.

[sigh]

It was stupid. Obviously it was. I just... I wanted to believe it. I want to feel like this planet can be a home to us. That we can be happy here, once this is all over. I want it so badly, so I just... I guess I'm trying to pretend it's already true.

[breathing for 5.3 seconds]

The truth is... that look they gave me?

[breathing for 1.9 seconds]

It almost broke me. I could feel it. Like a huge book being set down on a desk about to snap. My temper... my mind... is buckling beneath the weight.

[breathing for 3.2 seconds]

I've upped my dosage. I don't know what it's going to do to me, especially long-term. Maybe if Caldwell was here, I could ask him. He could give me some advice and help me get past this. But without him...

No. I didn't ask him. Not while he was here. And what's changed? It's gotten worse. No, I wouldn't have asked. Nothing would be different. I'd still be fighting, day after day, to stay in control. To keep my head on my shoulders. To be the kind of leader these people need.

[chuckles]

It's fine. We'll get the puncher placed, and then we'll do the next one. And then the next one. And the next. I can hold on that long. Maybe once that's done, we can hail the Votum. There's got to be a doctor on board that can help me. When the mission is done, I can ask for that. When my responsibility is lifted...

[breathing for 2.1 seconds]

When I've earned it.

TRANSCRIPT END

Day 14

It was different seeing the storm from the ground than from orbit. From the Votum, it looked massive. Powerful. Dangerous. Rhett studied the images of it that the Votum sent every time it passed over—thousands of them, by now, each one emphasizing its enormity and the impossibility of their task.

It didn't look like a storm from the ground. It was like the night. Like one final, horizon-spanning twilight that marched forward almost imperceptibly, but which carried omens of the inevitable, the inexorable, the ineffable. The dust that

CHAPTER 8

rose around it had no color, only shadow. The glowing, trembling heart of it was visible at a distance, radiating with naked malice.

"Do you really think they made that?" Rhett asked.

For once, Braaten didn't berate him. He glanced toward the horizon for only a moment before returning his focus to the SLOOP's controls. "It's like I told the old man. It certainly isn't natural."

"But do you think they made it?" Rhett asked. "On *purpose*?"

"I've been asking myself that. A lot, actually. Maybe the doc would have been able to figure out the how—we're close enough to get meaningful readings now, I think. But as for the why? The what?" He shook his head. "Maybe it was supposed to be a weapon. A nuclear option that went terribly wrong. Or, hey—maybe terribly right. For us, anyway. If we can do this... I mean. You know what I mean. We'll have a whole planet."

"Lucky us," Rhett said.

Braaten shot him a look. "It's not about the now, meathead. Nothing ever is. It's about our children and our children's children."

"Can't imagine a woman wanting to give *you* children."

Braaten's eyes narrowed from a smile hidden behind his mask. "I have a daughter, actually."

Rhett's eyebrows shot up. "On the Votum?"

Braaten nodded.

Rhett sent a disbelieving glance skyward, which got a chuckle out of Braaten.

"It's on the other side of the planet right now."

"I... knew that."

"Sure you did." Braaten chuckled again. He feathered the accelerator gently as the outer ring of the SLOOP began to lean with a gentle turn. They slowed as they reached the crest of a hill, stopping only moments before McNeary and Sarah's SLOOP rolled up beside them.

"It's closer than you said it would be," McNeary said flatly.

"I said it would be close," Braaten replied.

"And you think it's safe? I told you we should be minimizing our risks."

"It's a window of opportunity. Nuhalriu carries a lot of the planet's water in its wake. If we want to cross these floodplains in a safe and timely manner, we'll be better off when it's dry. Once we're clear of its path, we'll only be a day or two from the first deployment site."

"Mm." McNeary grunted, staring out at the looming expanse on the horizon. "How long do we have?"

Braaten consulted his navbrace. "Thirty-six hours? Plus or minus an hour."

"Thirty-six hours." McNeary blinked at him. "To cross a region over a thousand miles wide?"

"It won't be a problem. Even if we only had twenty-four hours, we'd barely need to be going over forty miles an hour."

McNeary did not look impressed. "And what if we don't cross now? How long will that set us back?"

"That's not really an option anymore. The ocean is too close in the other direction to allow us to escape the storm's path."

"So you trapped us," Sarah said.

"What? No." Braaten frowned. "We'll cross. It won't be an issue."

"And if it is?" McNeary asked, voice eerily calm. "If there's an engine failure? Another ooze field? Something else?"

"We'd see the ooze from orbit." Braaten bit off the words one at a time. "It. Won't. Be. An. Issue."

"We should go," Rhett said.

McNeary hesitated briefly, glancing between Rhett and Braaten. Finally, he dipped his chin. "You're right, Corporal. There isn't time."

CHAPTER 8

Day 15

```
PERSONAL LOG
RECORDED BY: Shamus McNeary, Captain
LOCATION: Mihaar Floodplain, Occassus II
TRANSCRIPT BEGINS
```

This is Captain Shamus McNeary, reporting from beneath the shadow of the storm. Thanks to some... flawed... calculations as to our navigation, we have been forced to make a dangerous crossing directly in the path of Nuhalriu. If all goes well, we should be clear of it in time, but given our luck so far...

I've allowed the team four hours of sleep before we keep moving. Exhaustion leads to mistakes as easily as rushing does, but we can't afford to dawdle. Every hour may count in the end, and the more distance we can put between ourselves and the very thing that killed this planet, the better.

[breathing for 1.3 seconds]

I... I'm about to run out of the sedatives. I thought I had more. I don't know what happened to them. Maybe I lost them. Or dropped them. Maybe one of the others found them and threw them away. Or could they... could one of them be in the same situation? Barely holding on, only keeping their grip thanks to a finite supply of chemical supplements?

[breathing for 4.9 seconds]

I'll be useless when they're gone. Worse, probably. Maybe a threat to the team. A threat to the entire mission. I can't... I can't...

[breathing quivers for 3.2 seconds]

I can't believe it's come to this. I thought I would have more time. I thought I would be of more use. I thought I could do some good for this world. For my team. For my species. But I'm...

[sniffs]

I don't think I've managed anything at all.

[breathing for 5.4 seconds]

I'm going to tell Rhett. I think... I think he'll be able to deal with me. Once it happens, I mean. Maybe when I take my last one, I'll tell him. The others don't need to know. They don't need to know what was wrong with me. They can just keep on believing... believing... that I was going to get them through.

Maybe he can make it look like an accident.

[chuckles]

Never thought I'd be here. Trying to plan my own accidental death.

[sniffs]

I wasn't any good to them anyway. They can... they'll do just as well without me. Better, maybe, so long as they don't put Braaten in charge.

It's...

It's fine.

It's better this way.

Probably.

McNeary out.

TRANSCRIPT ENDS

"I thought you said we had time," Rhett yelled.

"We did have time!" Braaten shot him a glare but had too much to handle with the controls of the SLOOP to hold it for long. "We *do* have—"

CHAPTER 8

A screeching clang ripped through the air as something dark and heavy struck the side of the SLOOP's outer ring. The whole structure wobbled for a moment, but the gyros saved them from completely losing control.

"Where's the old man?" Braaten hollered, his voice barely audible over the ringing in Rhett's ears.

Rhett tugged at the strap across his chest to loosen it enough for him to turn. Over his shoulder and through the transparent paneling of the SLOOP's cargo hatch, he could see the other SLOOP skidding along not far behind them. "Still alive."

"Would you *quit* saying that!"

Though their navbraces claimed sunrise was hours behind them, the SLOOPs moved through what felt like midnight shadows. Grey dust surrounded them on all sides like fog, limiting line of sight to a couple dozen feet. Rhett couldn't tell how Braaten was navigating aside from his frequent glances at the telemetry displayed on his forearm.

"You're sure you know where we're going?"

"Think I'd still be driving if I didn't?"

"You mean you'd stop if you were confused?"

"Shut up, meathead," Braaten hissed. "God *damn*."

The outer ring of the SLOOP dropped a couple feet suddenly before bouncing back up. Were it not for the three-foot suspension between the cab and the wheel, their spines might have shattered then and there. Rhett gasped a breath, earning him another glare from Braaten.

"Still alive," Rhett reported after glancing back again.

"You know I ha—"

Something struck the side of the SLOOP, sending them into a chaotic wobble. Rhett ground his teeth, waited for it to stabilize, but the scraping sound of metal on metal told him his hope was in vain.

"I don't think it's—"

"Shut up!" Braaten jammed his thumb into the release at his hip. The belt across his shoulder and lap leapt away. "You drive, meathead."

"What?" Rhett blinked. "What are you going to do?"

"Idiot."

Rhett slipped into the vacant seat as Braaten struggled past him. The controls shook in his hands, making them feel almost instantly numb as he tightened his grip.

"Can you fix it?" Rhett hollered over his shoulder.

"Can you *shut up*?"

"The others?"

"Doing better than we are."

"We should stop," Rhett said.

"See a good picnic spot?"

"The SLOOP's fucked."

"We're fine."

"Braaten, we're—"

"We're *FINE!*"

A loud crack. A second later, the wobble settled out again. The scraping sound was gone, replaced by a hideous whine that seemed to come from all around them.

"What did you do?" Rhett demanded.

"Drive!"

It was easier said than done. Every bump they hit shook the controls out of his hands, forcing him to snatch at them with increasingly numb fingers. With the amount of dust in the air, it was no surprise that it was gunking up the suspension, but it didn't bode well.

"How much longer?" Rhett asked.

"Whining already?"

"Braaten!"

"Another hour. We're passing through one of the spiral arms that formed as it reached the floodplain."

"This isn't the main storm?" Rhett asked.

"Is your skin melting?"

CHAPTER 8

Rhett's teeth rattled in his skull as they hit another divot, disrupting any attempt at a response. He glanced at his navbrace, trying to confirm their heading, but his mind felt too fuzzy to understand what he saw there. He blinked hard, screwing up the muscles of his face as he tried to focus, and looked again.

"Left, you idiot!" Braaten's hand reached into viewing, triggering a reflex to swat it away. Rhett jerked the controls to the left, the creaking of the SLOOP only just audible over the rushing howl of the wind.

An enormous darkness opened up less than a dozen feet to the right. It was hard to be sure, but it looked to Rhett like there wasn't ground over there. The edge of a cliff?

"Shit. Shit!" Braaten said. "Who's driving back there?"

Rhett felt the color drain from his face. "Are they okay?"

"Only just missed that edge. I thought it was the old man driving."

"This isn't really his element," Rhett muttered. He veered right after a glance at his navbrace, avoiding another edge.

"Just give him more warning," Braaten said. "And try not to get us killed."

Sure. Rhett glared out into the indistinct miasma of dust ahead. *Easy.*

"Is there a safe way down?" he asked.

"Down?" Braaten shook his head. "It's just a bunch of fissures. Nothing at the bottom. No way out if you fall. Left!"

Rhett turned, clenching his teeth as the outer ring of the SLOOP leaned around them. It was going to fly apart any minute now. He could feel it. Whatever Braaten had done... and this storm...

"There has to be a way through the fissure fields," Rhett said.

"Right!"

Rhett turned again, leaning hard into the numbness of his hands. "The others?"

Braaten glanced backward. "They're fine. They—SHIT!"

Rhett only barely heard the clatter of metal against stone. He turned hard, pulling back on the yoke to decelerate.

"What are you doing?" Braaten hollered. "We have to keep moving! They—"

"Where did they fall?"

"You're insane. We don't have time to go back. We have to—"

"WHERE?" Rhett roared.

Braaten pointed, but visibility was getting worse and worse. As the SLOOP rolled to a stop, Rhett realized they were only a few feet from the edge of one of the trenches.

"Sarah!" Rhett hollered, sliding down the ladder. "McNeary!"

There was no answer. Rhett stepped to the edge of the fissure, squinting against the dust and the wind, and peered down.

His stomach lurched at the sight of their SLOOP, fully on its side, wedged between the two sheer faces of rock by its outer ring. It was only about ten feet down, but with the amount of dust in the air, even that left most of the details to guesswork.

"They're down there!" Rhett yelled back at Braaten.

"I'm taking the driver's seat," Braaten yelled back.

Rhett rolled his eyes. For being so smart, the man was a moron. What was his plan? To drive off alone? Finish the mission by himself with only the two stormpunchers in their SLOOP? Somehow, Rhett doubted that had any chance of working out for him.

"Sarah," Rhett yelled down. "McNeary! Captain!"

"We're here," McNeary answered in a pained voice. "I... we... I'm sorry."

"No time! We're getting you out. If you can grab your punchers and climb out the door on your left—"

Sarah shrieked somewhere out of sight.

There was a pair of loud thumps.

"Door's bent in," McNeary said. "It won't open."

Rhett gritted his teeth, throwing a wary glance back at Braaten. The man hadn't moved yet, but his hands were poised on the controls. Would he actually do it? Leave the rest of them here to die if he thought it would mean his own survival?

CHAPTER 8

"Cover your eyes," Rhett yelled down. There was no time for caution. No time to think. He drew his Phi-8 sidearm and took aim for the edge of the precariously positioned SLOOP's window. If Sarah and McNeary were still vaguely in their seats, they'd be clear of the slug's path.

PRRTSH.

The window blasted apart in a shower of debris. There was a groan of metal as the captain and the translator struggled out of the newly created aperture and onto the side of the vehicle.

"Take this!" McNeary swung his arms violently and tossed a large bag up toward Rhett. It wasn't a great throw, but Rhett managed to drop his chest to the ground fast enough to snag the strap before it was lost to the oblivion below. Rhett hauled it up and tossed it toward the other SLOOP, hoping it would bait Braaten off the controls before he did anything stupid.

"Do you have rope?" Rhett yelled. If it weren't for the storm, they probably wouldn't have needed it, but with the amount they were having to fight just to stay upright—and not knowing how long the outer ring of their SLOOP would hold before snapping or slipping—it seemed like the safest plan.

"No time," the captain answered, lowering himself to crawl across one of the struts that connected the SLOOP's outer ring to the cab. Even now, he seemed strangely calm. "Sarah, you're going to climb on my shoulders."

"WHAT?" she yelped. "But what about you?"

McNeary said something Rhett couldn't hear, and Sarah nodded slowly and followed him out along the strut.

"Braaten," Rhett yelled over his shoulder. "Find some rope!"

He stretched his arm downward, clenching his teeth as a plume of dust hinted at a slip on the far side of the trench. Sarah climbed awkwardly up as McNeary's footing wobbled beneath.

Rhett grunted as he hauled her upward, helping her all the way until she was above the edge of the trench. She scrambled toward the SLOOP, muttering something utterly indecipherable over the wind.

"Captain," Rhett yelled down, taking his position lying flat against the rock with his arm outstretched once again. "You can make it. You just have to jump!"

McNeary just stared at him. After a moment, he looked away, shaking his head. "It's all right, Corporal. It's better—"

Metal screeched and rock crumbled as the SLOOP came loose from its place in the trench. The sound of it clattering into the depths might have been deafening had it not been for the wind.

Rhett lay there, head and arm reaching toward the now empty darkness, his mouth dry and wordless. He was gone. The man who was going to save them all—the man with the calm and the plan and the will to get them through.

McNeary was dead.

No time. Rhett hauled himself to his feet and stumbled back toward the SLOOP. Sarah had just managed to heave the pack up into the cab and turned to look at him as she reached the top of the ladder.

She stared for a long moment, but through the dust and the wind Rhett couldn't guess what she was thinking. She must have heard it fall. She must know what had happened. What it meant. She climbed into the back seat as Rhett reached the bottom of the ladder.

Once inside, Rhett took the controls without a word. Aside from Braaten's subdued directions, no one said anything. For nearly an hour, there was nothing more than the wind, the grinding of the SLOOP, and the oppressive weight of the loss to keep him company.

"It should have been fine," Braaten said weakly as soon as the SLOOP's engine fell silent.

Neither Sarah nor Rhett bothered to answer him.

"It should have been fine," Braaten said again as Rhett climbed down the ladder.

"It doesn't matter now," Rhett muttered as he reached the ground. "Now, it's down to us."

Chapter 9

Day 18

```
PERSONAL LOG
RECORDED BY: Sarah Galerkin, PhD, Xenolinguistics
LOCATION: Stormpuncher Basin, Occassus II
TRANSCRIPT BEGINS
```

This is Sarah Galerkin, recording on May 27th, 2272. Report given… report given in the place of Captain Shamus McNeary, who passed away a few days ago. Report inputted via the team's last remaining transmitter with a connection to the Votum, in a region we are calling Stormpuncher Basin.

I… I still can't believe he's gone.

I don't know if the boys have said a single word to each other since it happened. I don't know what I'm supposed to do. When Steven died, the captain was there to keep us together. He reminded us of our purpose. Reminded us of the mission. He didn't care about our egos or our presumptions—he only had a mind to get us all through. He was…

He was a leader. Right up to the very end.

[sniffs]

It should have been him that got out. Not me. I…

[chokes back a sob]

I should have made him go first. Maybe then we'd still have a chance.

[clears throat]

No. No, I don't actually think that. I mean, I don't actually *think that we don't have a chance. It's like the captain always said: possibilities, not odds. The odds have always been against us, right from the start. And yes, numerically, they are probably getting worse. But so long as at least one of us is alive, there's always a chance, isn't there? And that's what we should hold onto. Hope, not despair.*

It's what the captain would have wanted.

Maybe Rhett and Markus already have that figured out. Even if they're not talking, they both seem to know where we need to go. What we need to do next. One day at a time. One stormpuncher at a time.

Maybe once this first one is placed, I can...

I just want them to talk to each other. I don't want the last thousand words I ever hear to be ones that came out of my own mouth. I just... feel so alone. I know it isn't their fault. They need time.

We all need time.

[silence for 4.2 seconds]

I know Markus blames himself for what happened. Rhett blames him, too. And I... I don't know what to think. It probably doesn't matter, though. Even if it was Markus's mistake that got us here, we can't afford to be disconnected like this.

I have to say something, don't I? I'll never be like the captain... so easily confident. So easily in control. So easily able to earn everyone's trust and respect and get them to work together. But I... I have to try.

[silence for 2.9 seconds]

My analysis of Occassus remains largely unchanged. I maintain that there is a possibility that some of them have managed to survive this long somewhere in hiding, but now that I've seen Nuhalriu firsthand...

Maybe my certainty isn't what it was before. It's just... the destruction. The power...

I lived in Baytown back on Earth. I... I suppose if you're listening to this, you may not know where that was. If these recordings are passed down for generations, like

Shamus always liked to say... many of you probably never even saw Earth, did you? Huh...

Never mind.

The point is, I've seen storms before. Living in a floating city off the gulf coast gave me plenty of first-hand encounters to remember. There was a lot of rain, back on Earth. That was how most of the damage happened. Lots of water. A huge stormwall, doing all it could to sweep away anything and everything in its path.

There isn't much of a comparison to this. The winds were like I remembered, but I don't think a single molecule of water is floating in the air out in front of Nuhalriu. We weren't even within five hundred miles of its center. And the dust... Markus is still cleaning it out of every crevice of the SLOOP. To be honest, I don't think the thing is going to run for much longer.

[breathing for 3.5 seconds]

I don't think I have anything else to report. To whoever listens to this, I wish you well.

TRANSCRIPT ENDS

Day 19

The rock was nearly the size of a city block, stacked up like a monument long forgotten. Like much of the countryside surrounding it, it was encased in a thin layer of dust-glass, making it gleam like a beacon in the morning sunlight.

After all they'd been through getting to it, the fact that it had a smoothly graded slope leading up one side felt like a bad joke. They left the SLOOP at the bottom of the hill—Braaten muttered something about not trying it on a grade over thirty degrees—and started hiking just after midmorning. It only took them half an hour to reach the top, and only another ten minutes to find the most obvious spot for deployment.

"It's an automatic process, once you initiate it. The doc thought we should make it as intuitive as possible, in case..." Braaten trailed off, staring at the device in his outstretched hands like it had just spat on his face. He twisted his face partway to one side—the start of a head shake, maybe—before placing the tripod base of the stormpuncher on the tallest part of the outcropping. He opened a small panel on its side and pressed a switch, triggering the device's laser bores to irreversibly entrench it in the stone. The hiss and smell of melting rock was stronger than Rhett had expected, but the whole process was over in less than five minutes.

"See?" Braaten said wearily. "Easy as that."

"Even I could do it," Rhett said, half joking.

Braaten looked at him, but there was neither humor nor malice in his eyes.

"*We* are going to do it," Sarah said firmly. "All three of us. Together. To the end."

Rhett's brows furrowed. Where had that confidence come from? What happened to the worry she'd confided in him? It had to still be there. People didn't change that fast, if they changed at all.

But what was the point in arguing?

Rhett looked back at Braaten. "How far to the next site?"

"Four days."

"And... on foot?" Sarah asked.

Rhett and Braaten gave her matching frowns.

"I don't know how much I trust the SLOOP anymore," she admitted. "With all the damage it took from Nuhalriu... I wonder if it's a greater risk than it is a boon."

She had a point there. The last thing they needed was to crack their skulls after a cataclysmic failure. Rhett turned to Braaten, trying to gauge his expression. He was pensive for a long minute, then hung his head.

"You're right," Braaten said.

Just like that. No argument. No backtalk.

"One puncher for each of us to carry," Rhett said by way of agreement. "How far on foot?"

Braaten tapped at his navbrace. "Two weeks?"

"And Nuhalriu?" Sarah asked. "Any projected interference during that time?"

"It'll be a few more revolutions before it comes close to us again, Cap." Sarah stiffened, but Braaten kept right on talking. "We'll find ourselves somewhere to bunker up as soon as it's within a hemisphere of reaching us."

"Good," Sarah said. "Are we agreed, then?"

Rhett nodded.

Day 21

Sarah wasn't their leader, despite Braaten's newfound insistence on calling her 'Cap'. She didn't give orders, didn't give speeches. She simply shared her thoughts, asked Braaten and Rhett for theirs, and instituted a vote. Aside from leaving the SLOOP behind, it had only been trivial matters so far. Regardless, every decision had been unanimous.

As it turned out, all it took for McNeary to properly unify his team was to die.

They'd spent the morning climbing up and down through a region of shallow hills. An array of lakes that might once have been fresh, clean water were spread out before them, reflecting the red-brown sky without enthusiasm. It was a change from the sights of the mountains and the basin they'd just passed through, but that was all that could be said about it.

They stopped at the edge of one of the lakes to make camp for the night. Braaten was tinkering with some of the parts he'd salvaged from the SLOOP—making some other history-defining invention or other, Rhett was sure—while Rhett set the heating rack up for dinner. Sarah sat a short distance away on what might have been a petrified stump, turned away from them, and stared out across the meager scenery.

"Plaster's up," Rhett announced when the canisters' indicators clicked. Braaten came dutifully, but Sarah didn't move.

"You should talk to her," Braaten finally said.

Rhett pursed his lips. "Not sure what good it will do."

"Well, she needs talking to. I'm a good judge of that sort of thing."

Rhett suppressed the urge to retort.

"The problem," Braaten continued softly, "is that she most *definitely* would rather not look at me."

"The beard's not so bad. Must get itchy under the mask, though."

Braaten tried to smile. "What's your excuse? No testosterone?"

"A razor."

"Bullshit."

"Fine," Rhett said. "I stole the steel-snips from the tools stash on the SLOOP."

"Bastard. I've been needing those."

Rhett just looked at him.

"Well I don't want them *now*, meathead. You ruined them."

Rhett cracked a smile under his mask.

Braaten's chuckle barely reached his eyes. "This is what I'm talking about. You... she likes you. She'll listen to you."

Rhett very much doubted that. "We're doing fine. This is working."

"Working?" Braaten furrowed his brow. "Have you been watching her? Every night, she's on the brink of cracking like an egg."

"And you're doing better?"

"Of course not."

"Might help if you stopped calling her 'Cap'," Rhett said. "You didn't even call McNeary that."

"I'm showing her respect."

"You're being an ass."

Braaten ground his teeth, throwing a glance toward Sarah and back to Rhett. "Well, fuck. Never mind." He stalked away, retiring to his prefab despite the sun not yet being down.

Rhett took a long breath, trying to decide if he'd made some mistake. He took slow sips from the feed tube in his mask, managing not to grimace at the taste of the nutrient plaster now that he was growing used to it.

Maybe that was all he needed to do to make it through all of this. Get used to the plaster. Get used to the planet. Get used to the mask. Get used to the red not-plants. Get used to the threat of the storm. Get used to the people around him dying in terrible ways.

He glanced at Sarah, who sat like a statue on the lump of myco-wood. She didn't look like she was cracking to him, though he had never been the type to try to judge that sort of thing. But she did look tired.

Maybe Braaten was right.

Rhett approached slowly, carrying the last tube of nutrient plaster with him. He stood next to her and proffered it. Her eyes smiled at him weakly as she took it.

"You should go easier on him," Sarah said as she affixed the tube to the port on her suit.

"I don't know what you mean."

She breathed a slow sigh. "I know you're not as dense as he thinks you are."

"Kind of a low bar."

"What I mean to say is that I know you're not dense *at all*."

"I think the chance of that is… 'negligible'."

She showed only the slightest hint of amusement. "You know what I mean. About Markus. He… he hasn't been all right, since what happened to the captain."

"He was just saying the same about you."

She ignored this. "He blames himself, you know."

Can't see why he shouldn't.

The thought must have showed in his face, because Sarah gave him a look of disappointment and shook her head. "It doesn't matter. I thought you were the pragmatist. Can't you see it doesn't matter whose fault it is?"

Rhett's eyebrows furrowed.

"We still need each other. We need to trust each other." Her gaze grew distant. "More than that, we need to trust ourselves."

Rhett studied her in silence. "Do you?" he finally asked. "Trust yourself?"

She glanced at him.

"You've been having us vote."

"I'm not the leader."

"You've been having us *vote*," Rhett repeated. "On *everything*."

Her eyes narrowed a fraction. "No, I don't trust myself. I don't trust Markus. I don't even trust you." She looked away. "You let him fall, Rhett."

That stung. "I reached out my hand. He just...is it my fault if he chose not to grab it?"

"He *chose?*"

Rhett hesitated. He hadn't mentioned that detail yet.

"Are you telling me the captain wanted to die?" Sarah demanded.

"I... don't know," Rhett said. "He said... at the end, he said, 'It's better...'."

"What's better?" Sarah choked, eyes filling with moisture. "What did he say was better?"

Rhett shook his head. "He didn't. The SLOOP gave way before he finished. But I... I don't know. He didn't try to jump. He had time—a handful of seconds at least. He didn't take my hand. He..." A storm of emotions welled up from Rhett's gut. He wanted to puke. "I don't know. I don't understand."

Rhett flinched as Sarah wrapped an arm around him and pulled him close. They stood there for a few minutes in a somewhat awkward embrace, each silently struggling in the companionable evening air.

"See?" Sarah finally said, retreating a step. "This is what I'm talking about. I think we're all blaming ourselves. Markus for trapping us with the storm. Me for climbing out of the trench first. You for not being able to pull him out. But..."

She shook her head slowly, as if not quite believing the words coming out of her own mouth. "It was him. He made a choice. I don't know why. I don't think any of us can. But... he chose. We know he cared about the mission. We know he cared about us. He wouldn't want us to be ripping ourselves up like this. Blaming ourselves. He would want us to stay strong. Stay united. Keep running, like he said."

Rhett looked at her. "Maybe Braaten's right. Maybe you *should* be captain."

"I don't want to be. Voting... is better."

"Someone should have the final say."

"We have an odd number. Majority rules."

"Because we will only ever have two options?" Rhett asked. "What happens if we each have a different opinion?"

She took a deep breath. "I don't want to be captain."

"It can't be Braaten. And I *know* it shouldn't be me."

"Why not?" Sarah asked. "You're pragmatic. You don't hesitate when something has to be done. You don't get caught up in the battle of egos that Markus... *sometimes* gets into."

"I'm just a soldier. A meathead. I shouldn't be in charge of anyone."

"You know I know better," Sarah said, a measure of certainty settling in her voice. "I'll talk with Markus, then we'll put it to a vote."

"There's three options."

Sarah shrugged, wiping the streaks from her cheeks. "Oh, I think it will work out."

Rhett watched as she retreated to her prefab. A sinking feeling settled over him—the realization of a mistake he had made but did not fully understand.

"Fuck," he muttered. "Am I the captain now?"

Chapter 10

Day 22

PERSONAL LOG
RECORDED BY: Corporal Rhett Wethern, Security Officer
LOCATION: The Big Flat (Braaten's name), Occassus II
TRANSCRIPT BEGINS

They, uh...
   They made me captain today.
   [silence for 4.1 seconds]
   Idiots.

TRANSCRIPT ENDS

CHAPTER 10

Day 23

```
PERSONAL LOG
RECORDED BY: Corporal Rhett Wethern, Security Officer
LOCATION: The Big Flat, Occassus II
TRANSCRIPT BEGINS
```

Nothing major to report.

   [silence for 2.6 seconds]

   Well, nothing that I think is major, anyway.

   Sarah keeps giving me suggestions of things to report. I think she realizes I'm not going to ramble on these like she probably does. I'm sure the cap...

   I'm sure McNeary was very detailed in these recordings. Lots of... I don't know... 'historically significant' happenings. Sarah says it's the captain's duty to make these reports. Someday, someone's going to listen to all of this, and the more they can learn about what we went through, yada yada yada...

   [sigh]

   Listen. The way I see it, either someone's listening or they're not. I mean, obviously you're either listening or not. What I mean is...

   [silence for 1.4 seconds]

   You know what? Never mind.

```
TRANSCRIPT ENDS
```

Day 29

```
PERSONAL LOG
RECORDED BY: Corporal Rhett Wethern, Security Officer
LOCATION: Just west of the North Fungal Arbor, Occassus II
TRANSCRIPT BEGINS
```

Almost ran out of water this week.

[clears throat]

Braaten took the 'avoid the storm' plan a little too seriously, I think. We made a pretty significant detour through the region he insists we call the 'Big Flat', and surprisingly enough, a big desert doesn't have a lot of water in it.

We're out of the woods now, though.

[chuckles]

Or rather, we've just reached them.

They're calling it the North Fungal Arbor. It's like a huge forest—at least a hundred miles across—but it's all mushrooms. At least... they're sort of mushrooms. At first Braaten thought they were kind of like trees, aside from the fact that they don't make food from light. All the not-plants are like that here, he says. They've got roots going deep into the ground, and something down there is being used as food. But when he used his laser torch to cut into one, it turned out to be way stranger.

From what they can tell, the fungus has found a way to profit from the storm. It grows for a time, and when the storm comes around, it glazes the outside of the mushroom in dust-glass. Then, the fungus begins to digest parts of the glass—don't ask me how—and climb back out and keep growing. Apparently, it's using the glass as something like a layered skeleton to help it grow taller and wider than it normally would.

I'm not sure if I buy all of that, but the spirals of glass and mushroom meat were hard to argue against when we looked at the cross section.

[sigh]

I'm sure the scientists on the Votum will get a kick out of that when they wake up, but I'm getting tired of hearing about it. And if you thought Braaten's region names were bad, you should hear his species names...

[silence for 1.1 seconds]

We're going to enter the forest tomorrow morning. Depending on the density of the undergrowth, it may take us as much as a week to cross the Arbor. Shortly after that, we'll reach the deployment site for the second stormpuncher.

[silence for 3.2 seconds]

That's, uh...

I think that's it.

TRANSCRIPT ENDS

Day 32

"Something's definitely following us," Rhett said. They'd just broken camp for the morning and would be on the move again within the next few minutes. As he had every day since they'd arrived on Occassus, Rhett took a quick lap around the camp to look for any signs of movement.

"What makes you think so?" Braaten asked, hefting his pack onto his back. He hadn't so much as questioned Rhett in the last three days, a fact Rhett was hesitant to interpret.

"Pretty sure these are tracks," Rhett said, gesturing toward a pattern of strange indentations in a soft bit of soil.

Sarah came up to stand beside him, frowning down at the ground. "*We* definitely didn't make them. Or the wind."

Braaten arrived to frown at them as well. "They aren't very large."

"But look at the depth." To demonstrate, Rhett put his own boot beside the tracks and pressed into the ground. When he pulled his foot away, the imprint was perhaps half as deep.

"So it's heavy," Sarah said.

"Not *that* heavy," Braaten argued. "The marks are, what? Two inches across? Versus Rhett's foot? Pressure isn't just about weight—it's about surface area. They probably aren't more than fifty pounds."

"So the size of small wolves," Rhett said.

Braaten rolled his eyes. "*Very* small ones."

Sarah almost managed to let it go, but when they were just about done packing up their camp, she put her hands on her hips. "I think you guys are missing the point. We haven't seen any wildlife of this scale so far. Not since we landed."

"The ooze field," Braaten said.

"*Wildlife.*"

Braaten shrugged.

Rhett looked at her. "And?"

"The existence of an apex predator says a lot about the state of an ecosystem," Sarah said. "Namely about its stability."

"What makes you think it's a predator?" Braaten asked. "There's lots of mycotrees around to eat. These could be the equivalent of deer."

"It's an extant macrobiological specimen," Sarah said. "It implies that some ecosystems have found coping strategies for Nuhalriu. These creatures are successfully avoiding the storm—and if they are, others probably have, too."

Realization finally dawned on Rhett. "You're talking about the Occassi."

Sarah nodded.

"Not *that* again." Braaten rubbed at his temples. "We've been over this a hundr—"

A noise drew their attention, stopping Braaten mid-sentence. To Rhett's left, crouched along a branch of a mycotree some twenty feet away, was the shadow of a creature. Its form was indecipherable in the early morning shadow, but the sound of its breathing—a croaking, choking sort of noise—was impossible to miss. As Braaten had guessed, it wasn't excessively large, but Rhett knew better than to assume that meant it wasn't dangerous.

Rhett drew his pistol. "Sarah, grab your bag. We need to get moving."

Sarah glanced toward it, about ten feet away to their left.

Rhett took aim at the creature. "I'll shoot if it makes a move. Just grab the bag."

She nodded slowly. Hands raised before her—as if the creature was a mountain lion or bear—she moved toward her bag. The creature made no obvious movements, just kept up its raw, jagged breathing. Rhett squinted at it, trying to find the gleam of its eyes, hoping to gain some insight in finding them. Where were they? What was it thinking? How fast could it move? He could only guess.

Sarah reached her bag and lifted it slowly, awkwardly, onto her back. The creature didn't move. She backed away carefully, keeping her eyes fixed on the creature, until she was shoulder to shoulder with Rhett again. The thing remained motionless on the branch.

"Maybe it can't actually move," Braaten posited, turning away. "We really don't know—"

The shadow lurched out of the mycotree faster than Rhett would have thought possible. But trained as he was and aiming where he had, he landed his one and only pistol shot almost perfectly into its center mass. A spray of red followed the creature as it hurtled to the ground and lay there, motionless.

"Red blood," Rhett observed. For some reason, he hadn't expected that.

Braaten stared at the mass of flesh for a long moment, then shrugged. "Iron is a great oxygen acceptor."

"I guess I just thought aliens would be more…" Rhett trailed off as a chorus of ragged breaths broke out around them.

"Uh… Captain?" Sarah murmured. "How many shots do you have in that thing?"

Rhett scanned the mycotrees, trying to guess how many creatures threatened them. He could see only three, but the noise told him there had to be far more than that. "Not enough."

"Should have kept the SLOOP," Braaten muttered.

"And driven it through *here*?" Sarah said. "It wouldn't have fit under the—"

"I know." Braaten cleared his throat softly. "It's just… a lot faster than I am."

"Clump up," Rhett said. "We move together. Eyes out. Nice and slow."

"It's not going to work." Braaten's voice was shrill—something Rhett had never heard from him before. "They're surrounding us. How are we going to get *out*?"

"With a little show of force." Rhett picked a creature in the general direction they needed to go and took aim once again with his pistol.

PRRTSH.

The beast howled for a moment, then flopped over.

"Move," Rhett said.

It took them a minute to get the rhythm of the walk right. They moved back-to-back-to-back, a triangle of figures facing outward, their backpacks rubbing and bumping against each other with nearly every step. The sound of the creatures followed them.

"I don't think they have any eyes," Sarah said softly.

"What?" Rhett asked.

"I've seen a few of them. Some in partial light. There's no reflection from their face. Just… just skin. Or fur. I can't tell which."

"I still don't like the way they're looking at us," Braaten said.

Rhett dipped his chin in agreement. "How many miles to the edge of the Arbor?"

"We're still more than a day away."

Rhett pressed his lips into a thin line. They couldn't do this for an entire day. They probably couldn't keep it up for as much as an hour. What were they supposed to do? How were they supposed to get out?

"We could pitch camp," Sarah suggested. "Wait them out. They'll have to get bored eventually, and they aren't big enough to get into one of our prefabs."

"And if they try?" Braaten asked. "Even if all they do is chew up the wires, they could damage the filtration system. We'd be avoiding death today only to find it again when we can no longer breathe during the night."

"We don't have to deploy all three. It will be tight, but we can all fit in one. If it gets damaged..." Her eyebrows twitched as she considered where she was going with this. "We can find a way to share."

The eyes of his crewmates fell on Rhett. He took a deep breath. "I don't see another way. They have to sleep sometime—we'll try to move again once they do."

Braaten swore quietly but slung his pack down from his back and slid out the folded-up prefab. He flicked the deployment switch and stared nervously at the shadows surrounding them as the device set itself up. He adjusted the settings for its maximum filtration rate—better to keep up with three people inside—and ushered the others through the aperture.

To say it was cramped was an incredible understatement. Rhett had always found the prefabs to be uncomfortably small, even for just one person. For the three of them to fit inside at the same time, they sat side-by-side, knees against their chests, with their backs against one wall and their toes pressing against the other. Within three minutes, the air inside was musty and hot, a fact which the prefab's filtration system spun up to try to remedy.

"This was a stupid idea," Braaten said.

"You didn't give me any others," Rhett replied.

"We can't even *see* them. How are we going to know when they leave? Or when they sleep?"

"If you think we're enjoying this," Sarah said, "you'd be wrong."

"What do you think they want?" Rhett grumbled.

"Could be about territory," Braaten mused. "Could be predators, though."

"Hopefully not the latter." Sarah's hand had migrated to the thumb break on her sidearm's holster—an idle fidget she had come to use more and more in tense situations.

"Might be better for us, actually." Braaten shrugged, making a face at how little room there was to do so. "Sort of."

"What?"

"If they're defending their home, they may not stop until they've killed us all or driven us out." His tone was flat, matter of fact. Rhett had never heard him explain anything without inflecting a measure of derision. The man had to be absolutely terrified. "But if they're hungry, they might settle for only one of us."

Sarah grimaced. "Don't talk like that."

"Hey, you asked."

They waited for hours, exchanging a few grunts and even fewer words. It was unbearably hot, and after the first hour it didn't even bear remarking on. They heard nothing from outside the thin steel walls—a sign that might have been very good or very bad. Had circumstances been different, Rhett might have managed to doze off for a short while, but he sat at awkward attention, muscles rigid and back aching.

"We have to check," Braaten finally muttered. "Eventually."

"How long has it been?" Rhett asked.

The light of a navbrace was nearly blinding for its suddenness. "Nine hours, seventeen minutes."

Rhett nodded. "I'll do it." His muscles complained about being forced to move, but he knew they'd feel better for it soon.

"It should be me."

Rhett frowned at him.

Braaten rolled his eyes. "Do you think Sarah and I want you climbing over us? Door's right here."

Rhett exhaled sharply, then dipped his chin. "Be careful."

Braaten took a couple moments, then reached a hand toward Rhett. Rhett nodded, offering him the Phi-8. "Safety's still on."

"Not the gun." Braaten rolled his eyes again. "I want to shake your hand." Then, to Sarah, "Yours too, if you'll let me."

They shook his hand solemnly, but the mocking grin never fell from his face. "See? We'll all be friends before the end." With that, he secured his filtration mask over his mouth and nose and ducked out the little portal to the world outside.

He hunched for a long minute in the darkness—night had fallen since they'd taken shelter—clearly doing his best not to groan too loudly over what had to be intensely aching muscles. Rhett watched as his eyes panned around them carefully.

"You said," Braaten whispered to Sarah, "they don't have eyes?"

"Not like we have," Sarah said, "but that doesn't mean they can't—"

But it was too late. Braaten's navbrace ignited the area around the prefab with a sudden and blistering light, illuminating their surroundings in a tapestry of white and shadow.

"Fu—"

The word was swallowed by the sudden howl that rose all around them. Sarah jumped in her seat as something heavy was kicked through the doorway next to her.

"Run!" Braaten yelled. Taking his own direction, he sprinted off through the undergrowth.

"What is he doing?" Sarah stammered.

Rhett blinked hard, trying to get his eyes to focus on what had come through the door. It was about a foot and a half in length, perhaps six inches across, and housed in a soft-sided black case.

Braaten's stormpuncher.

"Giving us an out," Rhett said. "Hurry. That way."

"But Braaten—"

The screaming started then. Rhett tried not to think about it as he ushered Sarah out of the prefab and helped her put on her pack. He tried not to think about the extra weight of a second stormpuncher on his back—weight that could no longer be carried by the third member of their team. Tried not to think about the silence that followed or the unaccompanied patter of two pairs of feet.

When they finally reached the edge of the North Fungal Arbor, he tried not to think about what they'd left within.

Chapter 11

Day 33

PERSONAL LOG
RECORDED BY: Corporal Rhett Wethern, Security Officer
LOCATION: 1km east of the North Fungal Arbor, Occassus II
TRANSCRIPT BEGINS

Markus Braaten...
  [breathing for 5.2 seconds]
  Braaten was a good man.
  [breathing for 1.7 seconds]
  Smart. He...
  He and I didn't always... agree on things. From the start, we were... I don't know. He hated me. I can't say I cared much for him, either. But after what happened to Caldwell and McNeary... I don't know. I felt like we... understood each other.
  You know?
  Like brothers.
  [clears throat]
  Almost.
  He...

[silence for 2.2 seconds]

He didn't deserve what happened to him. He was brave, and without him...

[breathing for 1.7 seconds]

We were a day away from making it out of the Arbor. All we had to do was make it across, but...

Maybe we would have tried to go around it, if McNeary was still with us. I don't know how much time that would have added. Probably we should have done that. But we went through.

There were these... creatures. I didn't even get a proper look at them. We don't think they had eyes, but the way they responded to the light of Braaten's navbrace...

I just remember him screaming. Screaming... while we ran away.

He told us to run. Told us we had to leave him. It was too late for us to do anything to help him...

What was I supposed to do?

[grunts]

McNeary would have known.

TRANSCRIPT ENDS

Day 36

They hadn't waited as long before talking about Braaten's death. Rhett told himself it wasn't because they cared about him less. It wasn't that his loss was any less impactful than Caldwell's or McNeary's. It was just that, at this point, they'd grown so used to loss that it had lost a little of its sting.

CHAPTER 11

Or maybe it was that if they didn't talk about it, they wouldn't have anything to talk about at all. And since it was only Sarah and Rhett left, they both direly needed someone to talk to.

"We should signal the Votum," Sarah said for the third time in the last few days.

Rhett sat against the side of his prefab, staring at the transmitter that served as their only connection to the ship. It wasn't large, fitting easily in one of his hands, the short baton of its antenna jutting out of its main box. There was a small yellow light, little more than a pinprick at the tip of the antenna, which blinked with a slow, thoughtful cadence. It was designed to be as simple as possible, both for ease of use and for the preservation of its hydrogen-ion battery, which was promised to last for up to fifteen years. The fact that the promise would likely be tested—if either of them lived that long—was no comfort to him.

"What would we tell them?" Rhett asked. "There isn't another lander. The whole Votum was supposed to come down once the negotiations were done."

"They can engineer something. They have the materials. They have the time. We need help, Rhett. We can't do this on our own."

He didn't disagree with her. Even so, he simply stared at the radio and did nothing. Their path today had taken them through a series of rolling highlands, populated sparsely by mycotrees and other small shrub-like life. Though they hadn't seen any macroscopic animaloids (which Sarah was insisting they call them), the memory of their last encounter had made their journey arduous and paranoid.

"They'll die just like us," Rhett muttered.

"We'll die without them."

"They'll die just like us," he repeated. He looked at her, and the emptiness he felt inside stared out through the hollows of his eyes. "This was our mission. Our failure. We deserve... we deserve what we get. But them? They're still safe up there."

"They'll never wake up."

"Earth may send a ship," Rhett shrugged. "Eventually."

"If they ever get our signal. If there's anyone *to* get our signal." Sarah stood abruptly. "If they never wake up, it's not different from being dead."

He glanced up at her. After a long moment, he stretched out his hand to offer her the transmitter. She stared at it but didn't take it. Eventually, he lowered his arm and went back to staring at the pulsing light.

"Do you think Earth... is gone?"

"I think the Occassi survived," Sarah said. "It would be presumptively pessimistic to say humanity didn't."

"Takes some of the pressure off. Means we could just... not."

The kick wasn't graceful, but it was painful and surprising. It struck Rhett first in the shoulder, then in the side of the head, sending him toppling the short distance from sitting to lying on his side. He grunted, blinking up at Sarah as she hissed through her mask and glared down at her own foot.

"Ow! Fffff..." She shook her head, her gaze shifting back to him. "I'm not going to die for nothing, Rhett. Not for nothing. Is that what you want Markus's death to be worth? Or Shamus's? Or Steven's?"

Rhett picked himself up slowly, gauging whether she would kick him again. The radio had jumped out of his hand as he fell, and he picked it back up and brushed off a bit of red alien dirt. "People die for nothing all the time."

She studied him for a few seconds but seemed to understand what he meant. "This isn't a war, Rhett. There are no sides. No politics. It's just you and me and the planet. There are twelve-thousand people who need our help. We can't just ignore that."

He thought she was going to suggest they call for help again, but she didn't.

"What about Cyn?" Sarah asked softly.

Rhett looked up.

"You want to see her again, don't you?"

"Of course I do."

"If we... if you win, you can."

Rhett frowned. "You need to stop that. I'm no more likely to make it out of this than you are."

CHAPTER 11

She laughed joylessly. "Maybe."

"Sarah, I'm not going to let you die."

"You couldn't save the others. What makes you think you'll be able to save me?"

"*Sarah.*"

She shook her head, as if waking from a dream. "Why do you want to do this alone, Rhett?"

"I don't."

"But you won't call for help."

"It won't *help*," Rhett said. "We talked about this weeks ago, remember? Braaten said the transmitter only lets us send the green light. Even if he'd reprogrammed it to prevent the ship from landing, the people we wake up will have only a very limited time before the ship runs out of resources to take care of them. It was never meant to support its passengers when they were awake—only to prepare the way for us before the mission. The people we wake up? They'll starve to death before the storm has passed, even if we succeed. Ten years now, remember?"

She seemed to deflate. "I remember."

"I know it's tempting," Rhett said. "As a soldier, I want to call for backup. I want to know that someone up there has my back, has a plan, has contingencies in place. But this mission..." He trailed off for a long moment. "None of it was supposed to go like this. None of this was planned. If we signal the Votum, we'll be consigning who knows how many people to a meaningless death. And yes, being asleep isn't much better, but what if..." He wasn't sure where he was going with this, but his mouth kept moving anyway. "If we die, and the Votum stays up there for a decade, or a century, or however long. If the Occassi really did survive... they'll find it, won't they? When they find a way to fix their own planet, our people will still be alive up there. Still be safe. Cyn... she'll have to live without me, but so long as she's alive... so long as she's happy..."

"We lose no matter what," Sarah said darkly.

"Yes."

"No matter what we do. No matter if we live or die."

"That's exactly what I'm saying."

"But what if the Occassi *didn't* survive?" Sarah asked. "What if we're really it? The Votum's only chance? We still have to try, don't we?"

They stood in silence for a few minutes.

"Yes," Rhett finally said. "We have to try."

It wasn't a choice. It was simply a realization. A fact, however inconvenient. There was simply nothing else to do.

"So long as we survive," Rhett said. "We have to try."

Day 38

```
PERSONAL LOG
RECORDED BY: Corporal Rhett Wethern, Security Officer
LOCATION: Western Bank of the River Grey, Occassus
II
TRANSCRIPT BEGINS
```

I don't know how McNeary did one of these every day. I don't even do half of that, and I still don't know what to report.

[sigh]

Well, we're starting to get close to the second deployment site—the ruins of what must have been a large city. I mean, in the scope of things. It would only be a day or two away, if it weren't for the river here. The damn thing's almost a mile wide, and though it doesn't look fast, it is definitely deep enough and powerful enough to make a swim across impossible. Even if we didn't have bags and equipment, I mean.

So we're going around. There's a bridge a few days north of here, which satellite images confirm is at least mostly intact. We'll be backtracking a little to get back to the city, but Sarah and I agree the surest way is the only way. Like McNeary always said: no risks. We do this slow. We do this careful.

[breathing for 3.2 seconds]

I wish...

[breathing for 2.0 seconds]

It doesn't matter now.

TRANSCRIPT ENDS

Day 39

The bridge looked much better in the satellite images than it did in person. Though it was arguably standing and long chunks of it stretched out across the River Grey, the sound of it creaking was audible from over half a mile away. It was tall, standing almost a hundred feet above the surface of the water near its center, and the regular spacing of the support struts and cable reminded him of similar structures back on Earth.

"Doesn't look as sturdy as I'd like," Sarah remarked as they crested the last hill on approach to it.

"It doesn't," Rhett said. "But compared to how much weight it's bearing... will we really make a difference?"

They stopped at the edge of what must have once been a road—now coated with dust-glass a few inches deep. They looked at the bridge. They looked at the river. They looked left, then right, then to their navbraces for another crossing.

There wasn't another for a few hundred miles—and it brought them far too close to one of Nuhalriu's next passes.

"Is it a choice if there isn't a choice?" Sarah blurted out of the blue.

Out of the red, really. The sky on Occassus was very rarely blue.

"What do you mean?" Rhett asked.

"I mean this. We have other options than to try the bridge, but we don't *really* have other options."

Rhett blinked at her. "I'm not good at philosophy."

"I don't believe that for a second. But what I mean... I mean... if we chose wrong, but there wasn't a better choice... is it still our fault?"

Rhett pursed his lips inside his mask. "This isn't going to help us. Come on."

Surprisingly, she didn't argue. They stepped out onto the glass-buried street, watching with suspicious glances and listening with nervous ears to the slow shifting groan of the bridge.

"No cars. I mean—the equivalent," Sarah remarked, probably to distract herself from the noise around them.

"Would the storm have swept them away?"

She shrugged. "You'd think something would have gotten stuck somewhere."

It turned out she was right. About a quarter of the way across the bridge, pinned between a support strut and a tension wire, was the mangled remains of something metallic. There was no telling what shape it had once been, but the way it had been twisted suggested that it had been open inside—the chassis of some kind of vehicle.

They kept walking. The sway of the bridge became more apparent the farther they got, the stiff breeze pressing against them unwelcomingly, but without any real force. As they approached the halfway point, the real damage to the bridge came into view. Large chunks were missing from the center—holes large enough for the SLOOP or even the lander to have fallen straight through. The tarmac was discolored at the edges, sickly yellow when compared to the ashen red of the rest of the concrete. It was as if the materials had just... rotted away. By contrast, the steel struts and cables appeared generally unharmed—a sign which did something to reassure Rhett of their course.

"What must it have looked like?" Sarah wondered. "How old was it, before Nuhalriu?"

"Probably new? We haven't seen many structures this intact."

"Not necessarily. If they were like us, they probably went through cycles as a society. A focus on quality for a few decades, a focus on cost for another few. In some cultures on Earth, it was…"

She went on, and Rhett closed his mouth. It wasn't much use to engage with her, especially because he had no idea what he was talking about. She usually didn't say so openly—not like Braaten had—but there was a look she got sometimes when he talked. A subtle signal that whatever he said was about as correct as nutrient plaster was delicious.

Rhett studied her as she spoke. Getting her on a monologue was probably the best thing he could have done for her. She always seemed happier when she was teaching something—and though he absorbed very little of it, he did his best to seem attentive. With all they had been through recently, the least that he could do was—

Sarah's foot settled on a yellowed spot on the bridge, and before Rhett could open his mouth to say anything, she applied her weight to it.

When Rhett was a boy, his father had warned him about stepping on the drywall between the attic's studs. He'd been told it wouldn't hold his weight, but it had taken a bad step and a plummet through to the floor below before Rhett had actually understood what he meant.

This was much the same. The spot gave like a sponge, then tore away like bread. Sarah screamed, arms flinging upward, and Rhett lurched toward her, snatching for her midsection. One arm found purchase just below her ribs, which he felt as much as heard crack under the sudden pressure. The other was buffeted by the pack on her back, which smashed into his face as her weight landed fully in his grip.

After a harrowing struggle of what might have only been a few seconds, he wrestled Sarah and her pack back up to safety a few feet away from the new hole she'd made. For a while, she clutched at her ribs and stared at it.

"Ow," she finally wheezed.

"Are you all right?"

She glanced his way, but her vision wouldn't settle on him. Wouldn't settle on anything. She looked back to the hole. "It wants to kill us."

"What?"

"Occassus. It... it wasn't an accident."

Rhett rolled his eyes—a mistake, but at least she wasn't looking. "That doesn't sound like you. Not very scientific."

"Isn't it?" Sarah tried again to focus on him, this time with a little more luck. "We have lots of data points. Steven. Shamus. Markus."

Rhett suppressed a sigh. What did he know? "I guess."

"I told you, Rhett," she said, gaze growing distant again. "I told you I was going to die here. I knew it from the start."

Rhett shook his head. "And I told *you*. I'm not going to let it happen."

Her eyes snapped to his. "It's you against a *planet*, Rhett. Do you really expect to win?"

This wasn't helping.

"Can you walk?" he asked.

"I..." She took a few seconds to understand the question. "I think?"

He helped her to her feet. She winced on the second step, and it became immediately obvious that she was favoring her left leg.

"We can stop," Rhett said.

"No. Let's... let's get off the bridge. We'll look at it when we're on solid ground."

The rest of the bridge was a slow procession, broken up by a handful of breaks to catch their breath. Nearly all of the bridge had fallen away at one point, forcing them to grapple along the support strut and hope against a stiff breeze.

Fortunately, Rhett was still carrying a sturdy length of nylon rope, which allowed them the luxury of a backup line to hold onto as they shimmied their way across.

When they reached the far side, Sarah collapsed on the nearest available rock and twisted her leg to look at her calf.

"Definitely ripped through the suit," Rhett said, squatting next to her. "It's a simple cut, maybe four inches long. It isn't deep enough to be dangerous—it's already stopped bleeding."

"Still not fun to walk on."

Rhett glanced up at her. "Figured you'd want the good news."

"Yes, well..." Her brows furrowed. "Yes."

"We should make camp. Give you some time off the leg. Clean it out, get some antiseptic on it, bandage it."

Sarah nodded.

Rhett slid his pack off his back, then helped Sarah out of hers. He slid her prefab out of her pack and started the deployment sequence.

"Rhett?"

He glanced at her.

"Thank you."

Rhett shrugged. "I'm sorry."

"Sorry for what?"

"For..." He looked away. "For being weak. For wanting to give up."

Sarah stared at him pensively for a few moments. "We're all weak."

"Not McNeary."

She sighed. "Maybe not. But the rest of us? We're only human. We can't blame ourselves for our failings. All we can do is try to rise above them."

Rhett had nothing to say to that.

Chapter 12

The ground got softer about six inches down. Rhett had worried from all of his previous uses of the trowel that it would be next to impossible to dig a hole big enough. He had considered the laser cutter Braaten had designed but doubted the battery—or the nuclear equivalent that the thing operated on—would be happy about such an extended use.

He didn't mind using the trowel. Not really. There was a rhythm to digging. A sequence he could latch onto, like his practice with the Phi-8 in the firing range back on the Votum.

Ktchek. Swoo.

Ktchek. Swoo.

Ktchek. Swoo.

Ktchek. Swoo.

He wiped the sweat from his forehead every fourth toss of the soft-packed sand. It was a bit more frequent than he actually needed to, even with the evening sun shining directly on him, but the steady cadence helped him keep his thoughts organized.

The hole needed to be this long, just under six feet. He'd started with a shallow trench to get a sense of that dimension first. Since then, he'd steadily widened and deepened one side until the whole cavity was shaped vaguely like a teardrop, its long tail pointing toward the cave where they'd taken refuge for the past couple days. The cave hadn't been a perfect solution, but it had helped ease his paranoia about predators noticing them from afar. There were still too many unknowns on this planet, and staying still for long seemed like a risk without at least a few precautions.

His hands ached, but he picked up speed. He wouldn't finish before the light failed him. He should have known that, considering the tools he had and the size of the task, but he hadn't been willing to admit it to himself. The thought of sleeping in the cave while she...

Rhett dropped the trowel. Stared at it. Stared at his hands. He tried to move, but he couldn't. His breath came in shallow gasps.

Hseh-whh.

Hseh-whh. Hseh-whh.

Hseh-whh.Hseh-whh.Hseh-whh.

He tried to find a rhythm. Tried to regain control. His body shook, and he couldn't do anything but stare at the trowel at the bottom of the hole. That hole that he'd spent hours digging, arms aching, and it wouldn't be enough. Wasn't good enough.

He wasn't good enough. He hadn't been able to...

He couldn't...

His eyes shifted upward, to the mouth of the cave. The sinking sun cast a deep shadow over what lay within, but he could picture it.

He could picture her.

Day 46

I buried her yesterday.

[sniff]

I guess someone should know. Eventually. If you all ever wake up. If the captain was right and all these damn messages end up in some kind of history book. It will be important for you all to know...

No, I can't talk to all of you. I know the captain did it that way, but that's too big.

Cyn? I know others will listen, but these messages... they're for you. So you'll maybe understand what I went through down here.

If you ever wake up, that is.

[6.7 seconds of silence]

[clears throat]

Sarah Galerkin was our translator. She survived up until yesterday, the forty-fifth day of the mission. A few days ago, she got a cut on her leg. Damn thing swelled up so much she couldn't walk. We cleaned it and sterilized it over and over, gave her antibiotics, anti-inflammatories... nothing worked. We decided later it had to be that yellow mush from the bridge. Some kind of mold, maybe. It infected the wound. Maybe if we were on the Votum, the med bay could have synthesized something, but...

[2.8 seconds of silence]

Now I'm alone.

I thought it was quiet when we got here, but I always had Braaten's mockery. Caldwell's sage and snarky comments. Sarah's knowledge and melancholy. The captain's oppressive optimism. Now, all I have is this radio and its blinking yellow light, telling me it's still connected to the Votum somewhere in orbit. That little yellow light is all the connection I have to the rest of humanity. It tells me that when my job is done, I can send the all clear and be reunited with you.

[chuckles]

[sobs]

Goddammit, pull yourself together!

[series of thumping sounds]

I miss you, Cyn. But I haven't given up yet. We didn't lose the Stormpunchers with the others like we did with Caldwell. I still have four... enough to make it possible, but not fast. I'm less than a week away from where I'm supposed to deploy the next one—somewhere that used to be a city, from what the ship tells me. Doesn't seem like it's going to be empty anymore, so it will probably be dangerous. If this is the last message I send, I guess you'll know why.

[12.1 seconds of silence]

I'm going to sign off now. Talking to myself like this makes me feel... weird. Bye, Cyn.

[2.1 seconds of silence]

Talk... soon?

Day 48

Maybe he was right. Maybe it is good to try to sort out your thoughts this way. Out loud. Like I'm talking to someone who cares.

Well, I hope I'm talking to someone who cares. Even if you can't answer. Even if you never get these. It helps to know that I'm talking to you, and that you care. If it helps me to think, all the better. I could use a good head for planning down here, and I've lost the one I was using.

It didn't save him, did it?

[silence for 3.4 seconds]

It doesn't matter. There's still the mission. There's still work to do. I'm a soldier, and I know if I have a plan, I can complete it. I have my orders. My direction. My purpose. I can march toward it and hope for the best. Be as careful as I can. If I'm meant to complete it...

[silence for 6.5 seconds]

I hope this makes it to you.

I hope you are well.

I'll be in the city tomorrow. Maybe the next day. I can see it from where I'm camping tonight. Just a little smudge on the horizon. Right out here in the middle of nowhere.

[breathing]

I wonder what it looked like before. Were there farmlands out here, where I'm walking? Or suburbs? Maybe some factories? Restaurants? Shopping centers?

Whatever there was, it's gone now. Nothing left but low shrubs. Some grass. Patches where the dust-glass has gathered in little drifts like snow. I should give credit to the storm where it's due: the thing has completely deleted whatever Occassi society used to look like. If they were like us. If they were nothing like us. If we could have understood each other. If we could only have ever fought.

Gone. All of it, wiped clean by that gigantic fucking cosmic eraser. Smeared like graphite on a page. Unreadable. Useless.

[clears throat]

Sorry about that. Getting a little dramatic, I guess. I figure it's fine, from one artist to another.

[laughing]

Nope; can't take myself seriously.

[laughing]

[sigh]

Well, I'm not sure if these messages are going to help me think at all, but I guess a laugh at my own expense is a decent enough find. I'll try and be as consistent as I can. Try to remember to send them when things happen. When I think of things to tell you. You know, whatever.

Until then, Cyn.

I love you.

Rhett, out.

Chapter 13

Day 57

The city rose abruptly at the edge of the dust, reaching like a hundred hands for some distant and dying star. Its dead, stony flesh had begun to wear away. Twisted heaps of steel and other metals littered the space between structures, some still clinging high to walls, all of them battered into such submission as to make their original purpose impossible to discern. Dust had settled in some of the deeper corners, the drifts protected from the winds of Nuhalriu. A thin layer of milky glass had formed over the roads. Though it was near midday, the shadows of the surrounding buildings hid the sun, casting this whole ruined world in a murky malaise. He imagined a thousand unseen eyes peering at him from the rubble. Perhaps there were watchers above, waiting for him to turn his back. He couldn't care. He had a job to do, and there was no other way to reach his destination.

Armed with nothing more than a Phi-8 Mass Driver pistol and a bolstered suite of holoescent lamps he'd cobbled from the suits of his crewmates, Rhett Wethern stalked along the dust-blown trench between the structures. The Occassi, for some indiscernible reason, did not seem to believe in squares in their architecture. City blocks came in the shape of equilateral triangles, each one hemmed in by a trinity of roads whose junctions were as complex as they were strange. It was all littered with refuse now; he would certainly never understand it. Sarah might have liked to see it, though. And maybe Cyn... maybe she would find it an interesting subject for her paintings.

The silence deepened as he drew further from the touch of the wind. He stooped, leapt, ducked, and shimmied, moving as carefully and quietly as he could through the detritus. The only sounds were his footsteps and his heartbeats—both rhythmically pounding no matter how he bade them to quiet.

Rhett stopped at a relative clearing in the middle of one of the city's odd six-way intersections. He tapped at his navbrace, studying the layout of the streets around him. According to orbital topography, he wasn't far from the city's tallest remaining structure. While it wasn't terribly impressive compared to what a living society might have—barely more than 1000 feet—its endurance said something of the materials the Occassi had used as a society. It would, he realized, take him more than a day to climb, assuming it didn't have clear and convenient staircases.

Rhett scowled. He'd tried to pack light to help with his pace. He couldn't carry all of the crew's nutrient plaster or all three remaining stormpunchers at the same time, so he'd left them and the bulk of his supplies in the cave near where he'd buried Sarah. He'd packed what he expected to need for the trip to this deployment zone, but it was already clear he'd badly overestimated his travel speed. He'd lost a day to another one of those ooze-fields, this one twice the size of the first one they'd seen. Another two days had been spent crossing an enormous dried out rain basin that, for whatever reason, had generated enough magnetic interference to prevent orbital navigation assistance. Now, as he prepared for a climb he hadn't really thought through, he was already more than halfway through his supplies with no hope of a safe shortcut back.

"Maybe I'll find something here in the city," he muttered.

It was unlikely, to say the least, that more than seventy years after their apparent extinction, some morsel of Occassi cuisine would have been left lying around for him. Even if it was, would he recognize it as food? If only Sarah were here. Not only had she been a vital source of company, she would have made short work of the mysteries of the dead society around him.

He continued for a few more blocks, bemoaning how difficult it was to maneuver around obstacles with his heavy pack. "These dead societies never consider matters of convenience to the post-apocalyptic explorer."

CHAPTER 13

He tried to ignore that nobody answered him.

"Is it bad that I'm talking to myself?" he wondered.

"It's not like there's anyone else to talk to."

"Still, people might say I'm crazy."

He scoffed. "Sarah already thought that. Anyways, I must be crazy to believe I can actually finish this alone."

He shrugged. "Nothing better to do."

Rhett stopped, eyebrows furrowed, at an apparent dead-end. In two directions, heaped rubble and twisted metal formed what almost looked like a barricade. Up until now, he hadn't thought any of the damage appeared to have been arranged in a deliberate way, but this... this implied something about what might have happened here.

It might have been this way for more than seventy years. That was a long time for evidence to break down, or even for someone to come along and clean it up, depending on how suddenly they disappeared... or for what reason.

Was it a war? Could a war create a storm like Nuhalriu? It could have been a weapon gone wrong, certainly. It seemed more likely than it being something natural. But then... if they had the technology for destruction like that, would they really be constructing barricades to fight each other in the streets?

The tower was only two blocks away now. Rhett had to find a way over or around the barricades. He paused for a few moments, listening as he had so many times since he'd entered the city. Still, there wasn't so much as a breath. No signs of life, intelligent or otherwise. Perhaps it shouldn't have surprised him, but it felt ominous nonetheless.

"Maybe the water in the city is poisoned." He pursed his lips. "No water, no life."

He studied one of the barricades, thinking he saw a path of footholds he could use. With deliberate slowness, he stepped up to the first one. His bag leaned heavily against his back with his new angle, and he had to fight both its awkward weight and the haphazard danger of the barricade with every motion. No sudden movements, he told himself. With each step or shift of the hand, he waited for everything to settle before reaching for the next.

No shortcuts, like the captain had said. Just keep running.

Rhett peered over the barricade to find a street that looked the same as the one behind him. Nothing leapt out at him; nothing caught his eye. He pushed himself over the top of the pile, careful of a jutting piece of steel to his left. The descent was a little more difficult, since he didn't lead with his eyes to get a good look at his path, but he managed to reach the ground without slipping or cutting himself. He breathed hard for a few moments when his feet were finally safe on the ground, hating his mask for the way it limited his air supply. Better clean air than more air, he knew, but it still frustrated him.

He turned his eyes to the tower, which shot far beyond the reach of the buildings around it. It had been visible for hours, but he hadn't fully appreciated its size until he'd gotten close. To climb that thing... well, he certainly couldn't carry his whole bag that high. He'd have to stash it somewhere, only bring what he needed to survive the climb.

The entrance to it was, thankfully, obvious once he got close. A low archway, nearly collapsed on the inside, stood alone on one of the three flat faces of the building. The opening was narrow, but he could see more space inside, so he slipped off his pack and shoved it through the gap before slipping through himself. Inside, a large, decrepit antechamber greeted him. The ceiling vaulted high above him—nearly sixty feet, by his estimation—curving to a triangular three-way arch juncture at its center. A vast, swirling black and red mural had been painted on the walls, visible everywhere the rubbish didn't cover. He couldn't begin to guess what it depicted. Likely, it had once been far more colorful, but either from a period of radiation or perhaps the heat of the storm, the more delicate colors had faded away.

Paint, he thought. *These people painted*.

They didn't just have eyes, like Sarah said. They had *art*. They might be so much like humans were, and he'd never know it. It was as if he were walking through the skeleton of his own planet and had somehow failed to recognize it.

The differences... the triangular blocks and the strange creatures... this was all like a fugue dream overshadowing his knowledge of the death of his own world.

Rhett thought for a moment about his counterparts—the Occassi who might soon or had recently arrived on Earth. It was a feature of the treaty that embassy-reserves be established on both worlds for the members of the other. If Earth was dead, there might be other explorers there that, like him, were just discovering how similar they really were. What creatures on Earth might have taken over in humanity's absence? They'd already wiped out most of the large predators a century before the Votum left, so what might remain? It would depend on how humanity killed itself, he supposed. Same as here, with the storm.

So, then. How to go up?

Rhett scanned the walls closer to ground level. There were a few places where there might be doors, but most of them looked to be barricaded intentionally. He wondered at that. Both on the streets surrounding the building, and now within the building itself? What had they been trying to keep out—or in?

He'd already decided it best not to fire his sidearm unless it was absolutely necessary. Who knew what sort of creatures were silently hiding nearby? Discovering the barricades only reinforced that. On the off chance this was the Occassi's attempt to stop a creature, rather than an army, he didn't want to attract its attention with a loud noise. Even if it didn't have ears, he mused, a magshot's sound could be felt through the ground. Almost anything would notice that.

Rhett just had to decide, then.

He slipped off his pack, sorting through it for what he expected to need for the climb. Rope. Food. Some more water filtration tabs. A few other things. He slipped them into the various pockets of his suit, then turned toward one of the barricades. It took him almost half an hour to clear what appeared to be a solid steel door, and he realized shortly after that it had been sealed shut from the inside as well. Without slowing, he returned to his pack and rummaged for one of the devices Braaten had cobbled together before his passing—a handheld laser-torch that would, according to the man himself, cut through almost anything.

Just don't let it overheat, he'd jokingly warned. It seemed like ages ago. *The thing is powered by a micro-fission cell, so it should be used with care.*

Rhett ignited the beam, directing it toward a wide section of the door he had cleared. In seconds, the metal went from red to white, glowing as if with a deep inner fire. He moved carefully, directing the device with both hands to keep from wobbling. By the time he'd cut two long stretches—half of what he'd need to make a hole—the torch began to hiss in his hands. He set it aside for a few minutes, deciding it was a perfect time to have a meal. He made the same grimace he always did as the slurry slid down his throat.

"Watermelon flavor," he grumbled. "We didn't even have watermelons on Earth when I left. Why is it still a flavor?"

He flicked the spent plaster canister aside, listening to it clatter across the stone floor. Stone, not concrete. That was odd. They'd used concrete plenty of times that he'd seen, so it had obviously been invented. Why was this building different? With how much it dominated the structures around it, he would have thought it would be built out of their most advanced materials, not their most primitive ones.

Rhett returned to the steel door when he thought the laser-torch was cool enough. This time, he moved a little faster, a little more certainly. He had a sense now of the door's thickness and how long it took to burn through to the other side. Within twenty minutes, the metal began to creak, signaling him to give it a swift shove. It bent inward as if on a hinge on its left side, where he'd not yet cut the last inch or so of the metal. He smiled. Not too much noise; that was good.

Beyond the door, a wide and gently sloping ramp ascended to his left until it reached the corner of the building and twisted out of view. He wasn't sure why he'd expected stairs, but somehow the ramp still surprised him. It was so simple. So... antiquated. To build a structure so tall, with no sign of more sophisticated ascent methods, was almost unimaginable. Maybe the Occassi flew, either with technology or wings? Or perhaps there was a significance he couldn't yet guess about this tower. What if it was a sort of cathedral, and climbing it in this rudimentary way was part of some religious rite?

CHAPTER 13

Other than a generous layer of dust, the hallway was clear of debris. That didn't seem accidental, but he supposed he'd never really be sure.

Rhett stashed the laser-torch on his belt and drew his sidearm before beginning his long climb up the winding tower.

Chapter 14

Day 58

Rhett pitched his camp in another antechamber that was, according to his navbrace, not quite halfway up the 1000-foot ascent. The ramps, consistent in their angle and in their emptiness, seemed to go on forever. It had taken him hours to find a doorway to escape the endless winding, though it gave him no encouragement as to how far he'd still have to go. The ceiling vaulted once again, high overhead in its trigonal arch, and according to the navbrace's estimation, that would only be the second of as many as five such antechambers if the pattern continued.

The night hadn't been as quiet as he'd anticipated, but nothing came for him in his prefab. Instead, he'd done his best to sleep amidst the cacophony of chittering and buzzing that had to be the city's plentiful nocturnal insect population. When he awoke, bleary and unrested, the silence had returned like a blanket with the rising of Occassus's sun, Baitahili.

Rhett wondered at himself remembering the words Sarah had used. He normally wasn't one for language, but now... he supposed it was some little piece of her that he could carry on. Something to remember her by.

He donned his suit and mask and stepped out into the quiet antechamber. He shone his lights across all the surfaces around him before allowing himself a moment to stop and stretch. He considered breakfast, but with how low his supplies were already running and the amount of climbing he'd be doing today...

CHAPTER 14

it was probably better to go on an empty stomach than an upset one. He'd eat at noon, he decided.

Rhett packed up quickly, watching as the Personifab™ folded itself down for transport. He glanced at the radio where it hung at his hip, its ever-present yellow light continuing to blink like the heartbeat of all humanity. Then he strode across the antechamber and peeked up the continuing ramp to his left.

"Must have been a pretty serious religion," he decided, "to make its supplicants climb this whole damn thing."

Rhett began his ascent.

"Some kind of evil fitness gods, maybe."

He tried to smile, but the expression wouldn't fit itself to his face. He kept going.

The next antechamber took him a few hours to reach. His pace must be better now, or the subtle narrowing of the tower was making the climb seem easier. He stepped out into the antechamber, marking how the ceiling was not vaulted quite as tall as the previous two.

"I can do this," he whispered.

He crossed the antechamber, wondering once again at its emptiness. At least here there was one pile of… something. It was hard to tell what it was beneath all the dust, but a heap of rubble occupied one edge of the room, perhaps ten feet from the opposite corner's door.

Rhett shrugged. "Couldn't have been perfectly tidy."

He leaned through the far archway, sighing at the walkway sloping ever upward. They all looked the same now. Every hall, every turn, every inch he'd walked.

"I'm going to see this infernal ramp in my dreams." He pursed his lips, standing upright again. "Maybe I am dreaming. Certainly feels like I could be in one of those weird nightmares. All that needs to happen now is—"

Rhett ducked before his mind even registered something coming from his periphery. For a moment, he thought he'd dodged the object, but then he had the sudden sensation that his world was getting smaller. He reached for his pistol—his fingers touched but didn't grasp the weapon before a wide black membrane crashed down on his head, enveloping his arms and shoulders like a sack had been thrown over him. He yelped, mind whirling as his chest-mounted holoescent lamps blinked in and out of visibility with the moving folds of the thing entangling him.

Rhett threw his weight to the side, trying to unbalance whatever was trying to grab him. The sack gave a little, unwinding, if slightly. Then he crashed to the ground on his shoulder with a grunt, the pressure surrounding him. He reached for his sidearm again, caught it up with a pair of fingers as he was jostled about, then fumbled it out of reach.

"Fuck," he growled, throwing his elbows out against the membrane to no avail. It was still tightening around him, constricting his arms to his sides. Even if his pistol was still in his thigh holster, he doubted he'd be able to reach it. "Fuck, fuck, *fuck.*"

Rhett twisted, crushed arms fingering for the controls of the laser-torch at his belt. If he could turn it on... if he could only reach it...

A hissing sound alerted him to his success. The skin of his hip stung, but a burn wouldn't be so bad compared to whatever this... *thing* had planned for him.

Rhett's bonds loosened suddenly, and he was hurled across the floor. He skidded to a stop, the light of his lamps dancing. His mind caught up to him, and he switched off the torch, gripping it with his left hand as he came to his feet. He narrowed his eyes against the dimness, trying to discern what had attacked him.

Staring back at him—assuming it did indeed have eyes—was an enormous mass of roiling flesh. He saw tentacles, perhaps stitched together with something like webbing—that must have been the bag it had thrown over him. He couldn't see a face, nor how it moved, but he was fairly sure it was near where the heap of rubble had been. Had it been hiding behind it? Inside it?

The creature hissed at him but made no move to attack again.

Pistol. Pistol pistol pistol. Rhett swept one of his lamps over the floor of the room, finding the weapon nearly all the way in the corner to his right. He touched his thumb to the ignite button on the laser-torch and, keeping his eyes focused on the monster across from him, began shifting toward the pistol.

"Just waiting for me, ah?" he shouted, making a threatening gesture with his arms. "Think just because I'm alone I won't fight?"

The creature hissed again, moving in the strange way an octopus does toward the sidearm. Was it intelligent enough to understand that to be his goal, or was it merely mirroring his movements?

"I've got to say," Rhett spat. "If you're an Occassi, you're a hell of a lot uglier than I pictured."

How would he know? How would he even check?

The pistol was still ten feet from him. The monster was closer by half but made no obvious sign of looking at it. But how could he tell? Why did these aliens have to be so damn *alien*?

"Nuhalriu!" he shouted. It wasn't conversational, of course, but it was all he knew.

The creature didn't respond.

"Baitahili!" Rhett tried again.

Still nothing. The thing was right over top of the pistol now but hadn't moved to grab it. It looked as if it were posturing. Waiting.

It's an ambush predator, he reminded himself. *It will move faster than you expect.*

Then he'd move first.

He ignited his torch, shouted unintelligibly, and dove for the weapon. The creature let out a shriek, shrinking back at the warding light of the torch. It was just enough. Rhett snatched the pistol, fumbling with the safety for one harrowing moment, and leveled the weapon on the monster.

As if sensing its time had come to an end, the monster lurched toward him one final time.

PRRTSH. PRRTSH.

Rhett sank two solid shots into the central mass of the beast, his ears instantly ringing from the reverberations of the noise in the chamber. It shrank away for a few seconds, slipping backward while it left a sickly black trail of viscera in the dust. Rhett followed it, step for step, keeping his weapon ready. He raised an eyebrow as it sank back into what looked like a hole in the wall.

"None of that."

PRRTSH. PRRTSH. PRRTSH.

With one final series of flailings, the monster hissed its last.

For a few moments, Rhett stood still, breathing hard. He adjusted his mask, which had been knocked slightly askew in the fight, then returned his pistol and torch to their places on his suit and crouched to inspect the burn on his leg. The suit had been breached, but the wound itself wasn't bad. He slathered some antiseptic gel on it and patched the suit with a few adhesive strips.

"Could definitely be worse," he told himself. His voice escaped him in a dull, disinterested tone. "Honestly, not even bad for my first fight with an alien monstrosity. I have a few things to work on for next time, but all around pretty solid."

Hopefully he'd never have to fight another, but his luck hadn't been great so far. He stepped toward the carcass, eyeing where it had been trying to escape to. He nodded as he found the pile of rubble was still behind it, and a few of its tentacles had been shoved through a small orifice on its side. He brushed a bit of the dust from the heap, realizing at a touch that it wasn't stone or steel, but something organic.

"A cocoon?" He pressed on the fibers of it, finding them remarkably rigid. "It weaves its own hunting blind."

It dawned on him how fortunate he was. Not only to have survived the attack, but to have been attacked in the first place. *Hunting*, he thought. *Meat. Food.* He was low and needed enough to make it back to the cave. He studied the creature now with a new eye.

"Alien kalamari might not be so bad." He chuckled. "So long as it isn't poisonous."

It would have to wait. With the racket he'd just made, there could be any number of terrible things heading his way. He had to keep climbing. Had to complete the mission here, deploy the stormpuncher. If there was something left when he returned, he'd make of it what he could.

Rhett shuddered. But to let it go to waste?

"It would be even more wasteful to let myself die here," he reminded himself. He checked his leg one more time, then pushed himself to hobble toward the upward ramp. After a few steps, his gait leveled out. He could keep going.

The hours stretched on in the dark halls lit only by his puny artificial lights. He heard scuffling from below in the tower, but nothing came from above. When it was nearing midday, he emerged into a fifth, final antechamber that he could only hope was near the top of the tower. Light streamed in from a crumbling wall opposite the chamber door. That, he realized, was his next destination. The climb had only just begun.

Rhett afforded himself a pause for lunch. He'd need his strength if he was to continue. He considered giving himself a short rest as well but decided the risk to the carcass of the blind-weaver was too great. His living and dying could depend on what he could salvage from that.

Rhett's suit wasn't designed for climbing, but knowing both mountains and buildings awaited him, he'd managed a few modifications. That was to say, he'd cut parts of the protective paneling off to extend his range of motion, allowing him to grab anything he'd need to. He'd also cut a hole in one reinforcement ridge on his suit's right forearm, which allowed him to mount his laser-torch there. Though he wished for something fancier like electromagnets or a grapple launcher, he'd have to settle for what he had.

Rhett stepped up to the hole in the wall, breath catching even before he leaned out to look over the city below. And it truly was—the entire city was below him now. He stood on the precipice, as if he were almost flying, and the whole planet stretched before his eyes. His heart pounded in his ears as he imagined the fall. The crash. The splatter. How could he do this? How could he trust himself to nothing more than his arms to keep from—

Rhett stepped back, catching his breath. "So," he muttered, "looking down was a bad idea."

For some reason, the thought struck him as both incredibly funny and incredibly stupid. He laughed dryly.

"All right now." He clenched his eyes shut, trying to summon his courage. "I killed an alien monstrosity not a few hours ago. What's a little climb?"

Stepping back up to the ledge, Rhett reached up and out the aperture for his first handhold. Wind blasted against his face, forcing him to blink, but his grip held. Slowly, steadily, he shifted his weight onto the lip of the hole and found a second handhold.

He paused. The moment he stepped out with his foot, he was committed to this. Committed that this was the only way he could go about achieving his goals. Was there something he'd missed? Some other strategy that would prove safer, easier, or more certain?

Rhett shook his head. It was like the captain had said. No shortcuts. Keep on running.

He heaved himself out into the open air, setting his sight on his goal. Here at the top of the tower, the roof sloped steadily in the same trigonal archway he'd seen before. At its peak, a broken-off structure that could have been anything from a spire to a weathervane stood. He'd be able to secure the puncher to that.

Laser focus guided his hands and feet. Decades of weathering provided him with ample handholds, though they were smoother than he'd like from where it had turned to glass in some places. As they'd seen so many times before, the dust combined with the heat of the storm to make a sort of anti-freezing-rain. It needn't find sand where it was; it could deposit its own.

Rhett had always gotten a funny feeling when going into space. Some ridiculous part of his brain thought everywhere he could see was somehow under his control. As if just by achieving a lofty perch over the world, he could rule it. That feeling returned to him as his eyes wandered toward the distant horizon shrinking all around him. This time, however, it struck a new chord.

It was true, in one way of speaking. He was, as of now, the only living human on this planet. There were good odds saying he was the only *sentient* life on the planet as well. By simple default, he supposed, that made him a sort of king. Or

CHAPTER 14

emperor. Or god. This planet was his domain; he could come and go where he pleased, never to be disturbed by the fickle nonsense of other mortal men.

Rhett sighed, stopping his climb. What a lonely existence, to be a god.

It didn't help that everything on the planet wanted to kill him. If that wasn't the basest form of insubordination, he wasn't sure what was.

He kept climbing, mocking himself for his own thoughts. Emperor. An emperor without a court. Without council. Without subjects. Without power. Without... anything. He'd as soon believe that by climbing this tower, he could get all the way up to the Votum—back to Cyn. It was foolish. Insane.

The granite of the roof smoothed up ahead, still more than thirty feet from the top. Pockets of the mineral seemed to weather at different rates and under different circumstances, making the way ahead patchy and uncertain.

Rhett chuckled nervously as he leaned his weight into his grips, lifting his left hand from the stone to activate the laser-torch. It only then occurred to him that he'd be unable to turn it off as he climbed without a considerable waste of energy. He'd have to leave it on, beam firing at the stones and even into the sky above him between his directed applications to the stone.

"A beacon," he muttered. "I'm going to be a damn laser beacon on the tallest object for a hundred miles."

Every tactical fiber in his body recoiled at the thought. He would be so obvious. So vulnerable. But only if his onlookers could comprehend what they saw. If the Occassi were actually gone, he should have little to fear.

The odds were low, he knew. But the possibilities...

It didn't matter. This was the only way. He had to climb.

Rhett ignited the torch and set it to work against the granite before him, burning a good foothold in a matter of seconds. He watched it cool impatiently, then shifted his weight up and repeated the process. It was slow, but his grip felt even more secure now than when he'd first started. The sure way was the best way, especially when dealing with such heights.

Don't think about the heights!

If I fall, I will have a good long time to think about them, actually.

Stop it! Focus.

Rhett climbed. His arms ached. His knees began to buckle. But foothold by foothold, the angle of the tower began to turn inward, flattening to a point where his vertical climb was more like a steep hike. He switched off his laser-torch, lying flat against the granite with his knees locked to catch his breath. Against his better judgement, he hung his arms at his sides, letting the strain unwind like a worn-out spring.

He could do this. He could get to the top. The worst was behind him; he just had to finish what he started.

When Rhett reached the peak, he sat on the steep grade, wrapping his legs around the broken stump of the central monolith. He fiddled with the buckles that wrapped around his midsection, which secured the stormpuncher to his back. After a few minutes, he had it nearly in position on the spire. He activated the switch for the device's leg-bores and gritted his teeth as they worked their way into the stone. With a nod of satisfaction, the device's spring boots made contact, ensuring the device had a stable but flexible mounting.

It was done. Two out of four punchers had been deployed. He could move on.

Rhett secured his rope around the stump with a remote quick-release. The way back to the hole in the wall was an easy rappelling descent, and when he was safe back in the antechamber, he activated the quick-release and recovered his rope.

"And now, we can see about that feast." He stepped back through the door to the descent ramp, frowning after he'd gone only a few steps. "Walking downhill... there has to be something..."

He considered what he had on him, but nothing struck him as safe to be used as a sled. The time and energy he could have saved...

He shook his head. Walking, then.

When Rhett made it back to the carcass of the blind-weaver, he found a handful of small, fur-covered creatures climbing on it. For a moment, they seemed to look at him, as if glaring. They had no eyes, only a head shaped like that of a weasel, with two deep pits in the flesh at the ends of what might have been a nose. Apparently deciding he was no threat to them, they returned to their meal, gnawing at the open wounds the mass driver had made.

"Huh." Rhett approached slowly, squinting to study the odd creatures more closely. One of them hissed before scurrying away. They were bigger than he realized once he got closer. The largest might be all of ten pounds. It was a good thing they seemed to be scavengers. A pack of those things was not the sort of engagement Rhett's pistol was designed to be used in. He turned his focus back to the blind-weaver.

"Well." He pursed his lips. "Here's hoping you don't taste as bad as you look."

Day 59

Almost died yesterday.

[sigh]

Again.

I need to slow down. I know that. Need to be more careful. More aware. More of all sorts of things that I'm simply... not.

The good news is that the deadliest beasties down here are fairly tasty. This one almost tastes like chicken. You know, if chicken was singed over a laser-torch to cook it.

Yeah, really tasty.

[chuckle]

Someday, we're going to have these things in pens on farms or some nonsense. Monsters I can't even comprehend right now might be raised as feedstock by the time I'm old.

Hey, at least we won't all be eating nutrient plaster, right? Maybe I'll figure out some good recipes. You know, with my vast experience as a chef. Or at least as a grill-master.

[clears throat]

Grill-user.

Honestly, salt would be a good start. Since the plaster has everything you supposedly need, the lander didn't have any kind of seasonings or condiments on it. I'm sure there must be something decent that grows someplace on this planet, but who knows if I'll ever find it. Salt should be easier, though. Anyplace near the ocean will have it, and it's present in at least some quantity in mineral deposits all around the planet. The trouble will be figuring out how to extract it without also getting... other stuff.

Until then, I guess I'll have to live with bland alien calamari.

[chuckle]

Boo-hoo.

Day 62

Rhett left the city with the uneasy feeling that he was being watched. It could be the pitcats, he supposed. Even without eyes, they gave the feeling of watching, and he supposed the feeling had started only shortly after his descent from the apex of the trigonal tower. But the odd rat-like beasts had made no obvious move to follow him. Perhaps watching was all they intended to do.

He couldn't risk it. He set the Votum to track small-scale movement when it came around for each pass over him, but that would only cover seven minutes of every hour and twenty-two minutes. It wasn't a good shot, but it was something. Especially if whatever it was tried for a slow, careful approach.

CHAPTER 14

The wilderness accepted him once again with practiced indifference. Rhett was rapidly becoming a creature of this place. A being that belonged in these vast stretches of uncivilized emptiness. There were dangers here, certainly, but if he remained smart and vigilant... well, at least he had a chance.

The ES Votum pinged his navbrace to alert him of movement as it swung distantly overhead. He turned but saw nothing. Maybe it didn't matter. There was a series of rock formations up ahead; he could stage an ambush from there. He smiled grimly. It wasn't much of a plan.

Rhett checked his sidearm, noting its charge and the number of magnetopellets he had remaining. He'd be fine, at least until he reached the cave and could restock. Then again, with things like the blind-weaver around, perhaps he should be carrying more than he currently was. Should he make a detour all the way back to the lander itself? There would be more than enough there for as long as he was liable to survive.

Rhett climbed up between the rocks, adrenaline pumping through his veins. He checked each corner before he rounded it, keeping in mind the appearance of the cocoon the monster in the tower had built. In all likelihood, most creatures didn't survive their first encounter with the thing—any who did would learn how to identify and avoid their hiding places. He found a good nook that gave him a view of the path he'd taken without being too obvious to a pursuer. It would only take a moment for him to line up his shot. Hopefully this could buy him that much.

He blinked hard, raking his fingers through his hair as he tried to calm his breathing. His fingers came away caked in dust—he hadn't realized how ambivalent he'd become. He shook his hand out and settled it back into a stabilizing grip on his sidearm. It might only be minutes. Hopefully it wouldn't be longer than that. But what if it was? What if his pursuer decided to wait, to watch, perhaps suspecting he might try something like this?

These rocks could serve more than one kind of ambush.

Rhett cursed himself silently, wiping a bead of sweat from his brow. His pursuer could be anything. In the nearly two months he'd spent on this planet, he'd seen more than a dozen species he never could have dreamed of. Not once had one of them stalked him for such a distance.

He held his breath at a sound just around the corner. The creature would be visible soon—he'd have an opportunity to take his shot. Straining his ears, he wondered what it might be. There were no footsteps, so far as he could tell. Just a quiet, steady hum—like something breathing. It must have stopped, must be studying the place, perhaps suspicious of what awaited it. It knew. It had to. His chance to take advantage of his hiding place was slipping away; he could feel it.

Rhett listened for a moment more, trying to visualize where it would be standing. It wasn't more than fifteen feet away, an easy shot, depending on its size. He could do this.

With a deep breath, Rhett stepped out of his hiding place, pistol raised, eyes searching for his target. At a movement, his arms reacted, lining up the shot and squeezing the trigger.

PRRTSH.

His nerves tingled. He knew immediately that he'd made a mistake, but as his mind caught up to his body, he wondered how large a mistake it would turn out to be.

The thing that had been following him was not a creature. It wasn't even *alive*. As he stood over its ruined husk, mechanisms blasted out by a lump of super-sonic ferrene, he identified it as something altogether unexpected.

It was a machine. Roughly pyramidal, about a foot and a half to a side, it lay now as a hunk of scrap on the rocks. A few wires protruded, their appearance as familiar as they were strange. He couldn't fathom what technology propelled it; it had been floating some three feet from the ground when he'd shot it.

Rhett's mind scrambled. *This* was what had followed him? *This* was what he'd caught the eye of in the city?

He thought of the laser beacon he'd been forced to create on the roof of the high tower. It could have been that. But it could have been the noise of his Phi-8, too. He would likely never know.

A machine. What did it mean? Were the people who had built it still around? Or was it autonomous, still wandering the planet for... for what? Tactical surveillance? Some kind of scientific monitoring?

Rhett glanced skyward. There was another possibility. It might not even be the Occassi who had made it. It could be another species, perhaps in orbit right now, aware of his activities, of the state of the Votum. Had he just threatened them? Proclaimed malicious intent to an alien race that might hold the safety of his people in their hands? What if he'd just started a war? Or spat in the face of a group that came in peace?

He holstered his sidearm, rubbing his temples with his thumbs. There had to be something he could use on the machine, but there was no way he'd be able to interpret it. This was far beyond him; he knew it at a glance. He was out of his depth, floundering, drowning.

He needed Sarah. She'd know what the scrawled inscriptions on its surface meant. She'd be able to make heads or tails of the design from a symbolic perspective, probably clueing them in on who'd made it and when.

Braaten would have been able to analyze the tech. He'd be able to say what sort of other tech the species who'd invented it would likely have. He could probably have even estimated its age, giving an important clue as to whether it was Occassi or not.

Captain McNeary had always known what to do. Even in a situation like this, he would have been able to keep a level head—to make a decision. He would have advised caution, would have figured this whole thing out.

But all Rhett had was himself. Brash. Dumb. Afraid. Trigger-happy. A man to jump out and shoot and wonder why afterward. There were pieces here, but he could not place them. There were clues here, but he could not understand them. There were handholds here, but he had no way to grasp them. He was, to the uttermost, alone.

Why him? Why was he the one who had survived?

Rhett stared down at the blinking yellow light on the radio. The Votum was still up there. Those people were still depending on him.

Him. Just him.

There was no one else.

He screamed.

Chapter 15

Day 70

One of those not-bird... things... was sitting on a rock while I was eating breakfast this morning. It must have broken its wing or something. Was definitely holding it funny. It didn't seem to care for me watching it, but with a bum wing and nothing around for miles, it didn't bother trying to leave, either.

Okay, I'll admit it. I fed it a little bit. Made some jerky from something that never decided if it was a deer or a yak. Slow fellow. Good meat on it, though.

[grunts]

Oh, look. It's been following me, too.

Hey! You looking for more? Don't be sure you're gonna find it. I earned what I got. Killed it myself. What have you done?

[silence for 4.3 seconds]

Yes, yes, you've got cute eyes. At least you actually HAVE eyes. Too many things on this planet just have those damn pits on their faces. I figure they're like sharks, you know? But I guess eyes make more sense for a... bird. Have to be able to see to dive...

Or to steal from an alien stranger walking your planet.

[metal clangs against stone]

Go on! Find someone else to bother! Dumb bird.

[sighs]

I should really think of a name for them. Because they're definitely not birds. Wings are wings, I guess, but these things are somewhere between reptile and mammal, far as I can tell. Scales on the belly and around the eyes, hair most everywhere else. The wings actually have hairs, not feathers, but they're long and flat and kind of act like feathers.

[chuckles]

Imagine using your arm hair to fly. I can't even—

Hey! That's close enough. No. No. No. Go on, shoo! Hey... hey... hey! You get out of there! I haven't had fried squirrelhawk before, but you're convincing me I ought to try it.

Hey!

[finger snap]

I'm warning you. No. Nah-ah-ah. No.

Ok, Cyn. I've got to go. This thing is going to chew up my prefab's wiring.

Hey!

Day 82

Virgil's been getting cranky recently. I think it's the winter coming. I've seen other squirrelhawks flying south over the past week, I suspect as some kind of migration. He should go with them. If only he could. His wing never healed right. Best he can do is hobble around on the ground.

[chuckles]

Oh, Virgil? He's the squirrelhawk from... well, I know I mentioned him on one of my other messages. He's decided to attach himself to me. Follows me everywhere. I don't let him in the prefab, of course. I shored up the wiring on the exterior enough that I don't think he could ruin it and called it a day. Every morning when I come out, he runs around in little circles—sometimes trips on his bum wing. It's a wonder he hasn't broken something.

Well. Something else.

CHAPTER 15

He's good company, in an odd way. Doesn't make a whole lot of noise aside from occasional tapping he makes with the claw of his good wing. He doesn't even squeak, which seems odd because he has a mousey sort of face.

[sigh]

I can see it in his eyes, watching the others of his kind fly by. I can see how much he wants to join them. To be back where he belongs. With other creatures that understand him. See him for what he really is.

Hmm.

[silence for 5.1 seconds]

He probably has a girl up there somewhere, Cyn. A nest he's supposed to belong to. Someone who misses him. I haven't broken it to him yet, but... he's probably never going to see her again.

Day 85

Virgil bit me today. I swear he can't get any antsier. Teenage little punk.

[groan]

God, Cyn. I'm going to make a terrible father someday. You know, assuming I...

[silence for 12.4 seconds]

I know I said I didn't want to, Cyn. I hope that... I hope you didn't hold it against me. I just didn't want to put that strain on you, you know? Being a parent is a lot. They would have gotten into your paints. Kept us from going out, having fun. They would have... would have...

[silence for 3.8 seconds]

I don't know what the point in lying to myself about it is. It was about me, Cyn. It was always about me. It's stupid, I know, but I didn't want someone else to... to take you away from me. And not just you, but all the things we liked to do together.

Our hikes. Our backpacking. And with how little time I already had to spend with you while in the service...

   It was selfish. I know that. I hope... I hope I can make it up to you someday.

   [soft tapping sound]

   It's all right, Virgil.

   [tapping continues]

   Just go to sleep, Virgil. I know I'm keeping you up. I'll turn it off now.

   [sigh]

   Don't worry, Cyn. I'll transmit again soon.

Day 94

[breathing]

   I haven't seen him in a few days now, Cyn. It must have been sometime during the night. He just left.

   Maybe he's off to go find her?

   More likely he got picked up by something bigger. I should have let him into the prefab. He could have been safe.

   Sure, yeah. Safe while I roll over him in my sleep and squash him into paste.

   [sigh]

   It doesn't matter anymore. He wanted to go, so he went. He's been thinking about it for weeks. All the other squirrelhawks were going south, probably to the coast. I can let myself believe he made it there. That he's happy. That he found the one he was looking for.

   [chuckles]

   God, I sound like a child. He was a goddamn one-winged rat. Stealing food. Tapping on my prefab while I'm trying to sleep. He didn't do anything for me.

[sniff]

Cute, though. He probably made it, right? Right?

No.

No, Virgil's dead.

[chuckles]

I guess to live on this planet, you have to agree to die on it.

Chapter 16

Day 126

I've started to wonder if, when you've been alone for long enough, you start to convince yourself that yours is the only voice you've ever heard. What if I forget you all? Or my crew? When I remember the captain, I hear my voice speaking. Obviously it was different. But what did he sound like? What did Markus sound like? Or Sarah?

I can't forget your voice, Cyn. Can I?

I know I'm not supposed to. And I know it hasn't been that long... yet. All the same, I'm starting to worry that all I hear in my head is me. A lonely man in a lonely mind.

[silence for 12.8 seconds]

[breathing]

I don't know what else I'm supposed to say. I don't... I don't even know why I'm doing these anymore. Nobody's listening. Nobody cares.

I could just stop.

[silence for 4.7 seconds]

I could just stop all of this. I don't have to save us. No one will care. No one will even notice.

Who's ever complained about a bad dream they've never had? If I just... don't... you all will never have to wake up to this awful place. You won't have to figure out how to survive. How to rebuild. How to find satisfaction in the FUCKING. EMPTY. NOTHING!

CHAPTER 16

[breathing]

I'm not even sure I want you to join me. This world isn't good enough for you. And if I can't save you... I'm not either.

Fate decided that both Earth and Occassus should die this way. They died so close together. That can't have been a mistake. Did someone kill us? If so, then no matter what I do, they'll probably win. They'll finish what they started. My mission is doomed, no matter how hard I try.

And this mission. To save a planet. To save my species. And now, with no help? What a joke! Except I can't even pretend to laugh. Whoever thought this up... just... wasn't funny.

God? You're not funny.

Fuck, I'm pretending to talk to God through a radio.

[silence for 7.7 seconds]

Well, while we're talking. I guess I get it. We probably deserved it. I'm not sure about me specifically, but yeah, as a species, sure. Humanity has basically sucked since... well, forever. It was only a matter of time until we got what we deserved.

But what about them? Did the Occassi deserve it like we did? Did they build a world doomed from the start? Were they hateful, proud, conceited? Did they take without asking or thought of consequence? Did they destroy?

I guess I should ask the storm. The storm that never dies and never goes away. Did You make that storm, or did they?

No, don't answer. I know.

How can You destroy a thing like that? A storm that now, after they've died and gone, lives on to remember them by their greatest features. A lifeless avatar of destruction. Of hatred. Of everything that was wrong with... humanity.

Huh.

I bet we have a matching one on Earth.

Day 134

Rhett sat alone on the corner of his prefab in the pre-dawn light, staring at the sky. The radio blinked with the yellow heartbeat of humanity, his silent but loyal companion. All around him, the dead world stirred in its slumber, only to roll over and return to sleep. It would not awaken yet. Perhaps not ever. Or, perhaps, not until its appointed time.

He'd slept, but he was still tired. He was always tired. Tired of the mission. Tired of himself. Tired of this planet. The greeting of Baitahili only made a modicum of difference. At least now he knew he was supposed to be up. With the light of day, he could consider it safe enough to travel again.

He packed up his prefab in silence, ignoring the churning in his stomach that came from having been up for too long already. He couldn't go wasting food over things like that. His supplies were finite, and if he had any intention of making it the ten years after finishing his work deploying the stormpunchers…

He didn't need to think about that again. He had things to do first. Couldn't get ahead of himself. He could be careful with his supplies. Smart. Practical. But to begin the process of continual waiting-dread, he invited a new and unnecessary source of ennui.

No. He couldn't start that now. He still had two more punchers to place. It could still be more than a month, depending on the oozefield migrations. But at least he'd be delivering the third one soon.

Rhett checked his course on his navbrace again before setting out. According to it, the next city was just out of sight, built at the bottom of an upcoming escarpment only a few miles ahead. It was hard to believe, but as the early hours of the day slipped by, he did start to notice the horizon marching closer, its line

CHAPTER 16

shifting from the smooth clean edge of the planet's surface to the slightly bumpy one of a natural rock face. A few jagged shapes were discernable in the dust around him, but it was hard to tell if they were weathered rocks or actual ruins.

A short time later, a single spire began to rise above that horizon—a structure that he had no doubt to be his target. Dust blew past him; its flurries ceased forming dust devils at a certain point in the distance, instead falling off into the wide unknown below. Just an unseen edge, a tumble, and then gone.

Humanity had been like that. Alive and swirling one minute, the ground beneath their feet gone the next. What lay below?

Rhett stopped at the edge, studying the view. As the navbrace said, the city was built right up to the edge of the cliffs, but not above. Or perhaps it had been built above, but the storm had wiped that part out. He studied the stretch of clifftops to his left and right, but there was nothing but dust and rolling hills of glass. So little left to remember them by. Nothing more than these hollow shells of cities.

He used the laser-torch to burn a tie-down point into the rock above the ledge, then rigged his rappel line and remote quick-release. In what had become a well-practiced motion, he lowered himself over the edge, supporting his weight on his outstretched legs. He took a deep breath, considering his cabling and harness, the stone he had cut and the quick-release system. All such little things. Such little things that, for this moment, held the weight of humanity's last hope. Any of them could fail. It wouldn't even have to be his fault. He might not have been outsmarted, out gunned, or out maneuvered. Everything he hoped for could be erased with nothing more than a simple mechanical failure.

Rhett pushed the thought aside and began his descent. There wasn't time for thoughts like that. Not yet.

The cliff, worn smooth by the passing of wind and rain and rapturous heat, slipped by before him. The ground below might be another five hundred feet down, perhaps more. Maybe six hundred total from the top? A considerable height for this kind of landform, though still dwarfed by a few back on Earth. Since he only had two hundred feet of rope, he'd need to stop to re-anchor a couple times before he reached the bottom, but the laser-torch should make that relatively easy.

Rhett kept moving, remembering fondly the vehicles they'd had when they first arrived. The SLOOPs had been a bit uncomfortable, but to be able to sit down while moving several hundred miles day... That would be nice.

Almost as nice as having someone to talk to.

Rhett glanced down again, trying to gauge his distancing, then frowned. If he wasn't mistaken, the cliff didn't seem to go all the way to the ground. It just... ended. Was it some kind of cavern?

He came to the end of his rope and braced himself against the cliff side as he cut a new anchor point. A foul smell rose from the rocks as they burned—some kind of mineral deposit, he supposed. He ducked his head as the quick-release plunged past him, then flipped the switch on his climbing winch to wind it back up. When it had retracted enough for him to reach it, he clipped it to the new anchor and resumed his descent.

The nature of the cavern became obvious as he neared it. The city had not been built up until the cliffs and then on top of them. Instead, it had been built to the edge of the cliffs and then into and underneath them. He hadn't yet achieved an angle that would reveal the extent of the tunneling—perhaps it only went for a few of their odd triangular city blocks. But with every lope of his descent, his angle revealed more. The city just kept going. At last, he came to the end of the cliff face, still nearly three hundred feet above the ground. He shuddered.

"Yeah, totally," he grumbled as he cut another anchor point mere feet above the open expanse. "This system was totally designed to be used like this. What could possibly go wrong?"

Rhett paused for a moment, staring up the harrowing height back to the top of the cliffs. He could always climb back up. Find some other way down. It would cost him a fair amount of time, but what was that, really? Other than that damn radio, time was all he had out here. Would it be worth it to go back? Could he even climb that much cliff before wearing out? It was a risk. If he climbed and

CHAPTER 16

burned himself out, he might not be able to even make it down the way he was planning now.

He shook his head. Risks one way or the other. Might as well get this over with. He could make it down. And if he didn't? Well, no one would be asking after him anyway.

Rhett activated the quick-release again, gripping the stone hard. Somehow, with that maw of cavern just beneath him, the threat of the fall felt more real now than before. Perhaps it was because there would be no chance of him grabbing hold of something on the way down—though the rational part of him knew that wasn't likely before either. He held his breath as the climbing winch spun, only relaxing when he'd reconnected the line to his new anchor point.

"Okay." He blinked hard, trying not to look down. "No, that's stupid. I have to look down."

So he did. He feathered the switch, allowing the cable to lower him a few feet at a time. Unfortunately for him, he'd managed to place himself between buildings, so there'd be nothing convenient about touching down. As he watched the cable supply dwindled, the buildings still far below, he began to sweat. It was farther than he'd thought. Maybe even more than three hundred feet. There was no way the line would get him all the way to the ground.

A feeling like sinking into a bottomless ocean came over him. Tall Occassi towers reached up like an enormous hand trying to snatch him from below. How he wished they would. If he could only touch them...

His line ran out.

Rhett hung there for a moment, finger still feathering the switch to descend. The ground was... way too far. There were buildings around him, but none very close. The nearest, some twenty feet below him, was nearly thirty feet to one side. He swore. From here, he could see the full extent of the city in the vacuous cavern under the escarpment. Perhaps only a third of its area was exposed to daylight; the rest just kept going, farther and farther back, ending in a strange stone horizon. Did they tunnel all this out, or simply take advantage of a natural landform? What technology would even be required to move so much solid rock?

"Up it is."

Rhett threw the switch to winch him up, clenching his eyes shut as the machine sputtered and groaned. He lifted one foot. Two. The sound grew worse.

"Yeah, bad idea." It was designed to spool in climbing rope, not to lift a man carrying as much equipment as he was.

He stopped. Sighed. How did he always manage to get himself into situations like this?

There was only one way now—he would have to swing. To jump. To press the quick-release at the right time... and then he'd have to land, all without maiming or killing himself.

"Simple enough."

Rhett lowered himself the couple feet to the end of his line, then began swinging gently in the direction of the nearest structure. It had a flat roof, at least. And it was wide enough that he could land and roll without fear of hurtling over the far side. Still, he'd have to make it that far.

The wind brushed his hair into his eyes, earning little more than a grunt from him. He hadn't yet brought himself to cut it with his utility knife, but after this, he would have to. He couldn't let it get in the way at important times like this.

"Lack of planning." He swore at himself yet again. "The captain would have had something to say about that."

The city swept back and forth beneath him, steadily picking up speed. Rhett started a slow spin, which seemed to worsen each time he tried to correct it. He had to aim in spite of that? He could stop swinging, of course. But would that solve the spin? If anything, it would make it impossible to build up speed in the one direction he needed—the direction he already had.

His blood boiled even as he tried to calm himself. Here he was, hanging two hundred feet below the cavern ceiling, dangling from a thread he could only escape in the most dangerous possible way. And he just had to go for it. He could line it up; he just had to be careful. He had enough momentum now—just had to wait for the right moment.

CHAPTER 16

With an empty prayer, Rhett slapped the control for the quick-release, sending himself hurtling through the air toward the top of the structure. He cleared the edge of it, but he was still turning...

He landed flat-footed, facing sideways, but ducked into a ball to roll as best he could. After one rotation, he flopped over, skidding across stone on his belly. He clipped his nose on an unseen lip as he slid past it.

Rhett coughed as he came to a stop. Blood gushed from his nose, filling his mask, but he was alive. He stood with a groan, but even that told him no bones had been broken. It was a lot better than he deserved.

He pinched the bridge of his nose, trying to organize his thoughts about dealing with a blood-filled mask. He couldn't take it off out here, but if he could deploy his prefab, he could do something about it in there.

Rhett threw off his pack, becoming acutely aware of how small the space was inside his mask. If the blood got into one of the filters, the miracle of surviving the fall wouldn't get him very far. He flicked the switch to retract the climbing line, upending his pack while the little machine creaked. He'd have to see about a good cleaning and maintenance on the thing. It deserved that much.

Here. His prefab. He couldn't wait for its automatic deployment. He flicked the switch to manual, heaving its corners into their lock-snaps, only barely relaxing as the filtration system came on. Sixty seconds. That was how long it was advertised to take to ensure clean air within.

Rhett bent over, inverting his head to stop the blood from flowing. He grimaced, taking careful little sips of air as the hot fluid pooled around his upper cheeks and the bridge of his nose.

Finally, the click of a cycled system alerted him to the prefab's safety. He ducked inside, sealed the door, and sucked in one final gasp before taking his mask off. He held one hand cupped below his nose, the other pinching its bridge, as the system took another ten seconds to restore purity from the door being opened. He hissed his first breath through blood-soaked teeth, noticing now that one of them was looser than before. Still, it was a small price to pay.

His nose finally stopped bleeding five minutes later. He stared down at himself, grinning ruefully that he looked more beat up from the bloody nose than he had from his encounter with the blind-weaver just two months before. He'd have to find some way to clean all this up. With how uncommon a feature eyes seemed to be on the creatures of this planet, he suspected smell was a powerful tool for many of them. The more he stank of blood, the better a target he'd seem.

Rhett scowled as he peeled off his suit. Water was, as always, too scarce to waste on something like cleaning up blood. In fact, it was even scarcer now, given the water he'd lost in the blood itself. Besides, he'd need something chemical to remove the smell. That or some dedicated ultraviolet radiation…

Though he knew he'd bald over it, he raked his fingers through his hair once again. Better to let it dry for now. Let it dry, and then he could scrape it out of all the important places, like his filter system on his mask. After that, he'd see what was left.

He'd find a way; he had to. He couldn't squander the fortune of having survived this long.

"I'll nap, I guess?" He sighed, sinking into his seat after hanging the suit up to dry. "It isn't like there's anything else to do."

Chapter 17

Day 135

Rhett had done his best, and when dawn came, it was time to keep moving. This rooftop offered him no real protection, and the longer he stayed the greater the chance of something coming to check out the strange square metal rock that had shown up there.

His mask fans had acquired a new buzzing sound. He'd knocked them off balance somehow, or some gunk had gotten into the bearings. It would wear out before too long, but he might be able to get a replacement at the lander before that happened. Another gamble he'd be forced to make. Next time, he'd carry a backup.

"Sure," he muttered, watching the prefab fold itself down. "I'll just carry two of everything. That won't double the weight of my pack at all."

He secured the pack with its final magnetoclamp, then hoisted it onto his shoulders and clipped the hip belt in front of him. The roof seemed to be mostly empty, save a few rigid structures he couldn't identify. None of them appeared to be a point of ingress, but at least none of them were one of those damn blind-weaver cocoons.

Rhett strode to the edge of the roof and leaned out over the raised lip at its edge. It was probably another 150 feet to the ground. He had the option of rappelling down, but after the winch's mechanical failure, he wasn't sure he wanted to trust it before opening it up for a proper inspection.

He turned, considering. The existence of what appeared to be a railing suggested it had been accessible to the Occassi at one time. There had to be a door up here. He approached one of the rubble mounds, sidearm drawn. Though he couldn't make out meaning in the structure, he could clearly identify steel and broken stone beneath the outer sheen of glass. No inner darkness that spoke of a hole to some great *within*.

He approached the second mound with equal caution. This one was made entirely of crumpled steel sheets and framing. Useless.

Rhett paused as he turned to the last one, frowning. He could have sworn it looked different now than it did before. Did the color change? Or did—

No. There it went again. Back to normal, then back to different. A dim green flickering, pulsing every few seconds. A light?

His breath caught as he approached it, his mind flashing with memories of the drone he'd shot outside of that first ruined city. Was it the Occassi after all? Had he arrived on their doorstep, already an enemy?

"Getting ahead of yourself, Rhett." He approached slowly. "Just because there's lights on doesn't mean there's anybody home."

But hadn't Markus said it had been something like seventy years? For emergency lights to have stayed on that long, they had to have either a considerable power source or someone maintaining them. Either one might have their uses to him—and their dangers.

The rubble shifted as he neared. He clicked off the safety on his pistol but held his fire. It was so small. A stutter.

Rhett kicked at the edge of the rubble, watching as it twitched again. It didn't look alive. Didn't remind him of the blind-weaver or anything else he'd seen so far. But something *was* moving, or at least trying to. He shoved a large chunk of stone from the top of the pile, watching as the rest beneath it shifted and settled once again. Again, the movement came, this time giving off the faint hiss of sand sliding through an open crack.

"A door. There's a door buried right here."

He holstered his sidearm and examined the pile. If he could unbury what was here... well. If the door was still working, what might lay within? Would there be working technology? Artifacts of the Occassi that had survived their extinction event?

"If they even *are* extinct," he reminded himself. Even now, it seemed most likely that they were. But he'd come to agree with the captain on this one: possibilities were what to consider when there were so many unknowns.

It took him a few minutes of hefting, but as soon as the largest pieces had been moved away, the door managed to push its way open, upward from the floor, on squealing hinges. Below, a ramp led downward into a newly dust-filled gloom. The lights he'd seen seemed to emanate from a small panel opposite the door's hinges, which had since doubled its blinking frequency.

"Well, if anyone's watching, they know I'm here now."

Rhett switched on a handful of his suit's lamps and stepped down into the darkness. He found himself in a narrow hall that ended only fifteen feet before him, swerving off to the left. The walls were decorated with a simple but deliberate architectural motif—continuing the symbolic affinity the Occassi appeared to have for triangles.

Rhett still wondered about that. Was it something religious, or simply cultural? How long had it been going on? Sarah might have had theories. She would have loved to see this place. To talk about it, probably endlessly. Droning and droning...

Being here alone... Rhett wished for her rants. He missed them.

It would serve as something inspirational for Cyn. They weren't landscape material, he supposed, but the remnants of the Occassi were intriguing all the same. An artist had to appreciate that, didn't they?

Rhett peered around the corner at the end of the hall, the sharp angles of the triangular structure striking him as strange and aggressive. A long hall stretched that way, splitting off six more times before it came to an end. Would this building have a more expedient means of descent, or would that oppressive winding ramp show itself again here? He supposed if there was something more efficient, it would be damaged or otherwise nonfunctional, but he couldn't resist his curiosity.

He froze at an electric hum rippling through the structure around him. Sudden as a lightning flash, he was bathed in light from a series of fixtures overhead. He squinted, turning back and forth between the two halls, sidearm poised. But nothing came. He blinked, then glanced up at the lights.

"Incandescent?"

Two-hundred-year-old lighting technology. And yet, it worked. Something in this place was aware of his presence. Something was *responding* to him.

Rhett stalked down the hall, checking each corner before moving forward. The rooms were empty, save for dust and indecipherable refuse. Perhaps the place had been looted before the end? His ears were keen for any sound, but there was nothing besides his own footsteps and the steady hum of age-old filaments. How did they know he was here? Were they watching him right now? There weren't any obvious signs of cameras, but that might not be the only way they'd found to see from a distance. Or was it pressure on the floor?

He crouched abruptly, pressing his fingers against stone, but it was completely solid. There couldn't be sensors under there, could there? But if not that, then how?

"I'm missing the point," he decided. "It doesn't matter *how* they know I'm here. What matters is *who* knows I'm here."

And yet it was a question with which he was no more able to grapple. It didn't even have to be a person. Didn't have to be Occassi or some other alien species who'd beat them to the planet. It could be something artificial—a computer that had never gone completely to sleep after its makers left it behind.

Rhett turned down another hall, wincing as its lights flashed on. "Either way, I'm heading toward the belly of the beast."

What secrets might this city hold? If it contained the legacy of the Occassi, what would that mean for him? And what of his mission? If the Occassi weren't entirely gone, did humanity have any right to lay claim to the planet?

"It's the same as when we set out," he whispered, "We were always meant to share it. If we can find common ground again, there's no reason we can't coexist." His vision narrowed as a nearby door swung open at his approach. He jerked his weapon to point into the small room within, his hands trembling. "Assuming I don't manage to ruin it before better men get down here."

What was wrong with him? He wasn't normally this jumpy. He'd served his time back on Earth, had seen active combat in Imperial Zealand and the Sudan Confederacy. He'd always been smoother than this—more level-headed.

"This place," he grumbled, "is breaking my mind."

Rhett stepped through the newly opened door into a small, triangular room. His sense of direction told him he was essentially directly in the center of the structure just as the door closed behind him. An elevator, perhaps? But there were no obvious buttons, no controls he could use to operate it. In fact, he wasn't even sure he'd be able to get the door open again. Panic reached for him for only a moment before he felt the room begin to move.

"An elevator after all."

The descent was slow, the unseen mechanisms groaning with age and disuse. But still, they held, level after level. A series of blue illuminated symbols cycled past, one after another, on a monitor beneath his feet. After more than a minute, the room eased to a halt. For another thirty seconds, nothing happened. Rhett wondered if the doors on this level might be broken, but he had his laser-torch. He could cut through the steel to get out if he had to.

As he reached for the tool, the door behind him creaked open, coming to a stop with little more than a foot of width to fit through. Rhett eyed it nervously. Something so large and heavy could certainly crush him, even by accident. He'd need to take off his pack, slip it through first, then follow. Another risk.

"It's going to bite me one of these days."

With a fluid motion, he shucked his pack and shunted it through the gap, then slipped through himself. On the far side, another dark hall greeted him, taking a few more seconds to rouse itself and turn on the lights. One of them sputtered, then burst while the others hummed.

It suddenly struck Rhett that he could try to communicate with it... whatever *it* was. There had been two-way communication between humanity and the Occassi before their departure. If he didn't have Sarah, perhaps he could rely on her counterpart. What if one of the Occassi—or their computer system—could understand English?

He almost laughed at the thought, as if talking to anyone but himself now seemed ridiculous.

"My name is Rhett Wethern," He recited into the silence. "I'm a human from Earth. I came as part of a team, per the Extraterrestrial Embassy Agreement, to colonize this world. I have a solution to the storm that's circling your planet." He paused, waiting for a response. "I am bound for the tallest building in this city. I have a device I must deploy there. I would ask your assistance, but if I cannot have that, I must beg for your non-interference. My mission is for the good of both our kinds."

He heaved a breath, pausing again. There had to be something. Some indication that they'd heard. That they'd help. But the only answer was the steady hum of the incandescent bulbs over his head.

"Hmm," he muttered. "Just like talking to God."

At the end of the corridor, the artificial light began to mix with the natural streaming in from a crumbling wall. This was the ground level. Rhett vaulted through the crack and landed in the glass-blown street. Suddenly surrounded by the city's silence, Rhett turned to check the lights where he'd just come. They were off. Dark. As if they had never come on in the first place. He frowned. Were they gaslighting, or simply handling their power practically?

He'd had his own light sources, of course. Practicality was unlikely to be the reason. It seemed more plausible that the message of the lights and the elevator was simple: you are being watched. But what was there to do about that? They hadn't given him any indication of what they wanted. If there really was a 'they' at all.

Rhett shrugged, turning away. According to his navbrace, he was almost two miles from his destination tower. He stared down the rubble-strewn avenue

CHAPTER 17

toward it, noting its peak in the distance. That, at least, was clear. Occasionally, between all the feats of daring and uncertainty, it was nice to know where he was going and how to get there.

Still, he turned, gazing now into the darkening depths of the city in the cavern. He was certain now that he could see a light that way, blinking with a steady green pulse. An invitation?

"Or a trap." His eyes narrowed. Did they really want him to go that way? They'd been helpful so far, but that might mean little. A trap wasn't a trap without proper bait.

Their kindness—or at least their neutrality—seemed a very attractive attribute. What if they could help him further? They might have food. Water. Chemicals to clean his mask properly. Navigational guidance. They might have anything. *Anything.*

Rhett glanced back to the tower, so close, so attainable. He'd only have one after this, albeit up the side of a mountain. Another month, perhaps. Maybe two. Then the long wait. His eyes narrowed. What if they could help him with that? Help him get the fifth stormpuncher? Help him calculate a safer place for it?

What if he could have everything he wanted, but without so much misery?

The light flashed in the distance, its place indiscernible but its existence undeniable. That light might hold promise, but it might just as easily hold peril.

Rhett could go to the tower first. Finish this part of the mission before allowing himself a detour. But what if they had an easier way up? What if they took offense to him choosing his mission first? The invitation, now extended, could just as easily be retracted. He might return to this place, the stormpuncher deployed, only to find the light and its promise were gone.

What if he never had another chance to meet with them? What if they returned to the subtlety they'd demonstrated these long months, eluding him forevermore? So much would be lost. The tenuous bud of the relationship between humanity and these… somebodies… might be stamped out just like that.

Rhett took a step toward the light. Paused. But what if it was a trap? Right now, so far as he could tell, he was safe. He could place the puncher, then move on. Once he had the fourth one placed… well, that would be the time to take risks, wouldn't it? He could return to this city, take as much time as he needed. Could find the source of the light. Find whatever had been waiting for him here. If they'd been here for seventy years without the rest of their society, they could make it a few months more.

He stood frozen in the street, unable to decide. What would the others have done? Which way was even the more cautious one? The captain would say no shortcuts, but he also would consider the possibilities the Occassi presented. They had, after all, been the team's original mission. Sarah would want to make contact, but then again, it would have seemed much more reasonable to make contact if she were still with him.

Caldwell would have wanted to study them—xenobiology had always been his passion, despite his primary functions as a medic and navigator for the team. Braaten would want to study their technology, no doubt about that.

So that meant everyone would have been in favor aside from the captain, who at worst would have been neutral.

Rhett sighed. "I'm letting the vote of the dead decide my fate?"

But he didn't argue with it. The decision was one he could live with—assuming it didn't get him killed. He marked a point on the navbrace he thought might be the origin of the light just in case it went out during the approach, then started walking.

Chapter 18

Less than a mile after the cavern cast its shadow over the city, the look of the streets changed. No more were the buildings battered by dust and the streets full of rubble and glass. The silence remained, but the cityscape transformed from one of ruin to one that was simply *empty*. In some ways, it struck Rhett as even more eerie. Here was a place abandoned, but the reason for its abandonment had become distant and unclear. A ghost town. He walked with his sidearm drawn.

Doors began to open for him as he passed. He glanced this way and that, marking entry halls, greeting rooms, wide open spaces, each of them empty, yawning, hollow. He was not deterred. The light was still up ahead, still steadily flashing, awaiting his arrival.

For the first time, he thought he saw a glimpse of what Occassi society might have been like. It was a pale reflection without any of them to fill these placid streets, but he felt a growing sense of connection—of similarity. Here was a street of something like apartments. Little suites lined up and stacked up, efficient but spartan. Here was a street of workshops, storefronts, slots for what might have been market stalls or street food vendors. Here was a street of warehouses, hulking in their architectural auspiciousness, holding who knew what—perhaps nothing—within. He would come back to check. Even if everything had decayed or rusted, he might be able to salvage something useful as he continued his journey. Here was a large building, wide and shining, perhaps a place of government or religion. Or might they be one and the same for the Occassi? Rhett felt a sudden yearning for knowledge about them. What if it wasn't out of reach? What if some of them were still alive, just up ahead? Language would be a problem, certainly, but if they were like humans, they could overcome such difficulties.

Rhett could learn the origin of the storm. The nature of its heat. The events leading up to their species going silent—and with those, he could have a chance of understanding what might have happened on Earth. It might all be attainable. As if nothing had truly been lost. Maybe they could merely start again, right the wrongs, learn from past mistakes. This planet of Occassus could become the cradle of two peoples. Peoples who were now wise where their fathers had been foolish and learned where their mothers had been ignorant.

He could see the source of the light now, gleaming from a broad panel of wall as part of a larger display—the rest of which had broken down and decayed. As he stepped into the vacant courtyard beneath the light, he stopped to study his surroundings. The city ended here. The vast display before him with its one working part had been mounted directly onto a sheet of stone that stretched vertically for nearly three hundred feet. To one side, about twenty feet from the ground, a balcony appeared on the side of the cliff. A steel door sealed it from access, but its presence on an otherwise featureless wall was striking nonetheless. Beneath the light, shrieking now on decrepit hinges, a huge set of doors lurched open.

These doors seemed different. The others throughout the city were practical—steel, but thin, perhaps only half an inch thick. But the doors that opened the mouth of the cliff face were more than a foot and a half thick. As they opened enough for him to see, he noticed a series of vault-locking-pins surrounding the doorways edges, matching the slots cut into the door itself. He'd only seen doors like that in military installations back on Earth.

"Not a building," he murmured. "That's a bunker."

It made perfect sense. Some small subsection of the Occassi had seen their doom coming and had prepared for it. Any number of them—few or plentiful—might still reside in this place beneath the ground.

Rhett had found them. He'd *actually* found them!

He paused. It could still be a trap. Or a computer. Or robots. If the Occassi were still alive, why didn't they use their city? So much of it was still accessible, even functional. The storm only hit this region once every nine months. They could have an entire growing season for agriculture in that time. A breeding season for livestock. Time to hunt and forage for supplies. It was still possible they did all of those things; perhaps there were other ways into the bunker. Subtle paths in more convenient locations.

Still, there should have been some sign. Something they could have detected. Something the Votum would have caught and reported to him. How could there be nothing to show for their continued existence?

Perhaps it was the atmosphere. Perhaps almost breathable to humans was also poisonous to the Occassi. They might not have the same filter technology. Or perhaps their crops couldn't survive the conditions. Perhaps their livestock would be made unsafe to eat if they were raised out here. There could be any number of reasons.

Rhett kept his sidearm in hand as he approached the massive threshold into the cliffside. It still paid to be cautious. Just because they invited him in didn't mean they meant him no harm.

"If they *do*, though…" He sighed, considering the enormous doors to his right and left, then glanced at the Phi-8. "This isn't liable to save me."

The lights within flickered to life, revealing a long corridor of polished white stone ending in another massive door. As he stepped past the opening, the doors behind him began to groan once again. He almost bolted, then nodded in understanding. An airlock.

"Best hope whatever is normal air to them is breathable to me." He pursed his lips at the thought. "Or at least similar enough for my filter to manage it."

A final breath of air slipped through the door just before it sealed and the locking pins clicked into place. A fan cycled on somewhere out of sight, drawing the air in the corridor from his right to his left, then switched back off again. He could still breathe. No dizziness. No hypoxia. Another suite of motors switched on as he approached the inner door. His heart pounded in his ears as the light from overhead began to spill into the shadows beyond. When it became wide enough that he could slip through, the lights beyond began to cycle on.

"If the Occassi are here… why were their lights off?"

"Maybe they're just a bit farther in," he answered himself.

Beyond the second massive set of doors, a spiraling ramp stretched downward until the lights could not follow it into the gloom. A hundred feet? More? Rhett couldn't see the bottom. The incandescent bulbs followed him down, pinned to the wall at constant intervals. There must be places like this back on Earth, he supposed. It was a wonder how similar it must be, given the Occassi's apparent failure to invent triangular incandescent bulbs.

He chuckled to himself.

The lights ended when the walls around him did, but the ramp went on. On either side, support struts and railing kept him contained on his path, but out past those... there was only empty, black air. It tasted stale through his mask filters—as if none of it had been made to move for decades. Perhaps it hadn't. Rhett switched on a pair of holoescent lamps, raising his eyebrows when even their light could not reveal the walls of the chasm around him. How big was this place? Was the city built upon nothing but a dozen yards of stone and then thin air?

He kept going.

Minutes passed but stretched to feel like hours. The lights in the descent tunnel switched off when he was a dozen feet beneath them, making his world feel as though it had both shrunk to the size of the light of his lamps and grown to the size of the endless dark past them. A few minutes later, a glimmer of light began to grow far below him. From what he could tell, the shimmer had to come from a place at the bottom of the winding ramp—perhaps another descent tunnel like the one he'd left behind. Would that be where the path ended? Was that where the Occassi were now—and had been since they'd vanished from the face of their planet?

Rhett flicked his mask as the buzzing from the fan worsened, nodding nervously as it quieted again. The lander might be too far away after all. His only hope was the Occassi, then. They—or what they'd left behind—would need to be his salvation.

"A bloody nose," he grumbled as his knees and quads began to burn. "Killed by a damn bloody nose."

CHAPTER 18

It was like McNeary had said when Rhett suggested they split up: little things could become big problems when you're alone.

"I'll figure it out."

The darkness continued for what felt like forever. Rhett's navbrace informed him that he was nearly a thousand feet below the surface now. Certainly deep enough to survive a storm like Nuhalriu—or even a nuclear blast just outside their door. They would need to have systems for growing food. For power generation. For recycling resources they could no longer get from outside. Perhaps that was what they'd done. Perhaps it was simply easier to stay down here, safe and secure.

What if they had the capacity for more than they already had? What if he could summon the Votum to land, even before the stormpunchers were deployed? If there was room for some of the humans down here, he could have help with the rest of his mission. He wouldn't have to be alone anymore. Perhaps Cyn would be among the first to wake—

Rhett might not even need to finish his mission. He'd done so much. Been through so much. Surely there would be someone more qualified who could finish it for him. Some of those sleeping had to be soldiers. Scientists. Linguists. Navigators. People who would know what to do and how to do it.

He snatched at the metaphysical weight as it began to lift, pressing it right back onto his own shoulders. He hadn't even met the Occassi yet. He had no hints as to their numbers, their capabilities, or their generosity. Seventy years beneath the surface of their world must have changed them. They might want nothing to do with the humans. Might have no interest in helping them.

"Then why let me in?" He scratched his head.

"Maybe to kill me."

It would be an efficient plan, he had to admit. With him out of the way, they'd never have to deal with any more interlopers. Then again, there had to have been easier ways. For example, they could just as easily have trapped him in the airlock on his way in here. He'd have starved or run out of air eventually.

"So they want to give me a chance," he concluded. "Not a guarantee, but an opportunity."

Eventually, the light at the bottom of the spiraling ramp began to grow. As Rhett had predicted, it was another descent tunnel lined with incandescent lights. He welcomed their return with a sigh of relief, only now appreciating how oppressive the wide empty darkness had felt. It was only another forty feet or so to what appeared to be the bottom, a fact that also gave his legs some measure of comfort.

Rhett stopped when he reached the true ground, sipping a mouthful of water from the tube in his mask. The worsened buzzing returned until he slapped his mask again. Maybe the air was safe down here?

He consulted his navbrace for a minute, trying to remember how to make it sample the air. He smiled as he finally remembered, then watched the progress bar as it slowly trudged its way across the little screen. When the reading was complete, he stared at it for a moment. A little low on oxygen—nineteen percent instead of twenty-one—but otherwise the air was perfectly breathable. He switched off his mask, peeling it away from his sore cheeks and nose with a wince. For a long moment, he closed his eyes and simply breathed. This was what he'd been missing. Free, open air, not bound by the confinement of his prefab. Though he realized it was merely one large room full of air rather than a small one, it still felt better—even stale as it was.

He checked the time and was surprised to find it was only early afternoon. The darkness had cast him adrift when it came to time—if not for his navbrace, he would have completely lost sight of the shore.

"I'm stalling," he pointed out.

"Most definitely," he answered.

Rhett turned, studying the door that presumably led to all that he hoped for—and feared.

"I'll have to stop talking to myself. They'll think I'm crazy."

"I'm the first member they've ever met of a different sentient species. They'll think I'm crazy no matter what I do."

"Maybe they'll just think humans do this. Like we can't properly think inside our own heads."

CHAPTER 18

"Hey." He shrugged. "Some of us can't."

"Fair enough."

Rhett approached the door, sidearm drawn but safety engaged. He opened his mouth, as if to announce himself, but the electric hum of servos and the grinding of aged gears beat him to it. What might await him on the other side of the door? What might the Occassi look like? Would they be ready to speak to him, having brought a translator? Would they lock him up until they could determine if he was a threat to them? Would they be suspicious? Welcoming? Confused? Intrigued?

It all came down to this. It all came down to now. It might all be decided in these first few moments. First contact for the second time.

But when the door came to a stop, the corridor beyond stood empty. No one greeted him. No one arrested him. No one interrogated or interviewed him.

Rhett was still alone.

"Just not there yet," he decided. "This place must go on and on, deeper and deeper. It's a remarkable feat, really."

He stalked down the corridor, watchful for movement or signs of life. At the end of it, an archway opened up onto a balcony overlooking a large, spherical room. For a moment, he thought he might have wandered into a bizarre mirror of a beehive. Occupying nearly the entirety of the sloping floor and ceiling, hexagonal tiles interlinked with one another. At the center of each of the tiles, a triangular panel blinked with a short series of lights—three green, one blue.

Rhett frowned, trying to understand what surrounded him. The balcony he'd emerged onto ran the full circle of the room, occupying a strip of wall not occupied by any of the hexes.

He stepped up to the first one above him on his left, squinting to try to divine its purpose. The lights on the triangular steel panel continued to blink. An electric hum surrounded him. He could hear the whirring of tiny fans. The warm breath of a machine long and hard at work. Was it a computer after all? A massive computer, buried in a bunker beneath the city. Was that what had been watching him? Helping him? Even leading him here?

But why? Did it want something from him? What could he even give? Did it need repair in order to keep going? If it did, it should have chosen Braaten. He would have been far more capable. Or Sarah. She would have understood what it was asking her to do.

But it didn't ask anything. The room remained silent, save for the humming and the steady blinking all around him.

Rhett crossed the room slowly, following the rounded pathway of the balcony. At the far side, another archway led to a room that looked exactly like this one. Beyond that one, another. And another. And another. Room upon room, sphere upon sphere. There had to be thousands of hex tiles. Tens of thousands. The chain went on seemingly without end. The Votum had more than an acre of computer onboard, but this? It was more than twenty times that. The computing power of such a machine… Rhett couldn't even imagine it.

His mind circled around again to the only question that seemed to matter: why was he here? Why had this monumental machine led him to this place? If he could only—

A roaring sound like a radio squelch blasted him. Rhett toppled, dropping his gun and clutching his ears. The noise didn't stop—it was as if his hands could do nothing to block it. Was it even sound? Was it… was it being pushed directly into his brain?

The sound shifted for a few seconds, mutating from pure noise to organized buzzing, followed by a sound almost as if it were words in a language he couldn't begin to comprehend. It paused, allowing him to draw the breath he'd been awaiting for what felt like minutes. Then it returned, as clear as before, but its chain of sounds and syllables sounded altogether different. Another language? After a few second more, it stopped again, then restarted with a new flavor of gibberish. Was it looking for *his* language?

"My name is Rhett Wethern," he said. Maybe by speaking, he could help it find what it needed.

It paused again, as if listening.

"I am a human from Earth. I came as part of a team, per the Extraterrestrial Embassy Agreement, to colonize this planet. Please, I know you probably can't understand me... or maybe just not yet... but I just... I want to understand what's going on." He shook his head, realizing there were tears on his cheeks. "Where are the Occassi? Humanity's agreement is with them, and if it is still possible, we would like to uphold it."

A faint humming surrounded him, but no answer came.

"I have something to offer. We have a solution to the storm circling the planet. I've already begun deployment of the—"

[We need no solution.]

The voice, a garbled mix of a dozen different speakers, sang directly into his brain. Rhett collapsed at the feeling of it—not for the pain, although it *was* painful, but for the unspeakable relief of something to talk to.

It took him a long time to process its answer. He stood again. "We?"

The collective term seemed specific—unless it was just a quirk of the translation. What if humans had never addressed them in the singular first person before? Would they know the meaning of 'I'?

[The Occassi are here.] The tone shifted through its many voices. [The Occassi are safe.]

It had to be stitching together words and syllables from a series of recordings from their first contact with Earth. That it even made sense was remarkable.

"Here?" Rhett turned, studying the room around him. It only now dawned on him that its shape reminded him of the hypersleep pods on the Votum—lined up and stacked as far as the eye could see. "And who am I speaking to right now?"

[The Occassi greet you, Rhett Wethern. You have been long awaited.]

Rhett couldn't help but smile. Was peace an option, then? Could all of his missteps be salvaged? "I just... I am very pleased to meet you."

[You speak for the humans?]

"I... for now, yes," he answered. "The others are up on the ship, still in hypersleep. Until I get rid of the storm, they can't land."

[Then they are safe. That is good. And they are happy?]

Rhett frowned. "I... suppose so."

[It is good to be safe. It is good to be happy.]

"You said the... Occassi... are safe?" He raised an eyebrow, though he wondered if they could even see the gesture. "Are they happy?"

[Oh, yes. We are very happy.]

"Good. Is that why..." He raked his fingers through his hair, finally noticing his sidearm on the ground and re-holstering it. "Is that why you say you don't need a solution? To the storm, I mean?"

[Mmmmmmmmm.] The voices must have been made to sound contemplative, but the effect was not entirely delivered. [Are you happy, Rhett Wethern?]

Rhett hesitated. "I am now that I've met you. We thought you were extinct."

[Our existence is notable. But you do not answer the question. Rhett Wethern, who speaks for the humans, are *you* happy?]

He gritted his teeth as he caught onto their meaning. "I don't need to be."

[Mmmmmmmmm. Tell us about their hypersleep.]

Rhett wiped his palms on his suit, rolling his eyes as he recognized his gloves prevented him from clearing any sweat that had begun to build up. "It is safe. Effective."

[Do they dream?]

Where were they going with this? "I didn't."

[The Occassi dream all around you, Rhett Wethern.] Their tone softened, turned inviting. [Our words are brought to you through that dream. The machine-mind cares for us. Brings us happiness. Fulfillment. Answers to our many questions. It sates our hunger. Gives us freedom. And as we have said, it protects us from harm.]

"That's a hell of a sales pitch. I'm sure someday we'll get something of the sort. Perhaps when we make our journey to the next planet—"

[You plan to leave this one?]

"Well, no." He shook his head. "Not any of *us*. I mean eventually. Generations from now. When we're ready."

[But why would you want to leave? It is safe here. You can be happy here.]

"It's just... a baby chick from the nest, right?" He knew instantly how stupid the comparison was. Even if they did have something like birds here, they would have no idea what he meant.

[Rhett Wethern. *You* can be happy here.]

"I still have work to do." Rhett rubbed his temples, part of him considering what they had offered. "Once I get the last two stormpunchers placed, I suppose I'll have time to try your... dream."

[You've been working so hard, and you have made so much progress. Do you not deserve a brief respite? You could rest here, for a time. As you said, you are not far from your goal. What would be the harm in letting it wait a little longer?]

Rhett frowned, eyes wandering. They weren't wrong, were they? He did deserve some rest, at the very least when he was finished. But why not now? He was tired. He'd been going at this for a long time by himself. And part of his mission was to develop a relationship with the Occassi, wasn't it? If nothing else, it couldn't hurt to nurture that for a little while before he completed his other mission.

"If I accept, I have to know I can leave at any time. I am not done out there, and I will not stay here forever." He nodded, mostly to himself, eyebrows furrowed. "A little bit of rest might do me good. But my mission must be completed."

[Of course.] A mechanical whir and a sound like rushing air reverberated from the chamber beyond. [We wouldn't think of keeping you. You may come and go as you please.]

Rhett stepped through the archway, spotting the now open berth high up on the far left wall. Before he had a chance to wonder how he'd reach it, the balcony's shape transformed, sloping upward toward it.

Of course. Another ramp.

"You're sure... you're sure your dream will interface correctly with my biology?"

[We have full confidence. Your body is not so different from our own. The dream uses the same means through which we speak to you now.]

He stared up the ramp, realizing he had yet to take a step. "I want assurances that I can leave when I decide to. Can I meet one of you? If one of you could leave the dream, then I would believe that I could."

[Mmmm.] They seemed to consider it. [We wish it were that simple. You see, our bodies have been in stasis for a great deal of time. For one of us to awaken now... it would be very painful.]

"Seems like a design flaw."

[Only if you intend to leave.]

Rhett grimaced but found himself taking his first step up the ramp. "But I will be able to?"

[As soon as you desire it, yes.]

Perhaps it was worth the risk. Perhaps some solace after his hardships was exactly what he deserved. He'd already made so much progress; he could simply recuperate and then move on. What would be wrong with that?

He stared into the capsule, noting the array of... he wasn't quite sure what they were. A cot of sorts lay within at the center of it, wide and long enough for him to easily lay on.

"All right." He began to crouch, then stopped. "Wait. If I transmit a signal, is there a way you could boost it enough to reach the Votum—my ship up in orbit?"

[This is not difficult for us.]

"Okay. Don't worry, Cyn. I am coming back." Rhett closed his eyes, part of him still not sure if this was the right move. But he was tired, and they were right—he could use a little happiness. He unhooked the radio from where it hung on his hip, noting that the yellow light continued to blink, confirming he had a good signal, even down here. The Occassi were true to their word, then.

In and out, no problem. Just a short rest.

Everything would be fine.

You're not going to believe this, Cyn. But I found the Occassi.

Yes.

They're here in this city, where I'm supposed to deploy the third puncher. They have a vault deep underground. I don't even know how far down. They've been in hypersleep—or something like it—for nearly as long as you have. Theirs is different, though. More like a virtual reality, from what I can tell, that they get to live inside and control while their bodies are protected from the whims of time.

[breathing]

They've asked me to join them in it, for a little while.

Oh, yes. They do speak English. I mean... sort of. It's hard to explain.

They say it's safe to come and go. That I can take a break. I worry about it a little, but...

I deserve a break.

I think I'll be able to meet them in there. I haven't seen them physically yet, on account of the shielding of their pods. Apparently being in there for as long as they have makes getting out quite an ordeal. Or maybe they're just comfortable where they are.

[silence for 2.8 seconds]

What?

[silence for 5.2 seconds]

I understand. It will just be another moment.

[clears throat]

That was them. I imagine you couldn't hear them. They apparently are beaming speech directly into my head. Alarming, I know. I'm sure Braaten would have been beside himself wanting to study this place. And Sarah, too.

[sigh]

It's just a rest for me. Just a pause in the journey. I'll transmit again when I'm out. Tell you all about what I saw. I'm sure it will be amazing.

Anyway.

Love you.

Chapter 19

Day 1,942

Hello? Cyn? Are you there?

Hello?

Wait, wait. No. You aren't supposed to answer. You never answered, did you? No, no, that was... yeah. That was there. Not here. Okay. Hrr... uhh...

[silence for 8.4 seconds]

[sniffs]

Wait. No. That can't be right.

Shit.

Shit, shit, shit.

Nineteen... nineteen hundred? That's... that's, what? Four... no, five years.

I've been out for five years? That doesn't make any sense. I was just... I only... I only wanted to take a break. To catch up to myself. I was going to go in and just.... recuperate, you know? I didn't...

Did they do this to me?

[breathing]

[yelling] Did you do this to me? Ah?!

[silence for 3.6 seconds]

Did you now? Well, I don't remember—

[silence for 5.9 seconds]

You told me I could leave as soon as I—

[silence for 1.9 seconds]

I did?

I did.

[grumbling]

I... I can't really remember.

[silence for 4.3 seconds]

No, I do remember... well. I was happy there. And you were there, too, Cyn. At least... no. It wasn't you. Just a shadow.

[breathing]

Will you let me out now?

[silence for 5.8 seconds]

I don't want it anymore. It apparently took me five years, but I am sure of it now. It's empty. All of it. Your whole dream. Fake. There's a real woman up there on that ship. Twelve thousand real people who are depending on me. I can't just... but I already...

Am I too late?

No, no. I just need to get back to it. I just need to get back to work. Deliver the... what did we call them? The stormpunchers. I can't be too late. I was so close. I just...

Open this damn pod! Get me out of—

Wha!

[thud]

[grumbles]

Mask. Where's my mask?

[grunts]

Damn thing's broken. I guess I... I guess I knew that. Fuck. What do I do now?

[silence for 8.5 seconds]

[scoffs]

I'm not going back in there! Five years, don't you see? Five YEARS your dream took from me. For all I know, the work I've already done has been ruined. If the storm came around without all the punchers in place...

No. No, no, no. The lander! Caldwell said it would be clear of the path for a few cycles, but it's been much longer than that. All those supplies...

And what about the cave? There was still a stormpuncher in there. What if... what if...

God DAMMIT! Why won't my muscles work?

[silence for 2.6 seconds]

Fuck you and your atrophy!

[silence for 4.2 seconds]

Well, I'm not surprised they didn't use these words with you. They're words with very... niche applications.

[silence for 1.9 seconds]

Yes, like now!

[grunts]

Listen, okay? I'm sorry, but I have to borrow a few things. This pod has computer systems. Fans. Motors. I need some to repair my mask.

[scuffling]

[banging]

I'm coming, Cyn. I don't... I don't know how long it will take me. But I'm coming.

Day 1,945

Rhett emerged from the Occassi dream-vault as a sickly, weak, and frail effigy of a man. The climb through the dark gap between the worlds had taken him almost an entire day. He had to drag his bag—it was now far too heavy for him to lift. He thanked whatever excuse the universe might have for a deity that the Occassi had built with ramps instead of stairs. The trek would have been impossible otherwise. Still, it had been full of stops and starts. He'd puked half a dozen times. His bones were shaky. His nerves were shot. His eyes were blurry. His mind was foggy.

But he was awake.

He collapsed to his knees at the sight of the sunrise. The colors. The brilliance. It was all so real. It was all so *here*. Though his feet were insulated by his boots, his hands by gloves, his body by his suit, his face by his mask, it was perhaps the most holy thing he'd ever experienced.

But the feeling couldn't last. As he struggled back to his feet, the shadow of Nuhalriu introduced itself at the edge of the horizon. A quick check of his navbrace confirmed his fears—it was not more than a week from the city. He stared down the street toward the daylight, hemmed in on both sides by the hollow structures of the Occassi, trying to catch sight of the tower he had to climb.

"Yeah, sure," he muttered. "More climbing." He sipped at his mouth tube. Was there even time? Perhaps before, he could have made the climb and then found someplace safe to hunker down. But in this state...

And that assumed he didn't run into anything intent on killing him. If he came toe to tentacle with another blind-weaver, would he be strong enough to best it? If he tried to fire his Phi-8, would he even be able to keep his grip with the recoil?

Rhett stumbled, righting himself against a nearby wall. "Why did I do this to myself? I could have been done by now. I could have been done *years* ago."

"It was what I thought you needed."

"Oh, good. So I still talk to myself. Glad that's not cured."

"You'd be pretty boring without it."

He laughed grimly, hobbling toward the next building in the direction he needed to go. When he reached it, he leaned against it, breathing hard. It was only a few miles, but in his condition, it might as well have been on another continent. He was back where he started—no, worse than that. He wasn't even sure he was *capable* of completing his mission anymore.

"Shut up," he scolded himself, pushing off the wall. "It's the same as always. Progress is progress. One step at a time."

"I'm going to die here."

He stumbled and caught himself. "No. Not yet."

CHAPTER 19

The sun concealed itself in dust by midmorning, leaving Rhett cold and sweating in a city of shadows. His stomach gnawed at him, but he knew better than to feed it when he was taxing himself this much. Noon, he told himself. He'd have lunch and take a rest. He could keep going in the afternoon, at least until darkness fell. No risks. No shortcuts. Just sheer force of will.

Rhett stopped just before the sun reached its apex somewhere above the cliffs, his entire body shaking. Perhaps he'd already pushed himself too hard.

He sipped on the nutrient plaster carefully, minding the wrenching of his guts at the very suggestion of a meal. When he'd eaten half of it, he pitched his prefab and decided to allow himself a few hours rest before continuing.

Day 1,946

Rhett woke up coughing, fighting to draw breath. He spat blood, then checked the time, wincing to find he'd slept all the way into the following morning.

Yeah, maybe he had pushed it a little too hard.

He took a meal, glad that it took a fair bit better than the one the previous day. If he took it slow today, he might be able to start moving toward recovery.

"I don't have to beat the storm to the puncher," he told himself. "I just want to get into that tower. Figure out a way to hunker down for the worst of it. I can climb it after."

It delayed much of his plans, but the decision still took a weight off his shoulders. If he had a plan, all he had to do was follow the steps to complete it. One day at a time, one challenge at a time.

Rhett broke camp as soon as he was finished eating. He felt a little better than he had the morning before but cautioned himself against rushing. If the storm approached before he was ready, there would be time for panic. But for now, he would use his best judgement as he pushed forward.

He reached the horizon of the cavern above shortly after noon. The streets became harder to navigate, as he'd remembered, strewn now with rubble and other debris. It was treacherous work, and he slipped and cut open the leg of his suit as evening came. Fortunately, he didn't bleed much, and his medical kit had what he needed to set it right.

With any luck, that would be the worst that would happen to him.

Chapter 20

Day 1,948

Rhett wasn't ready when the storm came. Though a stiff breeze forced its way through the city streets in the morning, he decided he was close enough to the tower to make it the rest of the way there. It was a risk, and he knew it. But Occassus had yet to fully cure his brashness.

A harsh, splintering wind dug grooves into the skin of his face. Dust that had been a simple nuisance to trudge through became an unending assault of dangerous projectiles. He squinted, holding one arm before his face even as his other struggled to keep dragging his bag. Any one of the structures around him could shelter him from this wind—a temptation that was not lost on him as he pressed on despite the blood that had begun to trickle through his hairline—but to protect him from the eye of the storm? From the scorching heat of Nuhalriu, the Glass Storm? He needed something larger. Something huge and deep. He only hoped this tower would offer him the protection he needed.

No shortcuts. No giving up. He could still make it. According to his navbrace—which was rapidly losing signal as the stratosphere ionized—he still had a few hours until the heat would arrive. It wasn't much, but it kept him going knowing that as bad as it was right now, it was going to get a hell of a lot worse.

When at last he groped at the outer wall of the tower, his vision almost completely blotted out by dust and violence, he couldn't find an entrance. He circled the structure once, then a second time. There was nothing but smooth walls the whole way around.

Rhett collapsed behind a broken wall, which at the very least took the brunt of the wind and dust from his fragile body. He cried, knowing full well he hadn't the water to spare for it. It would end here, then. He'd failed. The true failure. The last failure. He'd never see Cyn again. Humanity would never reawaken. This planet was dead and would forever remain so. And he couldn't even spend his last days in the stupid ignorance of that happy sleep.

He should have waited. Should have been more patient. He could have left the dream-vault after the storm had passed. Could have at least checked to see if the storm was coming *soon*. He'd been so eager to get out. To get away from there. To put distance between himself and the thing he had done—the thing he had lost.

Haste. Haste. Haste. He'd always known it would be the death of him. He'd been playing against some invisible cosmic clock just waiting for him to make a fatal mistake. And here he was, a comet hurtling through the universe with a tail bright and brilliant, ignorant to the fact that he was nothing more than a clump of ice and dust that would melt away as soon as he'd caught some wrathful star's ire.

Rhett flipped through the pictures on his navbrace, lips quivering as he studied the one of Cyn. She was so beautiful. And in the picture, so very happy. He'd longed to see her that way again ever since they'd taken off from Earth. He remembered the nervous look she'd given him as they activated her cryopod—that image of fear and grief was still burned in his brain. This planet had never been for her, and yet she'd followed him. She'd trusted him.

Was she wrong for that? He'd been right about Earth. The planet had died, no different than this one.

But he'd fought here. There'd been a chance to save this world. If he'd stayed home, maybe they could have fought to save their own planet. They could have tried to fix the problems *there* instead of borrowing new ones here. He wouldn't have had to say goodbye to her, wouldn't have had to lie that everything would be okay. They could have been together in their last moments. Whether they were old or young wouldn't have mattered.

"I'm sorry, Cyn," he sobbed. He lacked the energy even to spit the dust from his tongue. His mask must be leaking. The shrapnel dust must have ripped through it somewhere.

Hours—he still had hours here. Hours to suffer. To wait for the inevitable.

Part of him wondered if he could use the laser-torch to cut through the wall of the tower, but he knew it was a vain hope. It was designed for thinner materials. If that structure was anything like the one in the other city, it would be multiple feet thick. Even if the laser-torch *could* cut through it, there was no way it would do it in time without overheating.

Rhett was still trapped. Still going to die. He had no other options.

He stared down at the sidearm on his hip. He still had that option, didn't he?

"Fuck," he rasped. "After all that, I'm just going to sit down and die?"

Spurred by a strength he couldn't explain, he heaved himself back to his feet. He scrolled back through the images of the city the Votum had sent to his navbrace. There had to be something in here. There had to be an answer. Buildings didn't just not have ways into them.

"Unless the Occassi built them that way."

"Not the time."

Rhett zoomed in on the clearest image he had, trying to discern the impossible from a camera view that would show him nothing. Unless... wait.

"A bridge?"

He looked up, remembering now that a shadow had passed overhead while he'd circled the structure. He'd thought it was just another building getting in the way of what little sun filtered through the dust, but no. That shadow was his *salvation*.

Rhett dragged his pack clear of the wall, feeling his way back to the stone face of the structure. His muscles spasmed, but he didn't let them slow him. He found the shadow a few minutes later and pushed out into the gale to follow it, his arm held like a blindfold over his face. He could find its source. He could find the entrance to the bridge—could find his way across. Slow and steady, same as before.

But not too slow.

Rhett hobbled through the dust, unmoored without a building to lean on. He winced every time he stepped outside the shadow, the light warning him that if he lost his way now, there would be no saving him. Every time he staggered back into the dimness, ears stinging, skin burning, he wondered if he'd gotten turned around. How could he be sure? There was so little time, and he might well be walking in circles hardly as wide as he was tall.

Finally, his outstretched hand found the source of the shadow. He felt his way around it—a small building with a grand-seeming entry ramp. His pace quickened as hope ignited in his chest. Passing through an archway, he entered the bridge, whose stone sloped in a gentle curve toward the tower. He tripped on a fallen rock and nearly fell through a hole in the middle of the bridge.

"Carefully," he growled, forcing himself back up.

When Rhett reached the far side, he found a massive steel door hanging open for him. He trudged through, his mind already reeling at the prospect of having to close it. It was far too large, far too heavy.

But when he was safe inside, the now forgotten sound of an electric hum and a massive system of churning gears reminded him the Occassi were still watching. The door slid slowly shut, sealing away the wind and the dust and their blinding, cutting, stinging claws.

Rhett held his relief until the locking pins clicked into place. Then he blinked, his skin still burning from where the wind had scoured it. It would probably be irritated for days, he realized. Tiny cuts tended to do that.

His prefab felt heavy in his pack. He fought to get it out, then wavered as he stood to watch it deploy itself. Would he be able to get back up if he sat down? Was he even safe in this room?

Rhett glanced around, finding the room pristine everywhere but where the dust had been blown in when he'd entered. In all the years the storm had swept over this city, it had never damaged this chamber. It wasn't a guarantee, but it was better than nothing.

He collapsed into his prefab and let sleep take him. His wounds... he could tend to them in the morning. If the storm took him while he slept, so be it. He had tried his hardest, hadn't given up even when it was the logical thing to do. He'd wavered, yes, but he'd pushed through it.

Though he'd lost five years to his mistakes, he might yet make up for them. He could find no shame in that.

Day 1,950

Nuhalriu heated the tower like an oven. According to Rhett's prefab's sensor suite, the air outside exceeded four hundred degrees at its height. He'd never heard the climate control system squeal quite so loudly, but it managed to keep him down at a comfortable one hundred and nine degrees for the worst of it.

When he emerged, he was in desperate need of water—and a shower. The first was comparatively simple, though in no way easy. The storm has whisked away any hint of water that might have collected in the city or the valley beyond. Though what he had might last him a couple days, he would need to find some very soon.

Rhett explored the lower levels of the tower slowly over the course of the day, massaging his muscles to ward off cramps as he steadily pushed himself harder and harder. He needed to be strong enough to carry his pack again, and this place was about as much protection as he would likely ever find for the task. It was grueling work, but he felt a certain kind of strength in it. He was back to having a plan. Back to the steps.

First, he would strengthen himself for the journey. Then he'd find water—in whatever form that came. He'd have to deliver his stormpuncher to the top of this tower soon after that, then he'd make for the cave and the lander to see what could be recovered. If he was lucky, he'd have a fourth puncher to work with and all of this would be worth it.

Rhett grinned ruefully. Progress was progress.

Day 1,952

Rhett woke just before dawn to a strange sound. It was steady, rhythmic, droning. He reached for his sidearm even before he pulled his suit and mask on. The noise didn't change. Didn't shift. Didn't articulate. It just... was.

He stumbled out of the prefab, checking each direction around it. The sturdy stone walls of the Occassi tower still stood in all three directions. Whatever the sound was, it was coming from *outside* those walls. A vague part of his memory flickered at it—a half-remembered something from a life long left behind. Had he heard it before? How long ago? What did it mean?

Curiosity overcame him.

"Open the door?" he requested, for a moment wondering if the Occassi were still watching him. When the mechanism responded, he had his answer. The locking pins unfastened, but as the door groaned against its hinges, it moved nowhere. Smoke began to rise from an unseen part of the mechanism, then a magnificent *crack* announced the final doom of the gears within. It hadn't moved an inch. It was broken, and now it was sealed.

"The glass," he thought aloud. The dust must have seeped into the hinges when it had opened for him, leaving it vulnerable to glassing from the inside when the heat of Nuhalriu came.

Still, the sound droned on outside. There was a word for it. He could almost taste it on the tip of his tongue. What was it?

Rhett ignited the laser-torch and got to work. The door was thick and solid—it would take him several sessions to make a hole wide enough to move through. It was best he started now.

The noise prodded at him as he worked. Teasing him. Mocking him. Why couldn't he remember it? It was from somewhere far away... sometime long ago... but how long ago? The hiss of the torch sharpened the noise, somehow bringing it more into focus for its steady certainty. It had been a thing he'd known well. A thing that bound him to a place—Earth, he thought—but the memory eluded him.

Rhett kept cutting, then paused to let the torch cool. Cut, then pause. Cut, then pause. The noise grew louder as he drew closer to it. It wouldn't be long now before he would breach the far side with his carefully drafted scorch hole. Would he recognize the sound the moment he heard it properly—without barriers between them?

A wave of air burst through the hole the moment he'd pierced the other side. His torch sputtered, somehow wet. A few droplets made it even farther, splashing across his face.

Rhett extinguished his torch and blinked at the strange coolness of the moisture. He stumbled backward, falling on his ass with an inglorious thump.

"Rain."

The word came to him with the sound of a thunderclap. He checked his navbrace, flicking though images of weather patterns overhead, then traced back from there in an attempt to understand. It seemed that everywhere Nihalriu went, it was followed by a crescent-shaped rain-front. It only made sense. All the moisture being yanked into the atmosphere by the passing of the planetary storm's heat had to feed into somewhere. Markus had told him about this, hadn't he? It felt like years ago.

It *had been* years ago.

Rhett blinked. He hadn't seen a single drop of rain since he'd left Earth. There were rivers on the planet, which of course implied precipitation, but he'd never actually *seen* it. It was as if all of this planet's weather was balled up into this one massive system. It was not only a force of untold destruction—it was the *only* force that nature yet wielded on Occassus.

That was what he was fighting. Not just a storm. A planet. A whole fucking planet.

"It's like a bad joke," he whispered as more water sputtered through the hole in the door and dripped down to the floor. "It doesn't matter how strong I get. How much I push. I am fighting against something utterly beyond my understanding."

But while his rational mind was drifting uncontrollably into space, the animal side was staring at the water. It was here. Right here. He didn't have to find it, didn't have to go and get it. The planet had *brought* it to him. Perhaps Mother Gaia was alive here after all. Perhaps she still cared about her children, even if they had only been adopted. This water meant he could go on. That he had another chance to succeed after so much time had been wasted. Though she'd tried to kill him not two days prior, she was now rendering succor in his time of need.

Rhett kept cutting, just enough for a healthy trickle to make its way down the door. He winced at the waste as he burned a bowl into the floor beneath where it dripped down. He lost some to the steam, but a pool would be easier to tap for purification. It only took a few more minutes for enough to accumulate.

He couldn't remember the last time he'd tasted such fresh water. Though caution forced him to run it through a purifier before partaking, the taste almost convinced him he shouldn't need to. It was so beautiful. He filled his suit pouches one by one, then his stomach until it was far too full. He didn't even care.

Finally, he lay back down in his prefab and let himself drift back to sleep to the melodious sound of the planet's only downpour.

Chapter 21

Day 1,954

I'm going to try tomorrow, Cyn. I'm going to climb the tower. I'm going to make this right. I've lost so much time... I hope you can forgive me someday. I hope that... if I can make it through all this... you won't remember me as weak. As selfish. As less than the man I was.

[breathing]

This tower isn't nearly as tall as the one in the first city. According to Braaten's calculations, it will still be tall enough to serve the purpose, but it won't be as miserable to climb.

Or wouldn't have been, anyway.

[silence for 6.8 seconds]

What are you doing right now, Cyn? Not right now, *now. I know you're still in hypersleep up there, like the others. I mean when you listen to this. What will things be like for you then? Will the communications officers deliver you these messages right away after they awaken to find them? Will they delay? Will they screen them? As if I would say something offensive. Something untrue.*

I don't think they'll care about any of that. I hope they won't. I hope it will only be hours for you. That hours after you wake, they will bring you these messages. That you'll hear my voice as one of the first to greet you after so many decades of silence. I hope that will comfort you, since I won't be there to do it myself. I hope you listen to these transmissions eagerly. That you mourn for my struggle but feel excitement for our reunion.

I hope we have a reunion.

[silence for 4.4 seconds]

What if we don't? What if I can't manage to get my strength back? What if I never make it to the top of this tower? What if I never make it back down?

Would three be enough? If five would take months, four would take a decade... would three do it? Perhaps in a century?

Would two?

[breathing]

I have to entertain the possibility, Cyn. If I don't make it to the top of this tower, if something happens to me... you might still wake up. In a hundred years. Or two. Or more...

You and the rest of the passengers might wake to a dead and empty world. You might have nothing more than these messages to guide you. To tell you what happened. How you got here. What you're supposed to do.

I'm not... I'm not qualified to tell you what you're supposed to do.

If that happens, Cyn. Or... or if you're not Cyn. If she ends up being one of the few who succumb to the quiet death that sometimes takes those in hypersleep... I want to say that I'm sorry. I want you to know how sorry I am. I want you to know I am doing everything I can. That I'm risking my life—

No. That doesn't mean anything. You know I have nowhere to go. I have nothing to do down here except try to survive. Try to make it safe. I'm trapped. Helpless. A fly in a web trying to call enough other flies to me that I won't have to die alone. In the vain hope that I won't have to die at all.

At least not yet.

[silence for 8.5 seconds]

Cyn?

I'm going to assume you'll survive. If anyone wakes up, the odds of you surviving are... much better than mine are right now. I know there's a chance you won't, but I can't accept that right now. I will hold onto the possibility that I will make it through this, and cling desperately to the odds being in favor of you surviving, too.

But if we never meet again, Cyn, you should know that I loved you. Deeply. Desperately. I know I did some things that frustrated you. I know I was dishonest about my transfer to this mission...

Did I already tell you about that? My memory... it's so fuzzy right now. I hope it will go back to normal once I've had more time out of the dream-vault.

[sigh]

The point is that I love you. That's the better way to say it. Love, not loved. Even if I am dead, I still love you. Maybe I'll try to haunt you, just to be with you. I don't know if you get to choose about that sort of thing. But if I get to choose, I will definitely haunt you.

Nicely.

[breathing]

No. You would deserve someone else. I bet they'd be better than me, anyway. Someone more rational. More spiritual. More creative. Someone who would understand you without having to try so hard. Someone who would never lie to you.

I've only ever been good at one thing, Cyn. You know I'd fight for you. I guess that's what I'm doing now. And if I fail at that... you'll know I tried. For everyone up there. For myself. And then I guess you'll know that in the end, I realized that fighting alone is not enough. That there has to be something more. Something deeper.

I hope persistence is that other thing. Right now, I don't think there's a single fight that I could win. But if I take my time... if I work to get stronger... maybe I'll get back to where I can fight again.

Wish me luck, I guess. In the past?

I know it doesn't work that way, but why shouldn't we try?

Day 1,955

Rhett's muscles fought him the whole way up. He paced himself carefully, choosing to cherish the fact that he'd yet to vomit. Apparently the ramps were a universal design philosophy among the Occassi, though what that implied about their anatomy, he couldn't begin to guess. Maybe they moved around on wheels?

He chuckled. "Now that really would be strange."

Though he remembered encountering many of them during his time in the dream-vault, he still couldn't put together a clear picture of what the Occassi actually looked like. It could be his memory—it was still milky and weird after what he'd put it through in that place—but he wondered if it was a quality of the dream itself. As with normal sleep, nothing was quite right in there. Nothing quite made sense. And now that he was out of it, none of it had stuck around.

Rhett stopped for a midday meal in a chamber with a house-sized hole in one of its walls, facing out toward the landscape outside the city. In the distance, he could make out the blue-purple bruise of a mycoforest a few miles to the east. Would it be any safer than the one he'd lost Braaten in, now years before? Though the memory stained his thinking on regions like that, he had once thought it beautiful. Unlike the trees of Earth, the forests here drew their nutrients from chemical processes in the soil. According to Braaten, their evolution to grow upward was simply an adaptation that served to widen the spread of their spores across the countryside. Their structure—which resembled some mushrooms from Earth—also lent them to provide significant shade to the biome below, creating a habitat that bred creatures that served the mycoforest's chemical needs in the long run.

CHAPTER 21

Everything in its place. Everything with a purpose. A game to play. Something to reach for. Like him climbing this tower. Was he not like the mycotrees? Reaching upward in the vain hope of spreading his kind across the surface of the planet?

"But at least they have company," he muttered, taking a sip from the plaster tube. "Or rivals."

Rhett stretched carefully before he continued, rolling his shoulders as he begrudged the weight of his pack. All of it was necessary, he knew. He'd left the expendable things at the bottom of the tower, same as last time. At least he hadn't needed to use his sidearm yet.

He smirked. Then again, the calamari hadn't been too bad, in the end. Maybe next time it wouldn't nearly cost him his life to acquire.

He kept climbing, slow and steady, studying the layout of each floor he passed. Unlike the previous tower, with its high ceilings and grandiose architecture, this one felt small, cramped, but built with more apparent purpose. Rooms lined every hall that sprung off from the central twisting ramp. In each one, a nearly identical suite of what must have once been amenities was arranged. The homogeneity reminded him of only one thing: an apartment building.

Perhaps the lives of the Occassi had once been as dull as the lives of humanity. Boring jobs. Boring apartments. Endless ramps. So many endless ramps. It was no wonder they'd fled underground to live inside a false reality.

Rhett considered the dream-vault again. It was obviously more than idle entertainment—an escape common and necessary for a world so much like Earth. It took absolute control. Absolute totality of the mind. There was no balance in the dream, no real life to mix in with the fake one. It was all there was. Absolute apathy, atrophying any possibility of purpose until there was nothing left but that easy, meaningless fulfillment.

He sighed. He'd fallen for it himself. He'd thrown away five years, and even now was suffering the consequences to his mind and body. Now he had to build his way back to where he was; then he could begin again at building toward what he could become.

It was all a means to an end. He had to make himself strong enough to complete his mission, strong enough to survive the ten years that would be required of him afterward. Strong enough to, after all that time alone, return to help society begin anew on this world. There was so much left to do, and in the shape he was in, there was no way he'd be able to do it.

"A worry for another time," he muttered. "For now, we focus on deploying the third puncher."

According to Rhett's navbrace, he was getting close to the top of the building. From the orbital images—and his awkward view from the ground—the roof appeared to be essentially flat, like the roof he'd landed on when he'd arrive in the city. That should make deploying the device easy enough, so long as he could figure out how to access it.

The ceilings grew taller on the last two floors. Luxury apartments, he supposed. Perhaps for the wealthy—assuming the Occassi had a concept of money—or perhaps for the politically or religiously powerful. He could feel a draft coming from somewhere but couldn't easily tell where. At the top of the seemingly never-ending spiral ramp, he came to a door that had been bent outward at the hinges, seeping cool evening air into the building. It only took a glance through the hole it left to confirm it was what he needed: roof access.

Rhett tossed his bag out, then slipped through himself, checking the perimeter carefully. He frowned. "Maybe a little too easy."

He started the work of deploying the stormpuncher, ears attuned for sounds of movement around him. Aside from the wind, there was only silence. On Earth, he might have expected pigeons to be roosting in a place like this. It occurred to him that he hadn't seen how squirrelhawks made their nests.

Rhett choked back an unbidden wave of emotion. Virgil had been gone a long time—a *long* time.

No. Now wasn't the time to be thinking about him.

He punched in the activation code and watched the sequence of lights on the stormpuncher that communicated it was fully operational. In minutes, it had bored its way into the stone and extended its electro-whatever arms so it could do what Markus had built it to do.

"Good." Rhett nodded to himself, turning back toward the bent door. He smiled. "Now to put *you* to use."

It only took him a matter of minutes to cut the door the rest of the way from its hinges. While its shape wasn't perfect—bent a little too sharply the middle to accommodate a comfortable seat—he was pretty sure it would prove a serviceable sled.

With a grunt, he shifted it into place, bracing it to keep it from sliding away without him. He positioned his pack in front of him, poised between his legs so it wouldn't fly off to either side. Then he settled in, took a deep breath, and let go of the edge of the doorway.

The descent was halting at first. The corner of the door kept getting caught on the edges of adjoining hallways. But after a few minutes of practice, he found he could spring off of the gaps with his foot smoothly enough to keep his momentum and even ease his rotation for the next one. What had taken thousands of steps on his way up would only take as many steps as there were hallways on the way back down. It would still be a few hundred, he guessed, but the difference was phenomenal. He couldn't help but cackle with glee as he bounced and bumped his way down the tower.

He skidded to a stop at the bottom, muscles suddenly frozen at the sight of what awaited him. A trio of strange creatures, nearly the size of wolves, picked through the pile of items he'd left behind for the climb. He fingered the safety on his weapon, hoping first that they somehow didn't have ears and wouldn't have heard him, then that they'd be afraid of the clamor and bolt rather than challenge him.

But one of them turned toward him, its wide iris-less eyes drinking him in with the pure malice of hunger.

PRRTSH.

Rhett's first shot hissed clean through the creature's skull—it had a skull, didn't it?—and crackled as it struck the stone wall far behind. The creature wobbled for a moment, its scaly mandibles quivering, then collapsed. The other two squealed, fleeing first in the wrong direction, then remembering the direction of the door.

Rhett shook his head as he stared after them. "Hope the noise doesn't bring anything," he muttered, nudging the carcass with his foot to gauge where it might have the most meat on it. It looked lean but well-muscled, certainly a pack predator of some kind. Where could they have hidden during the storm to have gotten here so fast?

"I hate wasting ammo on things I won't eat before they rot."

Day 1,969

Rhett sat across from the radio in his prefab during the deep hours of the night. He'd been disturbed by dreams of its yellow pulse suddenly going out—a sentence of utter futility pronounced across his entire existence. Every time the light flashed, he wondered if it would be the last time. Every time it went dark, pausing 3.6 seconds between every ping, he could feel his heart stop.

This time.

This time.

This time.

Every time it burst to life again, shining with the hope of dawn, he took a breath. All was well on the ship. Their orbit was stable. The hypersleep systems were not any more taxed now than they had been during the transit. Cyn was safe, only sleeping.

Like he should be.

This time.

This time.

CHAPTER 21

This time.

Rhett reached for it, wondering if sending a transmission would make him feel any better. He could tell Cyn about this. About how he didn't sleep like he used to—not since the dream-vault. About how he felt even more alone now that he had left behind the only other sentient life he'd found down here.

The light blinked again.

Tell who? No one was listening up there. They were all still asleep. No one would care what he said. No one would ask him what he meant when he said something strange. No one would tell him that they understood. That it would be okay. That all of this would be worth it in the end.

The light blinked again.

There was nobody out here but him. This was his planet. His lonely planet. It was true that perhaps someday others would join him. They would see what he'd done. What he'd saved. But would they ever actually understand? Would they picture these nights and think of him for all the moments when he wondered if it was even worth going on? Or would they see him simply as a hero? The man who had saved the human race. The man that brought them to their new home. Their promised land. Their guide. Prophet. Messiah.

The light blinked again.

If Rhett spoke into that radio, he was scrawling his voice across history. If he sent another recording, it would land among the annals which would define him for all the generations who might ever live here. Was it right for him to show them weakness? Was it good for them to see that he was simply a man? Weak? Broken? Tired?

So tired.

The light blinked again.

Why couldn't he just go back to sleep? The others were sleeping. How was that fair? Even the Occassi were sleeping, back there in their wondrous and artificial dream state. He could always return there. They would take him back. He could live out the rest of the eons in a lucid mirror of a world he never wished to return to. This savage planet could recede into the darkest corners of his mind, never to be called upon again. At least then he would sleep. And he would be happy.

Happy, but empty.

The light blinked again.

That blinking, like the pulse of all humanity, reminded him why he was here. It wasn't about him. It wasn't *for* him. He did what he did for the others. To give them a chance. To let them decide. It was not his place to decide for them whether to wake or to sleep.

That had to be enough. The knowledge that he was the only one able to free them drove him forward. This mission was his and his alone. No one else would do it. No one else *could* do it. This was his purpose. His destiny. His sole reason for being.

It was a weight, yes. It was a massive and incomprehensible responsibility. But like a lodestone, it could direct him. Give him clarity. Tell him every time he wavered that he was on the correct path: that pushing forward was the right and only thing he should be doing right now. If he failed, he failed. But so long as he'd been moving in the right direction, his trajectory and acceleration aimed to intercept the ultimate fulfillment of his life, he could die knowing he'd done all he could. That he had met his fate with dignity. That the things left undone could not have been done by him or any other.

The light blinked again, bringing Rhett a renewed sense of freedom. This radio was all he had. This flashing yellow call to action. A reminder that every time he stumbled, he did so for the cause.

Rhett would keep running. He would keep fighting. He would prevail.

Or he would die trying.

Chapter 22

Day 1,972

I've decided to start naming things.

[breathing]

Places, I mean. Sarah gave us a start—the supercontinent being called Miar. But with everything else... It's just me down here, and I've been growing increasingly annoyed by referring to places as 'the first city', 'that place where a squirrelhawk met me and then left me' or 'that mountain range near where Braaten died'. I figure if I can name them, I can keep them straighter in my head. Maybe move past what happened there and see the places for what they really are.

Did I ever tell you about my childhood dog? I was twelve at the time. My parents were—misguidedly—trying to find an animal that could keep up with the whirlwind that was myself. They decided a dalmatian would be able to run out my energy, and I could do the same for it. It didn't work out that way, but that's not my point in telling you. My point is that, at the age of twelve, I still decided that the appropriate name for a dalmatian was 'Spot'.

Yeah. I've never been good at naming things.

Maybe if I had gotten used to it at some time or another. Like for you, you always named your paintings after you were done with them. Mind you, some of your names didn't make any sense—

[whispering]—at least to normal people—

—but you always came up with one.

[chuckle]

I mean, your painting of that lake a few hours away from your family's home? You called it 'Sand Castles'. It was a freshwater lake. It was surrounded by dirt. There wasn't even any sand there. I know it was supposed to be some sort of artistic statement, but no matter how hard I tried... I just couldn't get there.

Hmm.

And your painting of the maglev station? It was the only painting you ever did that included people or, more generally, society. You always hated painting people. Said you never rendered them right. They looked fine. That painting... it was actually one of my favorites.

Do you remember what you named it?

'The Tomato Garden'.

[tongue clicking]

Nope. Never got there.

I'm going to use simple names. I guess like what I've been naming the creatures that I see enough times to bother. And I'll name some places after my crewmates. Pay them some respects. More than I've been able to, anyway.

I think they would've liked that.

Day 1,978

Dust scraped between boot and glass as Rhett crested the ridge over the Stormshadow Hinterlands. It was strange returning to the region, reminding him of all that had gone wrong in those first few months. A diplomatic mission to an alien world turned sour by extinction, the transformation of their mission into a fool's attempt at saving a planet, the deaths of his crewmates—his friends. He'd often wondered if the journey should have ended here, all those years ago.

Perhaps it still would.

CHAPTER 22

It was obvious long before he laid eyes on it that the region had recently been visited by Nuhalriu. Orbital images showed that the very center of the storm had passed over this spot, bathing everything in its path in dust and blazing heat. The ground itself glistened as it had the day they'd first emerged from the ship—blinding without the option of a glare-reducing visor. He held an arm up against the light, squinting each time he checked his footing and rechecked his heading. At least with the terrain so ravaged, he didn't have to worry about any hostile lifeforms out here.

He pitched his prefab in the lee of a glass dune, sleeping almost until first light. The wind was stronger in the valley beyond the ridge, the shape of the land and the smoothness of its features allowing it to build speed unhindered.

He didn't hear voices in that wind—whispered words from friends long dead. That would be crazy. And Rhett was not crazy.

First light found him as he slid down the last hill on the approach to the cave. From a distance, its mouth looked narrower than he remembered. Could he really have hunched so low while carrying Sarah's weight over his shoulder? It wasn't as if there had been much of a choice. When they found it, she had been barely conscious from the fever. Rhett hadn't thought finding a place to rest would save her, but he had hoped…

He found himself standing over her grave, a low mound that had long since been encased in a few millimeters of glass. It looked much the same as when he had left it. He still had that hope, foolish as it seemed. After all, what was hope if not the belief that somehow, things would turn out all right despite every logical indication to the contrary?

Rhett cracked a wan smile. At least she was still here, like she'd wanted. Nothing had come along and dug her up—a fear that had played out countless times in Rhett's nightmares.

What was he thinking? This wasn't where she wanted to be. Perhaps she had expected to die, and it had been her wish to be buried if it happened, but she had wanted to live. She had wanted to meet the Occassi, as Rhett had. To have a chance at making a new life on this planet.

Well, it was still to be seen if *anyone* would have that opportunity.

Rhett turned back to the cave. He was stalling, dwelling on the only emotion powerful enough to suppress his fear. But he had not returned to pay his respects to her grave. He had returned for supplies. For a stormpuncher.

He trudged to the cave's mouth, stooping through the squat entryway with a grimace. It had indeed gotten narrower, the glass layered in sheets upon the rock. He crouched to better keep his balance on the slick surface, the dread deepening as he clicked on his holoescent lamps to illuminate the space within.

For a long moment, he could not make sense of what saw. The cave walls—once muted grey stone—were streaked with nauseating colors in brutal, chaotic swirls. It reminded him of the subway graffiti back in his hometown, layer upon layer burying meaning in mesmerizing pigment. But there was no artistry here.

He kicked at the remains of a nutrient plaster canister, glued to the cave floor in glass, its contents blasted with heat until the pressure within could not be held back. Prior to mixing with water, the plaster was little more than a nutrient-rich powder, its vibrant color an indicator of its professed flavor. He'd been keeping dozens of canisters here, hauled out from the lander to this more convenient staging ground. If any of the canisters survived, he doubted they were safe to eat.

"Doesn't matter."

He'd hunted for food before, and he could do it again. The plaster wouldn't last him ten years, anyway. He would've had to find a better solution sooner or later.

Later was just no longer an option.

Rhett sifted through debris as he moved deeper into the cave. He'd had the sense to put his most valuable resources near the back, where the winds of a near-miss encounter with the storm would be less likely to damage them. But he'd never planned to allow the eye of Nuhalriu to pass over this place. Not without moving everything important first.

The Phi-8 batteries had exploded. No surprise there. The magnetopellets looked all right—they were solid metal and would take a lot higher temperatures

CHAPTER 22

to melt than even what the storm brought with it. He collected a few months' worth and stashed them in his pack.

Most of his replacement parts were ruined. The mask filters were nothing but puddles of black mush clogging up the bearings. Had he had the sense to take them out, maybe the rest of the mask would have… but no. The wiring was completely degraded. The sheathing had melted off of it, and some kind of amber fluid—a lubricant, maybe?—was leaking from the mechanical components.

When Rhett found the stormpuncher, he released a sigh that might have been the very soul leaving his body. The nylon bag he'd been keeping it in had partially fused to the casing, but the problems only got worse when he cut that free with his utility knife. Although structurally recognizable, each individual internal component was either melted, mangled, or exploded to some degree. If he had any notion of how the device worked—Markus had tried to explain it once or twice and had made sure everyone on the team had a copy of the engineering specs downloaded to their navbraces—he could probably give a reasonable measurement of where he was at on the scale from '1' to 'completely fucked'. But only knowing what he did…

Well. The scale just kind of maxed itself out, didn't it?

Rhett slumped against the cave wall, wringing the remains of a nylon strap between his hands. He stared sightlessly for a long time, grievous thoughts swirling in his mind. Even Markus couldn't have fixed this. It really was over. His mission. This planet. The whole damn human race. All of it was done.

Forever.

His eyes traced the pattern of plaster dust coating the walls, noting the way it had been layered into the glass. He should eat. Maybe deploy his prefab before it got dark. But that was a ways away. And what was the point? This thing he'd been tasked to do… it was impossible. Maybe it always had been.

"Fuck."

Rhett raked his fingers through his hair again, scowling as they came away bloody. The scabs hadn't fully healed yet, and he'd been doing that a lot today. If he wasn't careful, it might get infected. Then he'd…

Well. It wouldn't really make a difference, would it?

But there would be no one left to bury him.

Rhett began to sigh but choked and coughed when he realized he was not alone. An Occassi drone—like the one that had followed him out of the city where he'd deployed the first puncher—hovered just inside the threshold.

"What do you want?" Rhett muttered.

He had no doubt it had followed him here. How long, he couldn't guess. It hadn't been with him when he left the dream-vault. He would have noticed it trailing him, surely, given how much distance he had covered since then.

Then again, perhaps not. The drone was small, only slightly bulkier than his own head. It made little sound as it moved, and if it was able to keep track of him at a distance, it would have no reason to approach and reveal itself.

"*What* do you *want*?" Rhett staggered to his feet, snapping his sidearm from his holster and leveling it at the machine. "Are you here to gloat? To be proven right? Well do it, then!"

The drone remained where it was, apparently nonplussed. Rhett glared at it, gun pointed but finger against the slide. After a few seconds, it slid through the air toward one of the walls and began to pan around, perhaps inspecting the pattern there.

Rhett lowered the weapon, turning away to rip off his mask and vomit onto the ground. What right did they have to follow him here? To see him like this? He'd already lost everything. More than that. Every possibility of ever having anything ever again. Everything he'd fought for, everyone he'd lost, every day that he'd struggled and night that he'd suffered…

The drone said nothing, simply inspected the walls in a smooth, steady pattern at a distance of just under ten inches. Was it… scanning, or something? Constructing a map of the topography? What for? Markus would probably know.

"I want you to leave." Rhett managed to get his mask back on, his gun pointed at the drone once again. It seemed like the drone didn't have the same beam-speech-into-your-head ability that the Occassi in the dream-vault had, but he had to assume it could understand him. Even so, the drone continued its scan of the cave, approaching the remains of the stormpuncher where it leaned against the far wall.

"Wait. Can you...?"

The drone was obviously extremely advanced. If it analyzed the stormpuncher, perhaps discerned how it worked, could it—

The drone passed over the stormpuncher without pausing.

Rhett could take no more. He stumbled out of the cave, wincing at the light of the afternoon. His teeth wouldn't stop chattering, although it wasn't cold. The Phi-8 hung at his side from nerveless fingers, but after a couple tries he managed to get it back into its holster—if not to secure the thumb-break.

The drone followed him out. It positioned itself in front of him, one of the flat triangular faces pointing toward him. It didn't appear to have anything resembling an eye or camera on that side, but he was fairly certain there wasn't one on any of the other sides either.

"What?"

The drone slid a few feet away from him, to his left, then stopped. He stared at it, and after a few seconds it approached again. It repeated the gesture, sliding away through the air, then returning.

Rhett shook his head. "I don't know what you're doing."

The drone did it again. Then again.

"Is... something that way?"

He knew what it was before he even checked his navbrace. As he'd expected, the drone was indicating he follow it northeast. In the direction of the dream-vault.

"I can't..."

What couldn't he do? Couldn't go back? Because his mission was too important to delay any longer? The risk of failure too great if he were to return? There was no more mission, and he was nothing but a failure. What else was there for him except to return to the dream-vault?

But to go back... to admit to such abject failure...

Admit to what? He *was* a failure. His weakness at the dream-vault the first time was exactly what had gotten him into this situation. That was the reason he'd lost so much time, the reason he hadn't been here to move his supplies to safety before it was too late.

He could already be done. Instead, he'd never finish at all. This entire mission had come down to him, and his failure was entirely his own. There was nothing else to be said. Nothing else to be done. Perhaps the Occassi thought they were being kind to him. Offering him an escape after he came to realize that everything he'd worked for was utterly worthless. But to offer the dream-vault... the very escape that had caused this worthlessness...

But Rhett had been happy in the dream-vault, hadn't he? Sure, it had been happiness bathed in falsehood. A happiness that was and could only be artificial to its core. But compared to his alternatives... wasn't that happiness worth seizing? He could no longer claim that he deserved the real thing. Perhaps that sweet oblivion was better suited to him anyway.

The drone motioned for him to follow again. Rhett wiped at his cheeks, looking back toward Sarah's grave. She would want him to be happy. To find some modicum of comfort on this planet. Right? He wanted to go back. The more he thought about it, the more he wanted it. Perhaps the destruction of the stormpuncher was some kind of sign. A release from his duty to the mission, a writ of dismissal that carried both shame and solace. If he couldn't complete the mission, why should he try? If there weren't enough stormpunchers to destroy Nuhalriu, it wasn't his fault, was it? He'd accepted the price of ten years should he succeed with four after they'd lost their first, but now that there were only three, there was no way to—

He frowned. Then, upon further consideration, his frown deepened.

There *was* a fourth stormpuncher on the planet. He had no idea the condition it was in... but it did exist. Somewhere up on the slopes of that volcano, where they'd left Caldwell to rot, they'd left his stormpuncher as well. No doubt the storm had reached it by now. Or the volcano had erupted. Or the wind and rain had ruined its inner mechanisms. But if not...

"Not *everything* about this one is broken," he muttered. "If anything survived from that one, perhaps I could figure out how to get a functioning combination of the two..."

And if he needed more?

Rhett drew his Phi-8—

PRRTSH.

—and bolted the drone out of the air. It fell, suddenly just an inert chunk of metal and wires. He didn't know anything about the way it worked, but there were parts of it he recognized. Parts he could use. Parts that might just make the difference between a working stormpuncher and a dead dream on a dying world.

It wasn't much. In fact, it was so little no scientist would even bother measuring it. Negligible, Markus would say. Such a remote chance that it wasn't even worth considering. Every ounce of reasoning told him it was stupid. Far-fetched. Impossible.

No. That wasn't right. It *was* possible, but only just.

His final chance. His only hope.

His last desperate gamble.

Chapter 23

Day 1,991

I'm going back, Cyn. Back to where things first started to go wrong. Back to where Caldwell died. Where we left him.

Is that why it happened? Some kind of karmic justice for how we treated him after he died? We couldn't have gotten to his body. That's what we told ourselves. But now I'm headed back, and I'm going to do that very thing. I'm going to risk the same fate he suffered for a device that I'm absolutely certain will not work.

At least the Votum says there haven't been any eruptions on the continent while I was gone. There could be a chance, you know? Doesn't look like the storm got close enough to glass the area, either, though I bet it experienced a decent amount of wind. Who knows what I'll find. Who knows if I'll even be able to find it.

That's not the point anymore. This isn't about odds or chances or whether I'll survive. With everything that's happened, I can't rely on chance being on my side. Yes, I'll probably die on that mountain. I guess if that happens, I hope it will be like it was for Caldwell. Quick, if... violent. But it could be the volcano, too. Or some creature—there are more than enough bad ones around.

It doesn't matter. Either I find it and see what can be done, or I die and no one will be around to care.

I guess it's always been that way. Nothing's really changed, has it?

I'm still out here risking my life every day. Still pushing hard and struggling no matter how far I've come. It won't end if I get the puncher, either. I'll have to place it. I'll have to survive for ten years.

CHAPTER 23

Ten YEARS.

That's if Markus's calculations were correct. And it could depend on some margin of error. Maybe it'll be less, but maybe it'll be more. I might put up all four punchers and die eleven years after that and still have never seen you.

I...

I want to see you again, Cyn. You're all that's kept me going. All that's kept me recording these messages. All I think about when I see that flashing yellow light. I remember you and how much I want to talk to you again. To REALLY talk to you again.

To hold you.

To kiss you.

I could be an old man, Cyn. You probably won't even recognize me. I lost a lot of my hair down here...

Yes, I know you'd joke about it being the nutrient plaster, and yes, it's still horrible, but that isn't what happened. Back in Dreamhaven, I decided it would be a good idea to take a stroll while Nuhalriu was rolling in.

Yes, I know. Dumb. But, hey. It's me.

Anyway, that's just... well...

I could really use you right now, Cyn. If only for some company. It's been... It's been a really long time. I hope you're okay up there. Just sleeping, like you all have been. I hope you won't have to wait much longer, and that you'll forgive me for how much time this all took. I could have been faster. I lost so much time...

What if my food doesn't last, Cyn? Ten years is way longer than I have plaster for. What if it's something simple like that?

I just... I just don't know anymore. About anything. About any of it. I still have so very far to go. I've already been through hell, and now...

I just don't know if I have the strength.

Day 1,992

The hills near Caldwell's Rest looked the same as Rhett remembered them. It helped that he'd relived that day a dozen times in his nightmares, same as the days the others had died. This planet might be home to him and perhaps one day the rest of humanity, but it would always be the place that had first taken everything he had. Perhaps he should forgive it. Let the past be the past. Perhaps Occassus was like a strict parent, punishing not out of malice but love.

But what had the others done wrong? And what had he done to deserve all of this? He was a simple man. A simple soldier. Perhaps he was too simple. Too simple to understand, as a toddler could not yet grasp a timeout for doing something incredibly stupid or dangerous.

"It's a good thing I'm about to do something incredibly stupid *and* incredibly dangerous."

Rhett smirked, pausing to check the navbrace to get an idea where the volcanic minefield might be about to start. He had a plan, but it was a foolish one. He knew the trick with the geysers was pressure—too much of it was underground waiting for the right trigger to let it out. Rather than hoping he didn't do so on accident, he would do it very intentionally—like lancing a pocket of puss. His sidearm packed enough punch to get through a foot or so of rock, and with any luck, that would be able to release pressure where he wanted and when he wanted. If he could relieve enough of it before trying to cross, perhaps spots that would have been deadly before would be perfectly safe.

"This all assumes I won't just piss the volcano off and make it erupt."

CHAPTER 23

Rhett shrugged. There was no way for him to know that. He wasn't a scientist, and even if he had been, he'd run out of options. If this planet were ever to support life the way he needed it to, he needed whatever was left of that stormpuncher.

Rhett stopped at the edge of the lava field, sighing what he knew might be one of his last sighs. He still had miles to go, but this was where the difficulty really began. Any step past here could be fatal. Any wrong move—and he had next to no information on what moves might be right.

"No point in waiting," he muttered, drawing his pistol and firing it toward the ground thirty feet away. The thump of the magnetopellet striking the ground was subsumed entirely by the thunderous burst of steam that shot into the air. Rhett smiled ruefully; at least he'd thought to bring ear protection.

"Here it goes."

Rhett stepped out onto the smooth volcanic stone. He paused with his foot there, expecting something to happen. Of course it wouldn't be the first step. It hadn't been Caldwell's first step, either. They'd traversed more than a mile into the geyser trap before they'd set one off. He wouldn't know if his plan was working until he made it out safe on the other side. Everything until then was totally up in the air.

He chuckled darkly. "Up in the air."

Rhett took another step, then another. After twenty, he fired the sidearm again, wincing at the blast of steam that shot into the air. That could be him at any time. He'd never see it coming.

He pushed the thought aside. It wouldn't help him to keep imagining what could happen to him. It would happen or it wouldn't. He already had his plan; all he had to do now was carry it out.

Rhett pressed on, dismissing regrets and worries alike. There was something for him to do here. A chance to make things right. He couldn't let anything get in the way of that—least of all himself.

The day progressed with a deep, percussive rhythm. He had enough charge and magnetopellets to last him for hours, but would they stretch far enough for him to find what he was looking for? He got used to the rhythm—walking a short distance, firing into the ground ahead of him, then moving through what he hoped was now a safe zone. How long would it remain safe after he'd relieved the pressure? Hours? Days? Hopefully long enough that he could make his way back out once he found what he'd come for.

If it ever presented itself, of course.

His navbrace led him back to the spot where Caldwell had died within two hours of entering the lava field. To his surprise, he still recognized the place—as if not a stone had been moved since the day they left. He shot the ground twice before taking the last few steps to his old crewmate's remains—his skeleton still cooped up in his grey military issue envirosuit. Caldwell's bag was a dozen feet away, ripped up a bit by some small creature with claws, but most of its contents were intact.

Rhett emptied it carefully, taking inventory as he went. As much as he hated to think of it, this bag was one of the greatest troves of necessities he'd seen in years. It was a wonder so much of it still looked usable. The rocky terrain surrounding the volcano had insulated this place from the dust the storm usually brought with it, and perhaps the eye itself had missed by just enough the last several cycles to keep what little was here from turning to glass.

He breathed relief to find the stormpuncher there, mostly intact. A few dents in the casing, he noted. Probably a few wires to replace. All perfectly reasonable. All totally... possible.

"I have to admit," Rhett whispered. "I didn't actually expect to make it this far."

He glanced around, somehow certain something was sneaking up on him. He couldn't have made it so easily.

"Not done yet," he reminded himself. He still had to deploy it, of course. But what was a little cross-country travel to him now? It was just up a mountain. No city with blind corners. No volcano that might erupt at any—

Rhett frowned as the first rumble ripped across the lava field. He knew even before he glanced up what he'd see on the mountaintop. For a moment, it looked calm—just a huge chunk of rock jutting up from the ground. Then the scene around him was bathed in the light of a fire bursting upward like the blast of a nuclear bomb. He clapped his hands over his ears only a split second before the wave of sound hit him, knocking him off his feet. He struggled for a moment, reeling even as he knew exactly what was happening.

Of course. Of course it did. If there was a god up there, he was one spiteful motherf—

Another blast blew half of the mountaintop free from its base, hurtling like a massive and badly built rocket on a jet of lava.

Rhett stumbled to his feet, faltering with every other step as he tried to find the fastest way down in his panic. He reloaded his sidearm, firing a shot down the hill as he began to gain momentum. His pack pushed down against him, keeping him from fully stabilizing as he lumbered down the decline.

His next shot summoned a belch of magma along with its hiss of steam. He swore as he veered away from it, trying to predict now where the flow he'd created would track down the hill. He glanced to his right just as a massive chunk of rock crashed down less than twenty feet away. The ground beneath it buckled with a bubbling crunch, spurting forth its own stream of lava that spread at a speed he couldn't quite believe.

"Getting kinda crowded."

Rhett stumbled again and the weight of his pack suddenly became untenable. He reached out as he toppled, barely catching himself before striking his face on a rock. A twinge of pain shot through his right wrist as he wobbled back to his feet. He shook it gingerly, eyes sweeping about for his Phi-8, which had flown from his hand as he fell. He caught sight of it only a moment before a lava flow swallowed it.

"Shit."

He had to get out of here. Had to move, and fast. Perhaps with the volcano already erupting the pressure would be low enough. Maybe if he just ran, he'd be safe. It didn't really matter, though. The lava was closing in fast behind and around him, so he had no delusions about bumming around until he could come up with a better plan.

Rhett slowed slightly as he continued his descent. Another stumble could cost him more than just his weapon. His bag mattered more. The stormpuncher inside mattered more. He had to protect that most of all.

He considered stopping, emptying his bag of everything but his storm puncher and some food to get him through to his next hunt. But when would that be? Without a weapon, what on this planet could he reasonably kill? He would have to stop at the lander, but how could he guess what had survived his long absence? The spare sidearms his crewmates had been assigned were probably still there, maybe still intact. Enough food to make it there, then?

Rhett slid to a stop just as another huge rock smashed a hole in the ground to his left. His avenues of escape were quickly dwindling—soon to disappear. He slung his pack down, grimacing as he scraped each of his coveted items out of it and onto the mountainside. A dozen canisters of nutrient plaster and the two broken husks of the stormpunchers. Everything else... well, it wasn't worth his life.

He slung his pack back up and charged forward, suddenly conscious of the barbarian wail that was coming from his mouth. He didn't care if he sounded crazy. He *was* crazy. He was running down a fucking volcano while it was erupting behind him. On an alien planet. For the fate of all humanity. If that wasn't crazy, then there was no such thing.

Rhett sped up as he watched his last line of escape begin to close a few dozen feet down the hill. Two streams of lava had begun to flow toward each other, sure to intercept within a minute and leave him trapped between them. It was going to be close. Too close. He wobbled for a moment, his legs protesting the speed of the descent, but he kept his balance.

The moments passed as if each one took an age. Rhett could feel the shock of each footfall as it propagated through his skeleton. He could feel the burning sensation in his lungs of each labored breath, could hear the desperate whirring of his 'after-market' filtration system struggling to keep pace with his respiration.

His path narrowed. Four feet. Three feet.

Two.

CHAPTER 23

One.

Rhett held his breath as he committed to the final stretch, knowing full well he'd have to jump. It was the only way. He could do this. His body screamed at him as he pushed it even harder—even faster. Then, in one last burst of strength, he pushed off with his right foot and sailed over the radiant heat of the lava.

He landed on the other side with an awkward attempt at a roll, but he regained his footing before the hot tongues of flowing fire caught hold of his suit. He slid as the gravel beneath his feet gave way but kept upright and pushed off to land on another stretch of solid stone. He kept running as another blast sounded distantly behind him. A shower of stones crashed to the ground, prompting him to hold his arms over his head—as if that would protect him from a sufficiently large and super-heated rock. He kept running, hoping, praying.

When Rhett finally cleared the edge of the lava field, he afforded himself a glance back at the ruination that was left of the mountaintop.

"So I probably caused a volcanic eruption." He chuckled nervously. "No big deal."

Day 2,007

Sarah's Hope wasn't more than another day ahead of him.

Rhett sat atop his prefab in the pre-dawn light. The countryside had taken on a suite of hazel-reds during the warm season this year. While he appreciated the touch of color, it made him think of Earth and miss home more than ever. Would children born here on Occassus ever be able to imagine the wonder of an actual forest? A sea of green that completely surrounded you? The picture of Cyn in his navbrace showed it plainly, but perhaps the children would believe it had been modified. Certainly, the crops grown from seeds the Votum had carried would be green, as Earth's had been. But had there really been so many of them? Eventually, there might be a generation who believed that Earth was simply a place their elders had made up. A myth.

"Maybe someday. I guess it's nice to know that eventually all my struggles will be forgotten."

"Everyone's are," he reminded himself.

But on this particular morning, Rhett couldn't help but wonder about his struggle. About how much he still had left of it. Sarah's Hope was close, of course. There, he'd patch together what remained of the drone and his storm-scorched puncher to complete the one he'd found at Caldwell's Rest. It wasn't a sure thing that it would work, but he refused to consider that for now. The mountain where he would deploy it wasn't more than two weeks beyond that. But even once all of that was done, his work was only just beginning. He'd have to survive here. Maintain the punchers. And somehow, he'd have to never lose motivation for any of it.

Rhett sighed. He was running short on inspiration even now. Every day seemed harder. Every time he opened his eyes, he considered simply staying in his prefab for the day. After all, what was one more day in the face of the ten years he'd have to spend alone?

What if he simply stopped caring? He would likely die here before it was done anyway. Was it really worth all the time? All the effort? He knew what he had to do, knew the steps and how many he had left. But sometimes, he wasn't sure he even wanted to do them.

What was wrong with being alone?

Rhett considered the Occassi dream-vault again. There, he might sink away without care or worry. He could simply give in. Give up. No one would judge him for it. No one would even know. His life's potential, while unmet, would never be questioned. How was that any different than any other person? All humans died with unfinished business. All humans died with unfulfilled plans. It was the nature of man to make plans when the ones they had were completed. Always pushing forward. Always looking for that next thing. That was how they had gotten themselves into this mess, wasn't it?

And yet here Rhett was, staring at the opportunity to accept what he had. To accept the state of the world and universe around him. To stop challenging the norm, stop fighting the storm. He could choose submission, could choose sleep. He could choose to dream.

He could be happy.

Was that so wrong?

Rhett smirked. It was exactly that kind of thinking he'd been trying to prevent when he'd shot the second drone. Sure, he might end up needing the parts, but that wasn't why he'd done it. He'd needed to burn that bridge, to make sure there was no way the Occassi would accept him back so he needn't waste his thoughts on that possibility.

It had almost worked.

He sighed again, glancing now at the radio in his hands. Others didn't have this reminder. This little yellow light that flashed at them, reminding them they were supposed to have a purpose. That others needed them. That everyone was counting on them. Without him, they'd never see this world. They'd never explore its mycoforests or see the sunrise over McNeary's Ridge. They'd never know the bizarre cuteness of a pitcat or feel terror for a blind-weaver. They'd never share this planet with their children. Remember fondly their adventures here.

If he could not bring them safely down from the Votum, this whole world may as well not exist. They would sleep forever their involuntary sleep, never knowing what was here or what they might have seen. It was all in his hands. All in the strength of his arms. All in the resilience of his will. No one else could deliver them. No one else could bring them to this, their new promised land.

And here he was, pretending to be a damned philosopher. Of course he was the only one. That didn't make him special. It could have been any man. It could have been any world. Would they have done better? Would they have questioned their role? Questioned their purpose? Questioned the degree of their efforts?

Would they have been offered the siren's song of dreams? Would they have lost five years to its call?

It should have been someone else. It should have been McNeary. Or Markus. They wouldn't have questioned it. They would be done by now. They'd have figured out some better way. Caldwell, too, perhaps. He was a bit... old, but he had always believed in what he did. And Sarah? She had so much passion for her work. He doubted that candle would ever have dwindled, even in the face of all the waiting and the walking and the fighting.

But she had known she would die here. She'd told him that herself and asked him to bury her. To do it properly. A request he'd fulfilled with the discipline of a soldier... and the duty of a friend.

Maybe Rhett was supposed to be alone. Maybe that was just how this thing worked. The nature of purpose. The nature of a mission. The nature of destiny. Maybe it was always just a man fighting alone with his mind. A man choosing every day to get up, to put on his breathing mask, to climb out of his shelter, and to complete the grueling, the boring, the hard... the necessary.

That lent a sort of purity to it, didn't it? If this was everyone's plight—the very nature of mankind—to struggle and fight as much against oneself as against the world around them, then at least he was in good company. At least he wasn't crazy. And in some ways, thinking of it this way made him feel a little less alone.

It didn't matter if anyone ever saw his struggle. It didn't matter if anyone ever told him he'd done well. It didn't matter if he ended up in history books, religious texts, or among the countless great men now forgotten. What mattered was that he struggled. All men knew struggle, heartache, what it meant to be alone with one's thoughts—to see the shadow of self staring back at them and questioning everything they'd ever done. Asking them about their legacy. Demanding more of them. Demanding everything. It was not the place of any man to say, 'I struggled'. It did not make them special. It did not make them unique. It made them the same. It made them united. It made them *kindred*.

Rhett considered now that the Occassi were the same. They, too, were kindred. There must have been great men among them. Men who fought until at last the storm destroyed them all. Destroyed everything they'd ever built. Destroyed hope of a future and a legacy. Those who had survived had given up their fight, but they were not gone.

Perhaps one day...

Well, if they could be saved, Rhett would do what he could to save them. If they could be awoken, he would do what he could to wake them. But it was not his place to question their struggle. Perhaps he should look down on them for their choice—dream over reality—but he could not condemn them without first condemning himself.

Rhett stood, pressing the switch to activate the prefab's automatic folding mechanism. He closed his eyes at a faint breeze, bringing with it the smells of Occassus's wild grasses, which faintly resembled rosemary and cinnamon. This place could be a home. A good place to fight. To struggle. To go on.

So that morning, like every morning, Rhett decided to keep on running.

Chapter 24

Day 2,009

It worked, Cyn. I... I actually fixed it.
  All systems green. I just have to get it there.
  I just...
  [rapid breathing]
  Cyn, I think I can actually do this.
  I think I can win.
  I don't...
  [hysterical laughter]
  I didn't realize I didn't believe that until now.

Day 2,019

Victory Peak might well have been the most beautiful thing Rhett had ever seen on Occassus. Wreathed in the morning's mist, its massive stone faces shone with a blindingly blue reflection. It was a diamond against the grey sky, a shining beacon of hope and a promise of what this world had to offer.

CHAPTER 24

He knew it was just the glass-cover, of course. There were no blue minerals in the McNeary range, much less enough to make a mountain shine. As much as it took his breath away, his spectacular view here was simply a trick of the light as it shone on the evidence of this world's devastation. Everything was simply a matter of perspective, though. The auroras seen on Earth were simply evidence of the violent solar winds—something this world seemed to strangely lack. Even mountain ranges were evidence of the cataclysmic collision of massive plates of the planet's crust. Perhaps it wasn't uncommon for destruction to be beautiful, either through grim fascination or mind-blowing awe.

Rhett couldn't help but smile as the grade steadily steepened, bringing on a change from the occasional mycotree to a hillside covered in reddish bushes and grasses. Though all the colors were off, it reminded him of Earth—and of the times he'd spent with Cyn. Perhaps near here, she'd find the right sort of inspiration for her paintings. Maybe he hadn't brought her to a planet she could only ever hate.

It wasn't much, but it *was* something.

As evening approached, he found a bit of level ground overlooking the valley from which he'd come. He spent an hour trying to decide how to describe the view into the radio, as if he could paint with a thousand words anything nearly so beautiful as she could with oil or neoacrylic.

He finally put the radio down; she would see it for herself soon enough.

Rhett ran his fingers through his hair, tracing the fresh scar lines that crisscrossed his scalp. Another backpacking trip of theirs came to mind, through the mountains of Colorado. Though much of the tree cover had been burned out by industry decades before, they'd found a quiet tract of land on the western slopes of the Rockies that at least didn't have any people nearby. Their tent had been small, too cramped for the activities they had planned for their romantic getaway, so they'd settled for a soft patch of grass under the moonlight. They hadn't been together long, so Rhett had yet to fully grasp the eccentricities of the artist she was. When she'd told him that there, in the perfect light of the moon, they'd performed a holy act, he'd merely taken it as a compliment and moved on.

Only now, looking back, did he truly understand. It wasn't simply about being together, or being with nature. It was about being together *with* nature. Perhaps that was what mankind forgot that led them to this fateful place.

Rhett wished Occassus had a moon. The sky still looked strange without it.

He grunted, stretching his muscles that had already begun to ache from the hike. It was a good ache, at least. The ache of progress. The ache of growth. Of strength. It was the ache he hoped humanity would feel when it began to rebuild on this planet. The atrophy of their species from numbering twelve billion to merely twelve thousand was extreme, but it was also not insurmountable.

Rhett retreated into his prefab as darkness descended, turned on the radio, and simply talked. He told Cyn about what he'd seen, about how he was unable to properly describe it. He told her how he missed her, complained about the nutrient plaster, wondered about the Occassi and what she would think of them. He told her he wasn't far now; just a few more days and then the waiting would begin. He told her he knew he'd see her when it was all over, that they'd finally be reunited, that this long hellish nightmare would finally end. He imagined her answering him, engaging him, debating him, laughing with him.

It would be real soon. The first domino stood before him, and all it required was a stiff enough shove. He'd been winding up for weeks now—soon, he'd watch them fall.

Day 2,021

A soft morning breeze nuzzled Rhett as he heaved his weight up the final rise on his way to the summit. The air was growing thinner up here, putting greater strain on the filtration mask. His modifications in the dream-vault might have been the only thing that kept it running, he realized. He was at least grateful he'd paid enough attention to Braaten during the equipment briefings to pick up how to do that.

Dawn was not far behind him as he stood at his full height on the highest point of Victory Peak. The gleam of the glass-cover around him was still dull and dark, but its brilliance would soon be revealed by the arrival of the sun. If he could help it, he wanted to leave it behind him before it became blinding to make the descent with some measure of safety.

Rhett fetched his cobbled-together stormpuncher from his pack, saying a silent prayer as he punched in the deployment sequence. Though it complained as it bit into the glass and then the stone beneath, it ran smoothly enough and showed all green indicators within minutes.

"So that's it, then."

Rhett began his climb down, trying to make the meaning of what he'd said sink in. That couldn't be it. It couldn't be *over*. Was it really just the waiting now? It didn't feel real. Didn't feel possible.

"Let's not get ahead of ourselves." He chuckled as he almost lost his step. "Just because it's the end doesn't mean it's over. There's still so much work to do. So much persistence to have. I'll have to maintain these four, probably visiting each once a year to ensure they'll do their jobs. I'll have to hunt. Survive the storm. Keep up my strength. And if there is any way I can, I should try to settle. Maybe build something for myself."

He sighed, nodding.

"For us."

Chapter 25

Day 2,042
21 Days Post-Mission

Some days it's easier, Cyn. Some days I don't think about things as much. I just enjoy the miles that pass behind me. I don't wonder about what I'm going to do tomorrow, don't remember what I did yesterday. I don't try to plan for all the challenges we might face once we're back together. It's peaceful. Beautiful. Like I might be getting used to it all.

 [sigh]
 Some days, I still wonder why I'm doing any of it.

Day 2,182
161 Days Post-Mission

Winter is coming soon. The crew and I missed it the last few times because... well.
 Temperatures are supposed to be low, but not too low. Averages below freezing, but not a lot below zero. The prefab's climate controls have finally died, but as it turns

out, pitcat fur is extremely good insulation. I think I'll be fine. A blanket was easy enough, but I hope someday I might figure out how to line my suit with it.

Then again, it can get kind of itchy. Maybe I'll wait until I can figure out how to soften it a bit.

[silence for 5.4 seconds]

Systems on the Votum still seem to be fine. I've been checking religiously. Had a dream that the generator died, and all you guys...

Well. It occurred to me that if something did go wrong up there, even though you're so close, I couldn't get to you. And close... I mean relatively. Not like Earth. I can see the Votum on a clear night as it swings by overhead, like you used to be able to with satellites. Which kind of makes me wonder about the technological direction of the Occassi. They have a few hundred objects in orbit, but not nearly what we had on Earth. Maybe their rocket technology was just never up to snuff.

Which also makes me wonder if they really did send a ship to form an embassy-colony on Earth. I thought there might be some sort of symmetry between our species. Like we traded worlds somehow. But they just... it doesn't look like they got as far as we did—at least not in space travel. Maybe they intended to learn from us when we arrived, then send their own voyage after the fact. It would have been a violation of the treaty, but I can't really guess what their tech state or intentions were.

[silence for 7.9 seconds]

I bet it was that damn dream. When everything went south and we started looking out—trying to find our escape in the stars—they instead looked in. They fled down into their world, into the dream-vault, accepting an existence where they simply shut everything out.

[sigh]

I guess it worked out for them, depending on how you measure it. They're still down there. Still surviving. Still avoiding. For whatever that's worth.

Hmm.

Day 2,239
218 Days Post-Mission

I found an old novelty flavor of nutrient plaster in the supplies from the lander today. Licorice. I didn't know they even still made these—you know, when they were making them. I mean, what's the point of making a plaster flavor after a kind of candy that hasn't been around for a hundred years? Did they just dig up some old recipe and decide 'people will probably buy this'?

I guess somebody did. I know it wasn't part of the standard issue they sent us with, which means it had to be from someone's personal stash. Not sure who would go out of their way to order a janky flavor of nutrient plaster. Guess I'll never know.

I mean, I see the point in variety. The spice of life, yada yada. But come on! Licorice? It's like going so far out of your way to be unique that you forgot what it was like to be normal. Like some of the bodymods the kids were starting to get into when we left—the third eye, extra toe, retractable fingernail shit? I guess I get that, too. When I was a teenager, it was about cybernetics. Back in Caldwell's generation, I bet they... well... I guess that would have been during the alt-consciousness movement. Neuroregenerates and dopacyclers, if I remember right. I wonder if he was involved in that.

I can't really see him that way, but hey, a man can have a past. He can have secrets. Regrets. Other kinds of... formative events.

It was terrible, by the way. The plaster. Same as it always is. Could have at least had something good in your personal stash.

[silence for 2.6 seconds]

Whoever you were.

CHAPTER 25

Day 2,496
475 Days Post-Mission

I built a house.

[clears throat]

Not a very good one. More like a shack. A hut. Doesn't even really have a proper door on it.

[breathing for 1.8 seconds]

I know I haven't been transmitting as often as I used to, but it's for good reason. The batteries on this radio aren't going to last forever, even if they are subnuclear.

Anyway, the hut.

[silence for 2.9 seconds]

I had the Votum calculate the storm's path for the next few passes. Found a place where it will miss by just enough to matter for a few years. It's tucked away in a mycoforest, gets some sunlight but a bit of shade as well. Built it out of the damn things—weird to work with, let me tell you. Very far to the soft side as far as woods go, but strong and flexible. The wood is kind of tacky to the touch, making it pretty easy to just wedge things in place until you're ready to nail them in. Easiest bit of carpentry I've ever done on an alien planet.

[chuckles]

[silence for 4.2 seconds]

Starting to run low on ammo now. I've decided to conserve the rest for self-defense. I'm still... a long way from seeing the Votum down here. Been trying my luck at trapping instead, seen some success. Cutting steel spearheads from the lander's plating isn't as hard as I expected either. Picked up some good sharpening stones a while back and that's kept me in business for blades and edges and the like. Like the axe I made to help me build the hut.

My prefab sits in the corner. The hut doesn't insulate it much, but on windy nights I think it helps. The fact that the shine of its exterior isn't so open to catch predatory eyes also makes me feel a bit better. I'd paint it if I had the right stuff, but anything around here, I worry it would mess with the compaction tech. If I suddenly had to carry that thing around folded open... well it would be awkward, to say the least, even if it isn't all that heavy.

Hmm.

I know we wanted to buy a house someday. And, well, I don't think we'll have to buy it, but I think we will have one here. Maybe I'll build that one, too. I guess I have a while to practice my carpentry. If I have the fundamentals down by the time the stormpunchers finish their work, I should be able to teach some of the others, too.

[chuckles]

You always said I needed a creative outlet. I told you I wasn't like you. Didn't like making things. Didn't need to. As a soldier, I was far more used to un-making things.

You insisted we were the same. That all people just needed to find what was theirs. What spoke to them. What would make them whole...

[breathes]

Well, I'm not sure if it will make me whole, but it might just make us a house someday. Take what you can get, right, Cyn?

Day 2,527
506 Days Post-Mission

Well, the house fell down today. Nearly knocked my brains out, I think.

[groan]

Ah-ah... err...

Yep. Definitely concussed.

Maybe I'll wait on the carpentry until someone will be around to drag my stupid ass out of the collapsed monstrosity I built.

Day 3,002
981 Days Post-Mission

You know, my father sometimes used to say he never wanted kids. To our faces, usually. Especially when he was angry. Used to say, "This was never my idea! Your mother was the one who wanted you."

I'm not sure if it wasn't his idea at the time, but when we were actually around and he had to deal with us... it was true that he didn't want us. He was in it for my mother. He wanted to make her happy. Kids were part of that, even though he didn't know what he was signing up for. I don't really fault him for it now, but at the time... I felt like I had taken something away from him just by existing.

I never wanted to make any child of mine feel that way. Ironically, I thought the best solution was to do what he couldn't—find a woman who only wanted me, not them.

[chuckles]

That went well, didn't it?

Hmm.

I still want the same things, Cyn. I still never want to make a kid feel like he isn't wanted. When this is all over, I want you to know that I will never do that to them.

I... I will try to never do that to them.

I guess they'll probably listen to these messages someday, too. If we get that far. So I guess...

[clears throat]

Victor? You listen to your mother. And remember that Daddy loves you.

[chuckles]

[sighs]

We don't have to name him Victor. If it's even a 'him' at all. It was my grandpap's name. My mom's dad. He always liked us. Told us we were good kids. He's the one who recommended I join the service in the first place. He helped me...

Well, I'd say he helped me make something of myself, but look where that got me, eh?

[distant hissing]

[distant howl]

Ooh! Sounds like my trap's got something. Better go.

Day 3,187
1,166 Days Post-Mission

It's Christmas today.

   Apparently.

   Why my navbrace decided to inform me of that this year when it hasn't on any of the years before now, I will never know. Maybe it detected I could use some cheer or something?

   Yeah, I didn't think so either.

   [silence for 4.9 seconds]

   I remember when you brought me over for the first time to meet your parents. It was Christmas, but as I recall your family wasn't especially keen on the celebration.

Too much glorification of antiquated practices? I think that was the way your father put it. 'Stick in the mud' was the way I'd put it back to him.

The arguments only got worse from there.

You had to separate us. Your mother just backed off, too wary of a battle of strong wills in her household. Perhaps it was for your father's sake she retreated—not wanting to embarrass or undermine him. Or perhaps for yours, not trying to make your selection in men seem questionable. Or perhaps it was only for herself. She just wanted the conflict to go away so she wouldn't have to deal with it.

In any case, it was you who stepped up. The girl they'd brought up quiet, respectful, calm... their Cynthia. When you were with me, you became strong, assertive, defiant... my Cyn. You were what the situation needed, but still they questioned you. What happened to their little girl? Was this woman before them still her, or was she changed? Was she still the same girl, now merely revealed?

After we left... you cried. You were angry with me. I didn't understand why; I thought you wanted me to stand up to your father. I thought I was arguing on your behalf. Somehow, it didn't occur to me that I was part of the problem.

I saw a different side of you, too, that day. I saw a woman who not only wanted to have fun, not only someone looking for companionship, but someone who could run counter to me when she needed to. Someone who could change my mind. Someone who had a will and a strength and a vibrance of her own. Looking back on it now, I think that was the day I went from wanting you... to needing you.

Hmm.

Sometimes things change, when you've spent a little time with them. Or maybe they just reveal themselves. After all this time on Occassus... I'm seeing new sides to this world. In its barrenness, I once saw hostility. Desolation. Now I am beginning to see serenity. In its colors, so different from Earth's, I once saw only alien otherness. Now I have trouble picturing green grass... blue spruce... yellow wheat...

I've stopped wondering why this world isn't Earth, stopped wondering about all we'll have to do to make it suitable. To make it the way we remember. Yes, Earth was our mother. It raised us, nurtured us. Brought us to a place where we were ready to depart...

But we did depart.

We left her.

We need to change now, too. We need to stop looking for something that looks like wheat to make bread. There is a bounty here to find, if we simply accept what it is. If we can change to meet this world where it is. If we can complement it, not merely look to it for that which we had before.

This planet can be more than just where we live. If we let it, it can truly be home.

Day 3,458
1,437 Days Post-Mission

I built a new hut. This one should be safe from the storm for another year or two. Had to leave when the storm was due to hit the last one, which I was prepared for. It was basically the only deadline I had, you know? The only thing on my calendar.

I've started a little garden next to this one. It's spring now, and here in the foothills of Westercliff, a kind of fruit grows on a vine that is a little like a tomato. Purple, though. Stains your tongue something awful.

[chuckles]

I needed to do something like this. I'm on the last case of nutrient plaster canisters I managed to salvage from the lander. Won't last me another year, and I've got a while more than that still. But I'm doing all right. I've managed. It's hard, but since surviving is all I really have to do around here...

[silence for 2.1 seconds]

I shrugged. That was a shrug, just now.

Wow. You'd think by now I understand how this radio works.

[chuckles]

CHAPTER 25

I haven't decided yet if I am supposed to laugh at my own jokes. I mean... there isn't anyone else around to laugh at them. But then again, my laugh isn't a particularly good one. Not like yours was.

Your laugh...

[silence for 3.1 seconds]

Yes. I should try to describe it. Maybe it will help me remember it better. Remember you better.

Your laugh...

It was vibrant. Full of color. Somehow, the painter in you came through in your laugh. The way you saw things differently than everyone else did. Better than everyone else did. But you didn't want to keep that to yourself. You wanted us to see it like you did. To mark the humor... as you did beauty.

I swear, Cyn. Even if this planet wasn't beautiful—and I'm growing to believe it is—you could make it beautiful in one of your paintings. It took me years to see it clearly on my own. But you... I doubt it will take you a week. To you, it will be a new place, and though you will miss the old one, even long for it sometimes, you'll think it's exciting and intoxicating and magnificent. You'll show the others what you see. You'll help them make this place their home. Even if history remembers me as having brought them here, it will be you who made them accept it.

[sigh]

Only about four more years now.

[sigh]

I have some grey strands in my hair now. If I still had a full head of it, they might not be too noticeable. But with all the scarring? You can see it. Hell, the Votum can probably note it from orbital images if I'm outside while it swings over.

[chuckles]

Had to flush out my mask's filtration system again this week. It was definitely not designed for such extended use. I can hook up new batteries, replace filter sheets, and replace fan bearings all I want, but eventually the circuitry itself is going to die on me. I keep an un-modded backup on me, just in case. If I can figure out how to rig it up with all the extra gizmos again when the time comes, it might last me just as long.

Might not matter, though. According to the Votum, Nuhalriu is already showing noticeable weakening. At some point, the gunk it's been kicking up will settle enough that the air will be safe to breathe. It's still a few tenths of a percent off on a few ratios, so I bet our children will develop some sturdy lungs in childhood, but it will serve. If I get some lung scarring because my masks finally die on me when I have a year left to go...

Eh. It will probably be fine. I'll still be around to send the all-clear. That's what really matters.

[silence for 3.9 seconds]

Yes.

That's all that matters in the end.

Day 3,780
1,759 Days Post-Mission

So I know you have paints on the ship, packed along with your other things. But I was bored and found some berries with a really striking orange juice inside them, so I decided between them and the purpatoes, I could probably make a set of paints that would at least cover half the rainbow.

Let me just say I didn't understand how painting worked before, but now I REALLY don't understand it. It doesn't help that my brushes are just mycobark that I've stripped down to fibers on one end. It looks the part, but the way the fibers bend...

Maybe I just didn't leave enough fibers. Not enough bristles? It just gloops on and when I try and spread it around, I just end up with the 'paint' spreading up my brush. I'm like a first grader, I swear.

Actually, you know what? Maybe finger painting IS the way to go.

[rummaging sounds]

In case you're wondering, yes. I've finally cracked. I guess that's what happens when you decide to be an artist.

[clears throat]

Uh... no offense.

Day 4,143
2,122 Days Post-Mission

I'm moving the hut again. Well... 'moving'. I tore it down and salvaged all the hardware, is what I should say. The raw materials have to come from wherever I decide to build next, but the duraplastic rivets and the alumisteel brackets were all a giant hassle to make, so I take those with me.

It's a pretty good journey to the next safe zone. Two months, according to the navbrace. Then again, it might be still taking my atrophied self into account when calculating my average traveling speed. Still not sure if I'm offended by that. But with all the food I'm having to carry now—I am out of nutrient plaster—maybe the estimates should be regarded as correct? Definitely going to be carrying a lot more weight than I was before this time around.

[breathing]

Hmm.

[silence for 3.2 seconds]

Saw my first rain that wasn't connected to Nuhalriu last week. It was nice. Soft. Gentle. My garden looks better this season than it ever has. I have four different kinds of crops now.

Four!

I'm carrying seeds for each of them, but I can't be sure the soil or the temperature and whatever else will be as favorable as it was here. There's always the possibility it won't grow as fast, as well, as soon… I can only pack so much food on me.

Never mind that. Borrowing trouble there. There's plenty to go around without.

I'll be going back near where we lost the captain. I think I have a better route mapped through it than last time, so I think it will be safe, but there's always risk. There's risk in everything though, right? Certainly can't wait for the storm to come and get me.

Reminds me of our cross-country trips back in the day. Remember how we wanted to drive the trans-Atlantic bridge sometime? See the diners? The glass hotels? Feel a sense of borrowed nostalgia for a century of architecture come and gone?

We just never had a vehicle rated for the distance. They still only had electric charging stations along the whole length of it because of some international statute or other. Something about the protection of history. I guess that was the charm of it, though, right?

What do you think we'll build here? How long will it take us to get to where we were?

Should we even be trying to?

No, no, no. I'm done with philosophy. A man alone for a long time will at first resort to philosophy but will eventually become sick of it. I'm beyond sick of it now. If anyone asks me my take on the Degrasse-Keebler paradigm once you guys are all safe and down here, I'll have no qualms about punching him in the mouth.

Right in the mouth!

Hmm? Oh. There's the sun.

I'd better pack up. I don't want to waste any daylight. I'll transmit again soon.

CHAPTER 25

Day 4,298
2,277 Days Post-Mission

The new garden isn't quite as happy with where it is, but I found two new crops on the way, so who's complaining? I figure if these were growing here by themselves, they should grow fine under my care. Should know in the next few weeks.

It's chillier here. Navbrace is showing snow a few dozen miles north of here in the orbital images. Looking back, I think it's been there a few months, nothing new. Hopefully none falls here before I can get a good harvest in.

From where I'm at in the highlands, I can see one of the glass deserts to the west. At sunset, the sky is painted with it like a prismatic mirror. There are colors I've seen here that I didn't even know existed. Something about the atmosphere, maybe. I really think you're going to love it. I think you'll want to stay, not just be forced to. You'll want to watch this sunset again and again. Paint it once a year to see if you can ever render it just *the way you see it in front of you, like you did that island near your parents' house in Maine.*

[sigh]

My suit is finally trying to call it quits. Just goes to show that nothing lasts forever. Not even Diatan Polycotton^{TM}*.*

[chuckles]

Then again, their products outlasted the company itself by almost a century, so I'd count that as pretty impressive. And six years of continuous use, not to mention only rarely being cleaned?

Speaking of which, you are going to have to forgive the state you find me in when you land. I tried to make soap down here, but mineral lye is surprisingly hard to find. Some hygiene supplies survived what happened to the lander, but I ran through those ages ago. I decided to cut my hair as short as possible, thinking that might help it stay cleaner. It has helped so far, but I doubt it will be enough forever.

You're probably going to have to forgive me for a lot of things when we meet again...

Day 4,413
2,392 Days Post-Mission

Cyn?

Cyn?

I hear something. Something's coming. A lot of somethings, I think. But it's too dark for me to see anything.

I guess... God, Cyn. I don't know why I'm worried this time. I just have this feeling. This weight. My Phi-8 is loaded, charge seems good. Something about this—

There!

No, I don't see anything.

[breathing]

If I don't transmit again, Cyn... Just know that I love you. I'll always love you.

Day 4,415
2,394 Days Post-Mission

CHAPTER 25

Well.

[breathing]

I made it. I guess I... I guess I'll tell you about it when you get down here. Maybe I'll actually be able to make sense of it by then.

[breathing]

Then again, maybe not.

Day 4,577
2,556 Days Post-Mission

Bit of a feast tonight. Today is seven years since I deployed the fourth stormpuncher. A birthday, of sorts. Or a holiday. Probably needs a name; will have to think about that later. But that's not the point.

I made spaghetti.

Well, not real spaghetti. But the purpatoes make a decent sauce if you stew them properly and give them some salt. Another one of the things I've been growing—I couldn't think of anything better to call it than spaghetti melon. Kind of like a spaghetti squash—well, if you scrape out the meat of it right. You get the point. It's a lot grittier, and honestly pretty bitter, but with a good sauce that I've sweetened with mycotree sap, it comes together and almost tastes like food.

Definitely better than the nutrient plasters were, though.

Probably.

Also figured out that tepperdown leaves make a pretty nice tea. Kind of musky, almost a nutty flavor, but certainly a decent change from water. Now all I have to do is harvest some glass from the desert to see if I can't craft the pieces to make a still.

[laughing]

No. I probably don't need it. But some of the colonists are going to do it the first day you land, you can be sure of that. Hell, they probably smuggled the parts here from Earth, if I had my guess. And you know it's going to taste awful. It will be strong and tasteless and everyone is going to buy the shit out of it.

Hmm.

Buy.

Will we still... buy *things? We obviously came from Earth with some concept of currency and worths, but here? With no connection to what we left behind?*

No, no. I know better than this. It's not my place to figure any of that out; there's a whole suite of bureaucrats up there waiting to land whose job it is to figure out how a society should run on another world. Maybe they won't have to figure out how to regularly trade with an alien species, but I'm sure a society of just us humans will be enough to keep—

[beeping]

Oh, shit. Already?

I'm sorry, Cyn. The radio thinks it's almost out of battery. I'll see if I can stretch it, but I have to go for now.

Day 5,269
3,248 Days Post-Mission

I don't have long—have to conserve. Been pretending to transmit without actually doing it for a couple years, trying to make myself feel better about this whole thing. The Votum says one more pass through the stormpuncher matrix should do it for Nuhalriu. It will officially be deemed a non-threat.

[sigh]

Took fucking long enough.

CHAPTER 25

Day 5,598
3,577 Days Post-Mission

{incoming transmission}
   {authorization code 4815162342}
   {identification confirmed: Corporal Rhett Wethern}
   {processing}
   {processing}
   {processing}
   {ALL CLEAR RECEIVED}
...
{voice transmission activating}
...
[clears throat]
I...
[breathing]
[sniff]
   It's finally over, Cyn. I've sent the signal. The Votum will be making calculations for the next couple hours, but within the next few days...
   [clears throat]
   I'm finally going to see you again. We'll be together again. I don't know if the Votum will manage to put you near me on Miar, but it won't matter. However far I have to travel... I've already traveled farther. Longer. It will be nothing. Easy.
   I expect you'll wake up in the next day or so. Most of the passengers will need a little while to adjust to being awake again—even us military folks took a few days to get back to being right with ourselves. The good news is our hypersleep won't take

out of you what the Occassi dream-vault did to me. I guess in order to pamper the mind, they had to let the body suffer. But it still won't be easy. The others up there will need your help. They'll need your strength. Your confidence.

Just make sure that if you see anyone with veins showing on their neck or around their eyes, that you do not upset them!. Hypersleep mania is very serious and though it will wear off with time, people with it must be considered dangerous! Just based on the fact that there are 12,000 of you waking up, I expect there will be one or two people with it, but after more than a hundred years in stasis, who knows? It could be more than that.

Uh... I guess I should say that if you *are* the one experiencing those symptoms, that you should go to the med bay as soon as you can and ask for an oral sedative. A needle would work better, but I know how you feel about those. Like I said, we wouldn't want to upset you.

[sharp breath]

Anyway.

Hmm.

Well, if you get these messages and somehow manage to listen through them all before you begin re-entry, my navbrace still has enough charge to handle a few minutes of two-way video. Once you start re-entering, though, the signal will be shot to shit. We'll just have to wait for the grand reunion.

[chuckles]

[sniffs]

I'll see you soon, Cyn. One way or another. You can see the planet we're going to call our home. That our children will call home. And our grandchildren. You'll see the skies I wandered under. The steppes I crossed. The mountains I climbed. You may not understand me completely. I know that I've changed. I've grown. I've lost things. Maybe some of them are still here? Maybe not. But I think that through these recordings... through you joining me here...

I think we'll finally begin to redeem this damned earth.

Thank you for reading! If you enjoyed this book, would you consider leaving an honest review for me on Amazon? It helps so much more than you know and allows me to craft more stories like this one.

Here's a QR code link for your convenience:

About the author

A life-long lover of the magic of storytelling, L.A. wrote his first story at the age of 7 and has been writing ever since. Speculative fiction has always held a special place in his heart for the uniqueness of the places and the questions it can address. Though veiled by apparent strangeness, he has always seen it as capable of revealing deeper truth about our own reality.

L.A. graduated from Montana State University in 2015 with Honors in Biochemistry and a minor in Music Composition. This helped nurture his critical thinking and research skills which continue to be instrumental to his writing. During his collegiate years, he also met the love of his life, Julie, whom he later married. At once his greatest supporter and his staunchest critic (when he is wrong, which is more often than he'd like to admit), she has been an integral part of his creative process ever since.

In February of 2018, L.A. became the father of his first son, Griffin. His second son, Tiber, was born in December of 2019 and his third son, Malachi, was born in January of 2023. Though life has become considerably busier since he became a family man, L.A. continues to work on writing in what little spare time he can find. He hopes to one day pass on his love of literature to his sons.

If you would like to keep up with L.A.'s writing journey with a monthly newsletter, you can **subscribe at lamortonyates.substack.com**

You can also tune in for periodic short stories from L.A. and other Synthesis Press writers at **https://synthesisstories.substack.com/**

Otherwise, you can connect with him at:

Instagram – https://www.instagram.com/lamortonyates/

Facebook – https://www.facebook.com/authorlamortonyates

Or on our website – synthesispress.com

Also by

L.A. MORTON-YATES

A Shade. A Storm. A Soul.

Cursed with forbidden knowledge, 19-year-old Dela must hide her secret from her nomadic tribe or face exile into the frozen wasteland of the Bitters. When she becomes separated from her people during a blizzard, a mysterious and dangerous wanderer named Talon promises to help her find her way back to them. She quickly learns that nothing is what it seems, that her curse may actually be a gift, and that the Bitters are far more dangerous than she could have imagined.

Packed with unexpected twists, *Bittersouls* is a mixture of survival, adventure, and slow-burn romance that is sure to get your heart pounding.

Excerpt from Bittersouls

BY L.A. MORTON-YATES

The first time Dela saw the Jackal, it didn't try to kill her. It was a chilly night, but the little girl didn't notice. She was young, still so full of Warmth. The wind blew snow flurries around the camp, shimmering like stars in the firelight. She giggled as she kicked a smooth stone from snowbank to snowbank. The older snow had melted and frozen on the surface just thick enough for the stone to bounce instead of sink.

Her laughter was accompanied by the sounds of merriment behind her. The adults of the congregation were still hard at work on the fifth evening of the Festival of Three Flames, and Dela was long supposed to be tucked away with the other children in their beds. They couldn't hear her over the noise of their lively conversations, pumping bellows, and roaring flames. She didn't spare them much thought; they wouldn't even notice she was gone. She could watch as long as she wanted, then slink back to bed. No one would be the wiser.

She wasn't sure why she was awake. The other children didn't wonder about it, apparently. A feast involving weeks of arduous labor, held once every five years in this very spot. How could she not be curious? After all, she was practically grown up at almost five years old. It was right for her to wonder what this occasion involved, and why her parents and the others were so adamant about its importance.

But she hadn't wondered about it for long. She'd found the stone, then chased it as it skipped and slid through the snow-washed darkness. The fire was only fifty feet behind her, but in her mind it was already a world away.

Dela snickered as she kicked the stone again, pointing as if it had told a joke when it skidded to a stop. She skipped toward it, beaming as brightly as the moon high above the concealing clouds. The stone was glossy in her hand, shaved smooth by time and ice. She stared into it, her grin bubbling over into another giggle.

A warm wall of whiteness rose above her, blocking the wind and snow.

Dela looked up slowly, marveling at the creature's angular grace. It dipped its head, sniffing at her midnight hair. She gasped at the smell of its breath, like smoke and rosehips. It examined her with keen eyes, tilting its head slightly.

"Pu…" The word was lost in her wonder. "Puppy?"

She raised a hand to touch its snout, but it leaped away. Its limbs were sharp as bones, its ears pointed as knife blades. She'd heard rhymes about the creatures they called Jackals but had never seen one herself. It was beautiful.

She didn't wait for it to go. The adults would want to see it. It was so pretty. So regal. They had to know it was here to visit them. Maybe they would want to pet it.

She ran for the firelight, the rock she'd been chasing long forgotten. She hollered and laughed, plunging past the tent line and into the writhing mass of the congregation. The cold of the night fell away like a discarded cloak, replaced by the dry heat of the furnace at the center of it all. Some eyes followed her, but most were still too busy with their work. The bellows wouldn't pump themselves. Even for the interruption of a child long thought to be abed, the work could not be stopped.

A hand caught her arm, and the little girl whirled to find her father frowning down at her. "Adelaide," he growled, crouching to her level.

"Papa." Her smile widened. "Puppy!"

She pointed past the people and their festival, out into the dark and the cold of the night.

"What are you talking about, Adelaide?" her father asked, the quiet sharpness of a deep-seated worry taking shape in his voice.

"It's pretty, Papa." She jumped up and down, trying to get him to look where she was pointing. What if it moved? What if it left before he followed her? She lowered her voice, as if conferring an important secret to the man. "It's a Jackal."

"Oh, Rolf." Her mother appeared as if out of nowhere, putting a hand on the man's shoulder. "You know she's just making up stories, trying to find a reason to join us out here." She crouched beside the little girl, who pouted back at her. "Isn't that right, Adelaide? All the light and the noise and the excitement?"

"No, it's—"

"It's okay, Adelaide. I'm not angry." She smiled, warm and genuine. The girl almost folded at that. She loved her mother, and she knew the woman loved her, too. "Don't you think we should go back to bed?"

"But the Jackal," Dela whimpered. "It's so pretty. And nice!"

"That's nice, Adelaide." The woman picked her up, carrying her gently back toward the tent. "I'm sure it will still be there in the morning. Maybe we can meet it then."

"No, Mama!" The little girl fought against her mother's hold. Didn't they believe her? They had to believe her. "He's nice! He's come to be my friend."

"That's good, little cub." The woman stooped through the thick leathery flap of the tent, fastening it behind her. She set the girl down on the deep plush of her fur sleeping mat, wrapping her carefully in the extremities of the pelt.

"Don't you want to meet my friend?" the little girl pleaded.

Her mother's caring expression slowly grew stern as she studied the girl's face. Now she believed her, Dela could tell. So why wasn't she excited, too?

"How about a story, little cub?"

Dela didn't give up her pout, but nodded meekly. "What about?"

"Well…" Her mother tapped her chin. "You wanted to know about the festival, didn't you? How about a story about that?"

The little girl considered for a moment, then nodded again. "Okay."

"All right. Get comfortable, little cub."

She did so, wiggling and squirming until she'd found just the right position for sleeping. "Ready, Mama."

"Hmm. Have you heard anything about the Three Flames?"

Dela shook her head. "Not a lot, Mama."

"Well, long ago, the world was a beautiful, warm place. People lived together in camps that never moved, hundreds upon hundreds of them. The herds were always plentiful, and snow only covered the ground a small portion of the year."

"When, Mama?" The girl shook her head. "Was it like that when you were my age?"

The woman laughed. "No, little cub. This was a long time before that. A dozen Warmthtimes at least before I was born. There's been… I don't even know if they count anymore. Thirty Festivals since then?"

The little girl nodded.

"In those days, there was only One Flame that burned high and bright in the sky, uncovered by clouds and snowfall. People should have been happy, but they were not grateful for what they had. The great deceiver, Bale the Omnivolent, promised them they could have more. That if they followed his instructions, they could have not One Flame, but Three.

"The people of the world were foolish. They took his offer, not questioning what it meant. No light or life comes from nothing. Bale split the One Flame, giving to each man, woman, and child a Flame Within."

"But Mama," Dela said. "Isn't that where our Warmth comes from?"

"Of course, little cub." Her mother nodded. "Such a smart girl. But you have to remember, the world wasn't frozen in those days. We didn't need Warmth to live. But now, with the One Flame spread like ashes in the wind, every one of us must clutch at every bit of Warmth we can hold on to. That's why we need the Congregation."

The little girl nodded. "'We share our Warmth, so none may go cold.'"

The woman's smile widened. "You've been paying attention to your lessons, haven't you?"

Dela giggled, nodding.

"Well, that's good. Do you know what happened to the rest of what Bale stole from the One Flame?"

The little girl shook her head.

"He seeded the ground with the black salt of the Flame Without. Not everywhere, though. Only a few places have the salt, like the one we're camped around right now."

"But what's it for, Mama?"

"You know the blacksticks that all the grown-ups have?"

"The ones that help them start fires?"

Her mother nodded. "That's the third Flame. The Flame Without. This whole festival is our way of showing penitence for the mistakes of our ancestors. And by the mercy of the One, we can make the blacksticks here as part of our worship."

The little girl nodded slowly, then frowned. "But Mama, you said there were hund... hundre... lots of people. What happened to them?"

"That's why I'm telling you this story, little cub." The woman sighed, eyes falling to her lap. "The deceiver gave one more thing to some alongside the Flame Within. The Ministers have it mentioned in their texts as the Shadow, but most people just call it madness. When the Bitter Wind came and nature itself was changed, the people and creatures of the world grew frightful. Twisted. Corrupt. Not everyone found safe ways to live like we did."

"Mama?" Dela pursed her lips. "This doesn't seem like a very good story."

"It's not," her mother admitted. "But like most stories, it's told for a reason."

"What's that, Mama?"

The woman leaned close to her daughter, whispering carefully into the little girl's ear, "You need to understand that Jackals aren't animals. They aren't something you can turn into a pet, nor even something truly wild. They are *his*, Adelaide. Do you understand? They are mad, and they bring madness. If you ever see one, you must tell no one."

Dela shivered. She understood completely, so far as a little girl could.

"And if you see anything *after*," her mother added, "that is a secret you must keep until the day your Warmth runs out."

www.ingramcontent.com/pod-product-compliance
Ingram Content Group UK Ltd.
Pitfield, Milton Keynes, MK11 3LW, UK
UKHW041952230426
12048UKWH00008B/295